Here's what critics are saying about
The High Heels Mysteries:

"A saucy combination of romance and suspense that is simply irresistible."
- Chicago Tribune

"Stylish... nonstop action...guaranteed to keep chick lit and mystery fans happy!"
- Publishers' Weekly, starred review

"Smart, funny and snappy... the perfect beach read!"
- Fresh Fiction

"The High Heels Series is amongst one of the best mystery series currently in publication. If you have not read these books, then you are really missing out on a fantastic experience, chock full of nail-biting adventure, plenty of hi-jinks, and hot, sizzling romance. Can it get any better than that?"
- Romance Reviews Today

"(A) breezy, fast-paced style, interesting characters and story meant for the keeper shelf. 4 ½!"
- RT Book Reviews

"Maddie Springer is like a cross between Paris Hilton and Stephanie Plum, only better. This is one HIGH HEEL you'll want to try on again and again."
- Romance Junkies

BOOKS BY GEMMA HALLIDAY

High Heels Mysteries:
Spying in High Heels
Killer in High Heels
Undercover in High Heels
Christmas in High Heels
(short story)
Alibi in High Heels
Mayhem in High Heels
Honeymoon in High Heels
(novella)
Sweetheart in High Heels
(short story)
Fearless in High Heels
Danger in High Heels
Homicide in High Heels
Deadly in High Heels

*Hollywood Headlines
Mysteries:*
Hollywood Scandals
Hollywood Secrets
Hollywood Confessions
Twelve's Drummer Dying
(short story)

Jamie Bond Mysteries
Unbreakable Bond
Secret Bond
Lethal Bond
Bond Bombshell (short
story)

Tahoe Tessie Mysteries
Luck Be A Lady
Hey Big Spender
Baby It's Cold Outside
(short story)

Young Adult Books
Deadly Cool
Social Suicide
Wicked Games

Other Works
Play Nice
Viva Las Vegas
A High Heels Haunting
(novella)
Watching You (short story)
Confessions of a Bombshell
Bandit (short story)

DEADLY
IN
HIGH HEELS

a High Heels mystery

Gemma Halliday

This book is dedicated to all of the fabulous High Heels Mysteries readers who have written to me over the years. You are why I keep writing, and you are what keeps Maddie jumping into new dangerous, daring, and divalicious adventures.

A special thank you goes out to Kristine Zepf for picking the name of our island Tiki bar, The Lost Aloha Shack, and to Brandy Dewar Glaser for coming up with the signature drink served there, the Babbling Mermaid.

CHAPTER ONE

———

When I was a young girl I dreamed of being on the runways of Paris, Milan, and New York, strutting the most fabulous fashions known to womankind. Unfortunately when my height topped out at a less than impressive 5 feet 1 3/4 inches (yes, the 3/4 inches are important to note!) around eighth grade, it became painfully clear that a career as a runway model was not in my future. However I didn't give up hope on fashion! Instead I turned my hand to designing those coveted couture creations. More specifically, the fab footwear that did the strutting.

My name is Maddie Springer, and I design women's shoes for a living. And after four years of college at the Academy of Art fashion Institute in San Francisco, several more years paying my dues as the bottom rung designer at Tot Trots children's shoe designers (where I was in charge of not only the Dora the Explorer line of girls' sandals but also the SpongeBob SquarePants rain boots collection as well. I know, let the jealousy commence.), I was finally able to start my own line of designer footwear called High Heels Seduction. While my career as a designer was still in the early stages, not quite rivaling the likes of Choo or Louboutin yet, through lots of hard work and hustling on my part, new boutiques throughout Beverly Hills were displaying my heels in their pricey window displays. And I hoped to take this phenomenon from local to national with my latest client: the Miss Hawaiian Paradise Beauty Pageant.

Currently my footwear was slated to be worn by all fifty-one of the contestants on the one-week, nationally televised event. And if the exposure wasn't enough to have me happy-dancing in my slingbacks, the pageant had actually flown me out to the island of Oahu to style the contestants in person. Talk about a dream job, right?

"Miss Arkansas!" A tall, slim guy in a pair of skintight, white leather pants and a neon Lycra shirt shouted toward the group of contestants assembled before us.

A blonde with man-made breasts creating total side-boob in a tropical print bikini blinked her false eyelashes in rapid succession. "Yes?"

"How many times have I told you that you need to cross to the left, behind Miss Montana, not to the right, in front of Miss Delaware?" The guy in the leather pants threw his hands up in the air, shaking his head.

"Oh, sorry. Right. I remember that." The blonde nodded vigorously. I noticed not a single hair on her head moved with her. I made a mental note to ask her what brand of hairspray she used.

"Let's take it again from the top, ladies. Jackie, the music please!" Leather Pants waved his arms in the air like a conductor.

Immediately an upbeat 90's dance mix played through the outdoor speakers surrounding the Royal Waikiki Resort's pool, pumping a steady beat as fifty-one long-legged contestants crisscrossed between potted palms, chaise lounges, and mini waterfalls, rehearsing their perfectly choreographed opening routine.

"Isn't this just the most totes fabu thing evah?!" the guy lounging in the chaise next to me whispered.

"It will be," I told him. "If Miss Arkansas doesn't trip again."

"Amen, sister! I have half a mind to take that girl aside and show her how to walk in heels myself," he shot back.

I stifled a giggle. My companion, Marco, was slim, Hispanic, and more fabulous than a Lady Gaga impersonator at a Cher concert. His hair was a spiked bleached blond with trendy pink tips, his make-up was heavier than any of the Miss Hawaiian Paradise contestants, and his outfit today was a pair of hot pink Daisy Dukes, a white, mesh tank, and a bright, tropical print blouse (yes, blouse), unbuttoned with the ends tied into a little bow right at his belly button. He'd capped off the look with oversized purple sunglasses and a pair of hot pink flip-flops with rhinestones along the sides. I was pretty sure he out-blinged my own flowy, cotton shift dress and white kitten heels by about ten rhinestones.

"Honestly it's a wonder she hasn't been disqualified already," I noted, watching poor Miss Arkansas try to keep up as the girls broke into a dance number. While she was a striking blonde with model-worthy features that I could easily see beating any of the other contestants in the beauty department, she had the grace of a water buffalo. In stilettos.

"You know Dana's too charitable for that. That girl would have to take out the entire first row of viewers in the auditorium before she would disqualify her."

Marco was right. My best friend Dana Dashel was a television actress, girlfriend to one of Hollywood's hottest movie stars, and currently making enough of a name for herself in the entertainment industry that the Miss Hawaiian Paradise Pageant had jumped at my suggestion to have her as one of their celebrity judges. With Dana judging the pageant, and my footwear front and center, we had agreed that the one week in Hawaii from the start of the preliminary judging to the pageant's live televised show, would make the perfect girls' vacation away. Something we both sorely needed. Dana had lately been working long hours on the set of her television show, Lady Justice, and I had been running on fumes, juggling my budding fashion career with raising my pair of twin toddlers, Max and Olivia. Luckily my husband had some vacation time coming, and he'd agreed to take the time off to spend with the kids while I took the time off to spend my days lounging in the sun and awaiting the mai tai cocktail hour. (You can see why I married him.)

And of course Marco, being one of the girls himself, had insisted on cashing in his vacation hours at his job as a swanky salon receptionist and tagging along.

I shot a glance to the judges' table, where Dana's eyebrows were pulled into a frown of concentration, her eyes focused on the contestants' steps as her pen hovered over her scoring tablet. Beside her sat the two other celebrity judges: Ruth Marie Masters, whose claim to fame was being Miss Hawaiian Paradise 1962, and Jay Jeffries, a daytime soap opera actor.

"No, no, no!" The man in the tight leather pants threw his arms up in despair again. "Honey is there something wrong with your ears? Can you not hear the beat?" he shouted at Miss New Mexico.

The leggy brunette with hair that was almost as tall as I was blinked at him, shaking her head no at first, then re-thinking that answer and nodding instead.

"It's one-two-three, one-two-three. Emphasis on the third, got it?"

Miss New Mexico nodded her head up and down like a bobble doll.

"Take five, everyone, while we re-set. Again," he yelled, waving his hands in the air.

I'd only just arrived in Hawaii that morning and had been afforded the briefest of introductions to the exasperated pageant director, Simon Laforge a.k.a. Mr. Leather Pants. He had given me my official itinerary and the pageant personnel contact and informed me that footwear fittings were not scheduled for two more days, at which time he would instruct me on what I "needed to know." I suddenly felt like I was in a bad Bourne movie parody, but considering he was my boss for this job, I went with it and made myself scarce, lounging by the pool until fittings.

"Geez, he's being a little hard on her, dontcha think?" Marco whispered to me.

I nodded in agreement. I hadn't actually seen anything wrong with Miss New Mexico's steps.

While the choreographers wrangled all of the girls back into their starting positions, powder compacts and lipsticks came out, and Dana stretched her legs, sauntering over to our chaises on the edge of the action.

"Oh, man, is it happy hour yet?" Dana sighed, eyeing the sleek glass bar in the far corner of the pool area.

"Want me to order you something?" I offered.

But Dana shook her head. "Not until we're done with this segment. I have to stay sharp and focused. You know the dance number is one-third of the first half of the preliminary score."

I couldn't help but grin. If Dana was talking fractions, she was taking her job very seriously.

"Well hopefully we're almost finished with this number," I agreed. I'll admit, I'd been eyeing the bar myself.

"If Miss Arkansas can ever get her steps right," Marco snarked. "I swear that girl is as clumsy as—"

"Stop!" Dana immediately stuck her fingers in her ears and started shaking her head. "I can't hear this! I need to be objective to judge."

Marco rolled his eyes. "You can be objective, but you don't have to be blind," he mumbled to me with a grin.

"Places! We're going again in thirty seconds!" Laforge shouted from across the pool, waving his neon-clad arms about him.

Even with her fingers in her ears, there was no way Dana could miss the signal. "Duty calls," she said turning back toward the judges' table.

"All right everyone. I want you to watch Miss Montana," Laforge shouted over the click clack of heels returning to their positions. He gestured to a tall, willowy girl with alabaster skin, big blue eyes, and hair so pale blonde that it almost shone silver in the bright sunlight. She gave him a dainty smile then executed the choreographed steps around the tropical birds of paradise, lava rocks, and waterfalls with the grace of a trained ballet dancer. With moves like that, and looks like hers, it wasn't hard to imagine Miss Montana taking the title.

Not to mention it seemed as though she was the director's favorite.

"See? Is that so hard?" Laforge asked, shooting pointed looks at the other contestants. "All right, let's take it from the top. And one, two, three..."

I groaned. It was going to be a while before I got to those mai tais.

* * *

By the time all fifty-one girls had finally executed their steps to Laforge's satisfaction, the sun was starting to burn a bright orange just above the blue Pacific, my arms were starting to get the first pink tinges of sunburn, and Marco, Dana, and I were quickly making our way from the pool area back up to our rooms to change. We followed the landscaped trail around the back of the resort to the hotel's main lobby.

Only we didn't get much farther than that, as a woman in faded denim jeans, work boots, and a black T-shirt that read "Fashion Kills" stepped in front of us, blocking our way to the elevators.

"Shame on you!" she cried.

"Excuse me?" I asked, hoping she had accosted the wrong person.

"You and your so-called 'beauty' pageant." She thrust a Barbie doll, clutched in one un-manicured hand, toward Dana. (Summer Beach Barbie, if the likeness to my daughter's toy was any indication.) "This is what you're teaching young girls is the ideal woman. Fake parts, sticky tape, and spray-on tans. A completely unrealistic version of womanhood."

"Uhh…" Dana's eyes bounced side to side, looking for an escape route.

"Do you know what the anorexia rates in the United States are?" the woman asked, shaking Barbie hard enough to knock a tiny plastic shoe loose. "One in four! Thanks to these shams of competitions where one living doll tries to outdo another, girls in this country are starving themselves to death!"

"I—I'm sorry?" Dana squeaked.

Only the apology didn't seem to calm the angry protester any. She opened her mouth to argue further, lunging Barbie-first at Dana.

Luckily she didn't get far, as a guy in a Hawaiian shirt with the word "security" stitched next to the lapel suddenly appeared at her side.

"All right, you've been warned already. Take it outside and off hotel property."

"You're afraid to hear the truth?!" the woman shouted. "The truth about what's really happening to our young girls!"

"Oh, you can tell us all about it," the guard said. "From the twenty feet away from the door that's on your permit to protest peacefully." The guard sent us an apologetic smile over her head as he steered her toward a pair of glass double doors at the front of the lobby.

I let out a breath I hadn't realized I'd been holding. "That was scary."

"Seriously," Marco agreed. "I mean, did you see how thick her eyebrows were? Ever heard of tweezers, dahling?"

I shot Marco an elbow to the ribs.

"She might be right, though." I noticed that Dana's forehead had pulled into a little frown as we stepped onto the elevator.

"Right?" I asked.

"Well, I mean I know she was a little over the top. But…she has a point about the contestants creating unrealistic expectations."

This coming from the 5'7", 110 pound, strawberry-blonde movie star who had spent the better part of the last ten years in the gym.

"Everyone knows how much goes into looking like a beauty queen," I assured her. "I can't imagine anyone thinks these contestants haven't put a *lot* of work into their appearance." Though I had to admit, that anorexia statistic niggled at the back of my head when I thought about my own perfectly pudgy little toddler girl at home.

"I guess," Dana agreed, though her frown remained.

"Puh-lease," Marco said, smacking the button for the twelfth floor where our rooms were located. "You cannot tell me the world would be a better place if we all dressed in combat boots and decided to forgo eyebrow threading!"

I sent him another elbow. However I had to agree that I would not be giving up my own grooming rituals anytime soon.

We split off when we hit the twelfth floor, Dana and I heading to our rooms in the east wing, while Marco made a sharp left to his room. The pageant coordinators had secured the entire twelfth floor of the hotel for the contestants and the various staff, such as yours truly, associated with the pageant. All of the male staff were currently residing in the west wing, presumably to maintain the chaste standards of the Miss Hawaiian Paradise reputation.

I keyed my card into my door then quickly showered and did a blow dry and mousse thing with my hair before putting on a fresh round of eyeliner, mascara, and Raspberry Perfection lip gloss. While it was nearing evening, it was still a balmy eighty-one degrees outside, so I slipped into a pale blue sundress with a halter neck, pairing it with low-heeled silver sandals with a cutout detail along the straps. I still had a few minutes before meeting Marco and Dana downstairs, so I grabbed my cell and dialed home.

Three rings in I heard my husband pick up.

"Hey, babe."

I smiled at the sound of his voice. As much as I was looking forward to our girl time, I had to admit a part of me had hated the idea of an entire week away from my guy.

"Hey, yourself."

"How's paradise?" he asked. I could hear him shifting the phone as a small, toddler-pitched voice squealed for attention in the background.

"Fabulous. It's..." I looked out my window at the view of the waves gently crashing against the white, sandy shore, the setting sun creating a dusky pink wash over the entire scene. "Horrible. Ugly. You'd hate it."

My husband chuckled on the other end. "Nice try."

I grinned back. "And how was your day?"

"Piece of cake," he said. Though the squealing in the background had turned up a notch, so I wasn't sure if I 100% believed him.

My husband, Detective Jack Ramirez, was a member of the LAPD homicide division. He had a big gun, a big tattoo of a panther on his left bicep, and a thin white scar running through his eyebrow from a long-ago fight. His dark hair was just a little too long, his dark eyes could pierce a confession right out of a perp, and I'm pretty sure he could bench press me. While I was as girly a girl as you'd ever want to meet, my husband was a man's man to the core. Which is why I had just a teeny tiniest bit of trepidation about leaving him alone with the kids for a whole week. A carjacker in Inglewood, I'm sure my husband could take care of without a second thought. A pair of sticky-fingered, sippy-cup toting, terrible almost-twos? That I had my doubts about.

"Did my mom stop by to take the Livvie to Gymboree?"

"Yes," he answered.

"And your mom dropped off Max's buggy bear?"

"Yes."

"And Livvie got her ear infection drops?"

"In both ears."

"And Max has had his—"

"Why do I get the feeling that you don't trust me?" Ramirez cut me off.

I thought about lying for a second, but I knew my husband would be able to sniff that out in a heartbeat. "Because I don't."

Ramirez laughed on the other end. "We'll be fine. We've got a case of Pull-Ups, we're stocked on string cheese, and I've got nothing to do but watch Elmo for the next seven days. Trust me. I got this."

I bit my lip, holding back the rest of the interrogation I'd had planned. Hey, if he said he had this, I had to trust him, right? I mean, what was the worst that could happen?

I decided not to dwell on that thought as I told him to give my love to the kids and that I missed them all. Then I hung up, grabbed my purse, and made for the door. I was in paradise, my husband said he had everything under control at home, and those mai tais were calling my name.

* * *

The air was just starting to turn warm by the time I awoke the next morning. I rolled over on my side to look at the alarm clock. 7 AM. Normally I wasn't what you would call a morning person, but I was still on California time. I closed my eyes, pulled the blankets over my head, and tried to tell myself there was no reason to be up at dawn. Ten minutes later I decided it was useless.

I pulled myself out of bed and contemplated joining Dana downstairs in the gym. For about half a second. My feelings on going to the gym were about what they were on wearing Crocs—if a gun was to my head, I'd do it. But no way would I like it.

However as a concession to last night's drinks (not to mention the pineapple teriyaki pork kebabs and the chocolate lava cake that went with them) I decided swimming a few laps in the pool might not be a terrible idea. I slipped into my new purple one-piece with turquoise hibiscus flowers along the front and tossed on a white-cover up round my hips. In lieu of heels, I grabbed a pair of wedge sandals in a white wicker that would be moisture resistant and made my way to the elevators.

At this time of morning, the pool area was largely deserted, the lingering scents of sunscreen in the air only hinting at what the day ahead would bring. In fact it looked as though there was only one other patron at the pool this morning, lying on a chaise lounge a few feet away.

I immediately recognized the long legs and pale silver-blonde hair of Miss Montana. She wore a pair of dark sunglasses over her eyes, her head lulling to the side under a big floppy hat as if she'd dozed off.

I looked up at the sun. Even this early in the morning it was already starting to get warm, and I could easily imagine Miss Montana's pale limbs turning an unsightly pink if she snoozed too long.

I wondered if I should wake her. Being of Irish decent myself, I knew how quickly fair skin could burn in the harsh sun. That was the last thing a beauty queen wanted before going on stage. There were many flaws that one could hide with makeup, but a deep sunburn was a toughie. I paused, contemplating the cool water or the burning queen. In the end my own fair skin wouldn't let me walk away, and I made for Miss Montana.

"Excuse me?" I called quietly, not wanting to startle her awake. "Did you put on sunscreen?"

Only the girl didn't answer.

I reached out to gently shake her shoulder, but instead of rousing her, the movement served to jar her sunglasses to the ground.

And that's when I realized something was wrong.

I blinked, my pre-coffee brain slow to register what I saw as I looked into the wide, unseeing stare of Miss Montana's glazed-over eyes.

This beauty queen wasn't sleeping. Miss Montana was dead.

CHAPTER TWO

———

"Name?"

"Maddison Louise Springer."

"Place of residence?"

"Los Angeles, California."

A pair of bushy eyebrows puckered down suspiciously in the weathered face of the homicide detective before me. "You're from the mainland?"

Considering I had already told the two uniformed officers who'd arrived first on the scene that I was a patron of the hotel, I thought that was rather clear. However I nodded. "Yes, I'm here with the Miss Hawaiian Paradise pageant."

"You're one of the contestants?" he asked. I could hear the skepticism in his voice.

I pulled my cover-up a little closer around myself. Maybe I wasn't in the same model-material league as Miss Hawaiian Paradise hopefuls, but I didn't like the insinuation that it was completely outside the realm of possibility that I might be a contestant. "No," I conceded. "I'm designing the shoes for the pageant."

A hint of a grin tugged at his thin lips. He was a tall guy, slim, about sixty with skin that looked like it had seen the sun every single one of those days. His face and his arms, exposed from the elbow down beneath his tropical printed shirt, were generously freckled, and the network of lines along his face took more twists and turns than the Hana Highway. He'd introduced himself as Detective Kalanihankuhihuliha. Which, at first I thought was one of those "say that five times fast" jokes, but he was deadpan about it.

"So you knew the deceased?" he asked, nodding toward the pool, where a team of crime scene techs were busy taking pictures and bagging items. I averted my eyes. When the ME had arrived on scene and taken off Miss Montana's big, floppy hat, I'd gotten more than an eyeful of the poor girl. The hat had been covering a bloody gash at the back of her head which, if I had to guess, had contributed to her current state.

"I knew *of* her," I clarified for the detective. Having just arrived in Hawaii the day before, I had yet to personally meet all fifty-one of the contestants I'd be fitting.

"Okay, what did you know *of* her then?" he pressed.

"Only that she was Miss Montana."

"Her name was Jennifer Oliver. And from what your friend over there told me, it sounds like she was the front-runner in this competition."

I glanced nervously behind me. Marco was standing beside Dana at the edge of a line of crime scene tape spanning the perimeter of the pool area. Word of the dead beauty queen had spread through the hotel at lightening speed. For the last hour the detectives had been splitting up members of the pageant party and hotel guests into small groups to question them. Lucky me, they had saved me for last. Maybe because after finding Miss Montana's body, I'd been shaking so hard my teeth had been rattling together.

"She was doing very well," I agreed. "But none of the preliminary scores were in yet."

"I see," Detective Whatshisname (I was so not trying to pronounce it) said noncommittally, a pen hovering over a notepad. I noticed that in contrast to the electronic notebooks the homicide detectives in my husband's unit used, this guy was using an old-school Bic ballpoint and a lined paper.

"You're staying on the same floor as the deceased, correct?"

I nodded, feeling my hair bob up and down on my bare shoulders in the sunlight. "Yes, all of the women are in the east wing, and the men are in the west. Most of the contestants are doubled up in the rooms."

"Right. It looks like the deceased shared a room with Desiree DiCicco."

I shot a glance over at the group of contestants assembled on the other side of the crime scene tape. Even in the wake of such surprising and devastating news, each and every one had taken the time to apply false eyelashes and copious amounts of lipstick before appearing on the scene. "I'm not sure," I replied honestly. "I only arrived yesterday. You'd have to check with the pageant director."

"Oh, I will," the detective promised. "Did you happen to see or hear anything last night from your own hotel room, Ms. Springer?"

I shook my head. I'd fallen into bed exhausted the night before. The combination of jet lag and mai tais had lulled me into a deep sleep almost immediately.

"Well here's my card." He handed me a small square of cardboard with what looked like a coffee stain on the corner. "Let me know if you think of anything else that might be pertinent to our investigation."

I nodded, slipping the card into my beach bag. Honestly, though, I didn't think there was much more I could tell him. I hadn't known the deceased. I'd only had the misfortune of being the one to find her dead.

After being released by the detective, I quickly made my way back upstairs to my room and traded my swimsuit and cover-up for a pair of white, linen straight leg pants and a violet wrap top. I did the bare minimum mascara and lip gloss and slipped on a pair of simple pumps before making my way back downstairs. By then, everyone associated with the pageant had been gathered into the ballroom, mingling in small groups and speaking in hushed tones. I spotted the two other judges deep in conversation with Laforge. Most of the pageant contestants were standing together awkwardly, as if not sure what they should be doing now that we'd gotten off the pageant's normally airtight schedule, and various costumers, choreographers, and pageant coaches were all wearing the same tightlipped, somber expressions. As I threaded my way through the groups, most of the conversation seemed to center around the question of whether the pageant would continue or not. Most of them seemed to hope it would. I couldn't say I totally blamed them. I knew how much time and money each of the contestants had put into this pageant. I'd overheard one of them at the rehearsal the day before saying that her talent outfit alone had cost her over $2,000.00.

Tables of impromptu snacks had been set up along the ballroom walls: doughnuts, pastries, coffee, and fruit. Of course, considering the swimsuit competition was scheduled for later that afternoon, no one was actually eating snacks.

Except me. What can I say? Finding dead bodies made me seek comfort food. I grabbed a doughnut and made my way to the back of the room where I spied Marco and Dana chatting with some of the contestants. I recognized one as the unfortunately uncoordinated Miss Arkansas, her blonde extensions trailing down the back of her spaghetti-strap dress. Beside her were a mocha-skinned woman with cheekbones to die for and the brunette with the big hair I'd seen chastised at yesterday's rehearsals, Miss New Mexico.

Dana nodded a hello as I approached the group and eyed my doughnut with a frown. But she wisely didn't say anything. She'd long ago given up trying to convert me to the dietary habits of an aerobics instructor turned actress.

"Did you know her well?" I heard Marco asking the three beauty queens.

"Well, you know how it is. We all get to know each other pretty well on the pageant circuit," Miss Arkansas answered. "Especially here, living in such close quarters."

"She was your roommate, wasn't she?" Marco probed turning to the brunette with the tall hair.

I raised an eyebrow. That would make Miss New Mexico Desiree DiCicco. I took another bite of my jelly doughnut as I listened carefully to her answer.

"She was." She paused, wiping a non-existent piece of lint off her floral printed skirt. "God, it's weird to talk about her in past tense."

The other queens nodded, murmuring quietly.

"Did you see what time she left her room?" I asked. I'd overheard the crime scene techs saying that Miss Montana had to have been dead for several hours by the time I'd found her.

Desiree shook her head. "I'm a heavy sleeper."

"Maddie this is Desi, Miss New Mexico," Marco said, quickly making introductions. "I don't think you've met Whitney,

Miss Delaware, yet?" He gestured to the girl with the cheekbones. "And Maxine, Miss Arkansas," he finished.

Quickly wiping the powdered sugar from my fingers onto my thigh, I stuck out my hand toward each of the girls. "Nice to meet you all."

"I am so excited to meet you, Ms. Springer. We all just love your shoes," Miss Delaware gushed as she shook my hand. Though I wasn't sure if she was being sincere or trying to win some points with my friend the judge.

"Thanks, I'm excited to be here."

"Us too. Even under the circumstance," Miss Arkansas said. Though her comment served to bringing a somber tone back over the conversation.

"Tragic," Dana said, shaking her head. "She was so young."

"Any ideas who could've done that to her?" Marco asked the girls.

I felt my eyes narrowing as Marco's voice took on that scary Fablock Holmes quality, like he might pull out a deerstalker hat and magnifying glass at any second. I silently sent him do-not-pry vibes. The last thing the pageant directors wanted was dealing with fifty hysterical beauty queens claiming there was a murderer amongst them.

"No, of course not," Delaware said, her teeth nibbling on her pink lipstick, unnaturally long eyelashes fluttering up-and-down like spiders having seizures. "Everyone loved Jennifer."

Miss Arkansas nodded in agreement. "We all did!"

"It seemed to me she was doing very well in the competition," Marco countered.

"No scores have been turned in yet," Dana chimed in, clearly trying to play neutral. "I mean, everyone is still on even ground with all of the judges."

"But you all must've noticed how well she was doing, right?" Marco pushed.

Arkansas shrugged. "I guess. But I think we all felt she whatever points she was getting. I mean, she was just, well, kinda perfect, you know?"

I was about to open my mouth to protest that even perfect people can make enemies, when Miss New Mexico snorted beside her.

"You disagree?" Marco asked, arching one perfectly groomed eyebrow. (If I didn't know better, I'd say he'd done some extra plucking since last night.)

New Mexico shook her head. "Oh, sure, she *acted* all perfect, but she was really a perfect brownnoser."

Arkansas gasped beside her, her eyes darting to Dana. I could tell she was mentally picturing Miss New Mexico's chances at Miss Congeniality quickly slipping away.

"Why do you say that?" Marco pounced.

"She was always playing everyone's friend, but nobody can be that sweet all the time, especially not a beauty queen. I mean—let's face it—to get to the national level pageants you've got to be competitive."

"You can be sweet and competitive," Arkansas argued.

New Mexico snorted again. "Not if you want to win."

"Do you think any of the other contestants felt the same way about her?" Marco asked.

"Wait—" Delaware put up one manicured hand. "You're not suggesting that one of the other contestants would want to harm Jennifer, are you?"

Delaware was a smart cookie. If I knew "Marco Holmes," that was exactly what he was suggesting.

Arkansas's eyes went big and round, a hand going to her lips.

Marco opened his mouth to speak, but Dana rode right over him. "Of course not," she quickly said, shooting Marco a look. "I'm sure no one associated with the pageant had anything to do with the tragedy."

Marco shut his mouth with a click. I was pretty sure he was thinking the exact opposite.

"Who could've done it then?" New Mexico asked.

"Do any of you know if Jennifer had any friends on the island? Family? A boyfriend maybe?" I asked.

Arkansas looked to Delaware. Delaware chewed on her lower lip again, and I could see flakes of lipstick starting to stain her upper teeth.

"Well, we know she had a boyfriend," Arkansas finally piped up.

"Oh reeeeeeally. A boyfriend." Marco leaned in. "You know what they say about the boyfriends."

"What?" Arkansas whispered.

"They are always guilty."

I elbowed Marco in the ribs. "Ix-nay on the ilty-gay, Sherlock," I whispered.

But Arkansas had already taken the bait. "Ohmigosh, you think? That would be terrible!"

"Did you ever hear her talking about any problems with her boyfriend?" I asked. Hey, if Marco had already opened the door, I might as well step through it.

Arkansas shook her head violently from side to side, her extensions whipping behind her like a tail. "No, everything that Jennifer said about her boyfriend was always so positive. I mean almost to the point where he seemed..."

"Nauseatingly sweet," New Mexico finished, smirking.

Why did I get the impression that there was no love lost between New Mexico and the dead girl?

"So you heard her talk about a boyfriend too?" I asked.

"We all did," Delaware finally chimed in. "But everyone talks about their boyfriends here, you know? I mean we all miss our guys back home."

"Did she say anything specific about him?"

"She was always talking about the stupid ring he gave her!" New Mexico rolled her eyes.

Arkansas elbowed her in the side, her eyes again cutting to Dana.

"Do tell?" Marco prompted.

"She had this ridiculous 'promise ring.'" New Mexico made air quotes with her fingers. "She went on and on about how it was the perfect emerald color to match her sweetheart's emerald eyes. Gag. I mean—really—what are we in high school? Promise of what? Seriously, this guy couldn't be all that if he couldn't commit already and get her an engagement ring. A promise ring is just a cheap piece of jewelry that says, 'I like you but not enough to buy you a *real* ring.' You know what I mean?"

Marco snickered. "Oh, I know what you mean."

Dana frowned, looking down at her own multi-carat engagement ring on her left finger, courtesy of her movie star boyfriend, Ricky Montgomery. While the sparkling jewelry had been gracing her finger for several months now, Ricky had yet to set *the date*. A fact I knew was beginning to bother Dana.

"If they were really that serious, I can't imagine the boyfriend having anything to do with her death," I quickly changed the subject.

"Well, I don't know if they *were* that serious," Delaware argued.

"Why would you say that?" I asked. I had a feeling that Delaware was holding something back

"Well," she hedged, her eyes cutting to the doorway where a uniformed police officer was posted. She paused, doing some more lip chewing. "Look, please don't tell anyone I said this, but I saw her leaving her room last night."

"What time was this?" I pounced.

Delaware nibbled more lipstick. "Around twelve thirty. Maybe one."

"Impossible," Dana cut in. "She couldn't have gone out after midnight. Miss Hawaiian Paradise Pageant rules clearly state that no contestants are to leave their rooms after the midnight curfew."

Delaware shot her a look like she'd got her hand caught in the cookie jar. "I—I couldn't sleep, so I went out to get some water from the vending machines at the end of the hall. And I swear I saw Jennifer leaving."

"To meet a man?" Marco asked.

She shrugged. "Why else would she be sneaking around in the middle of the night?"

She had a point. "Did you see which way she went when she left her room?" I pressed, thinking of the men's rooms down the west wing of the hotel.

Delaware nodded. "She got into the elevator."

Dana pursed her lips into a thin line. I could tell that had Miss Montana not already been dead, she'd be losing major points right now.

"So you saw her leaving her room last night about twelve thirty, heading down toward the pool."

But Delaware's eyes cut to mine, her head shaking back and forth. "No, not the pool. When I got back from the vending machines, I looked out the window and saw her heading toward the beach."

I heard my own confusion echoed in Marco's voice as he asked, "Who was she meeting on the beach?"

Delaware did some more head shaking. "I don't know. But whoever it was, I'm guessing it didn't end well."

I had to agree with that one.

I was about to ask New Mexico if her roommate had made any previous middle-of-the-night excursions, when Laforge's voice piped up from the ballroom's double doors.

"May I have your attention please?" he asked, addressing the room at large. Dozens of coiffed heads turned his way. "The police have finished processing the scene and have concluded their interviews for the day. The other directors and I will be convening with the local authorities shortly to discuss the future of the pageant."

Murmurs of speculation ran through the crowd.

"We hope to be able to have more information available for you soon, however in the meantime I would suggest that you enjoy the hotel's many facilities."

I raised one eyebrow in his direction, wondering if that last line had been in their sponsorship contract. In case of unexpected murder, please plug the Tropical Tryst Buffet and the Hula Hibiscus Day Spa.

The three beauty queens excused themselves from our group, whispering together as the crowd in the ballroom began to disperse.

"So what do we think of the Midnight Mystery Man angle?" Marco asked, leading our trio toward the lobby.

I shrugged. "It could be a bit of a leap to say she was meeting a man, but I think there's a good chance that whoever lured her out of her room last night might have had something to do with her death." I knew it was stating the obvious, but I also knew that unless I stated it, Marco was going to keep Sherlocking-it.

"That is, if Miss Delaware was correct in identifying Miss Montana as the woman she saw heading toward the beach,"

Dana jumped in. "I mean, it was the middle of the night. Delaware might have been mistaken."

"Well, let's go find out!" Marco offered.

I raised an eyebrow at him. "As in…"

"There is a fabu little tiki bar down on the beach. Maybe Montana was heading there? Maybe someone saw her meet up there with her Midnight Mystery Man."

"You're going to keep calling him that, aren't you?" Dana asked.

Marco paused to contemplate for a moment. "Her Randy Rendezvous?"

Dana and I did a simultaneous eye roll.

"Come on," Marco whined. "Surely someone saw her. Right? It's at least worth interrogating the bartender?"

While I was hesitant to get involved, I had to admit that after the morning's events, a mimosa didn't sound altogether terrible.

"Okay, but we're just *asking* a few *questions*. Not *interrogating*," I said, pointedly looking at Marco.

He batted his eyelashes at me. "Whatever you say, Watson."

* * *

The Royal Waikiki Resort was conveniently located directly ocean side. While all beaches in Hawaii were public property, the Royal Waikiki had several of their resort amenities located just steps away from the Pacific. We walked from the pool area down a small stone pathway that lead to both an outdoor dining area, where the nightly luaus were held, and the "Lost Aloha Shack" tiki bar. The actual bar itself was constructed of native looking bamboo and palm fronds, giving it a classic, rustic feel. To the right of the bar was a stage where I could easily see Don Ho impersonators with their ukuleles or fire dancers lighting up the evening. Currently, however, the stage was empty, and there were a scant, few patrons.

While the look of the Lost Aloha was island-rustic, as we took up stools at the polished wood bar, I could tell that the construction was on par with the rest of the swanky resort. In front of us top-shelf liquor lined the back wall, along with trays of glasses sporting little pink umbrellas and embellishments ranging from classic martini olives and onions, to festive pineapple slices and mango kebabs.

A guy with long, shaggy blond hair and at least a day's worth of stubble on his chin walked up. While he clearly wasn't of Hawaiian descent, from his deep tan I put him as a local who spent a fair amount of time in the warm Hawaiian sun.

"'Sup. What can I get for you?" he asked in an accent that was pure California surfer.

"Mimosa, please, Dirk," I said, reading the nametag pinned to his floral printed Hawaiian shirt. I didn't usually drink before noon, but after having found a dead body, I thought I could justify the alcohol content. Plus, mimosas were *almost* all orange juice anyway. That was healthy, right?

Marco ordered the same, though Dana opted for a mango pineapple smoothie instead, saying she was still "on call" as a judge.

Dirk nodded. "You got it, chicas," he said, then turned to grab three glasses from behind the bar.

"Say, were you by any chance working here last night?" Marco asked, as the guy tossed half a banana and some mango slices into a blender.

I steeled myself, hoping that Marco stuck to "questioning" and not "interrogating."

Dirk nodded, shouting over the sound of his mixer. "Yeah, I pretty much run this place. The only times I'm not here are Wednesdays and Fridays. I teach surfing those days." He gave us a lopsided smile as he set three full glasses on the bar.

I took a grateful sip of mine, enjoying the bubbly sensation on my tongue from the refreshing mixture.

"Hey, if any of you feel like catching some waves on your vacay, give me a ping." Dirk slid his card across the smooth top of the bar toward me. It had a picture of Dirk giving a hang loose sign with his pinky and thumb, the words "surfing with Dirk" below it next to a cell number and Twitter handle.

"Thanks," I said slipping the card into my purse, "but we're actually here with the pageant. So I'm not sure how much downtime we'll have."

Dirk's face suddenly transformed from jovial to solemn. "Oh, man, I heard about that pageant girl. What a bummer, right?"

"Total bummer," Dana agreed, taking a sip of her smoothie.

"One of her friends said she saw the girl heading this way last night...?" Marco fished.

Dirk nodded. "Yeah, that police dude asked me the same question earlier. She was the blonde chick, right? Super long hair?"

I nodded. "Jennifer Oliver. She was competing as Miss Montana in the pageant."

"So she *was* here having a drink last night?" Dana asked. I could see disappointment marring her features, tiny lines she'd yet to give over to Botox forming along her forehead.

But Dirk shook his head, his blond hair whipping back and forth. "No way, man, not drinking here. I know those girls got curfew going on. I see any them down here, and I'm supposed to report right back to Laforge. He left me a good tip for that—you know what I mean?" Dirk grinned.

"But you did see her?" I asked.

He nodded. "Oh, yeah. Like I told Cop Dude, I saw her, but she wasn't drinking here. She was down the beach. There." Dirk pointed to a spot about a hundred yards down the white sand. Currently it was occupied by a pair of little boys making sand castles with plastic buckets.

"What was she doing?" I asked

Dirk shrugged. "I didn't ask. I was slammed with the duck people."

I gave him a blank look, wondering just how reliable of a witness the bartender was. "Duck people?"

"The insurance group," Dirk clarified. "You know, they've got that duck in all of their ads? He's, like, totally funny, dude. Anyway, their annual convention is sharing the hotel with you pageant peeps this week."

Ah. I had noticed a large number of men in suits roaming the lobby of the hotel.

"Anyway," Dirk went on, "like I told the cops, those duck dudes can totally drink. I was slammed last night. Besides,

I've learned to keep my questions to myself. Most people checking in here go with the what-happens-on-the-island-stays-on-the-island motto, you know what I mean, chicas?"

Unfortunately what had happened on the island to Miss Montana was definitely *not* staying on the island.

"Was she with anyone?" Marco asked. "When you saw her on the beach?"

Good question. I sipped at my mimosa again as I watched him answer.

Dirk's head bobbed up and down, his bangs jumping on his forehead. "Yup, totally."

"Who?" Marco and I asked in unison.

Dirk shrugged. "Search me, man. There's zero light down there after sunset. All I could see from here were two figures."

"But you're certain that one of them was Miss Montana?" I asked.

"Oh, yeah. I saw her walking from the resort. I got a good look as she passed by, because we had fire dancers on the stage. Totally lit up the bar, you know?"

"But you didn't see her companion walk by?"

He shook his head. "Sorry, like I said I was slammed. It was just dumb luck I happened to look up when the dead girl was walking by."

"Could you tell if the figure you saw was a man or woman?" Dana asked, clearly still wanting to think the best of her contestant.

Dirk paused for a moment, sucking in his cheeks and staring off into space. "No, sorry. It was too dark to see. I kinda got the impression it was a dude, just by how close together they were standing, but I wouldn't, like, swear on my life—you know?"

A patron at the end of the bar waved a hand, signaling for Dirk.

"Hey, give a holler if you need anything else…" He trailed off, leaving to take the other order.

"So Jennifer *was* meeting a guy," Marco said slurping noisily through his straw, a note of I-told-you-so heavily lacing his voice.

"We don't know that for sure," Dana hedged. "You heard Dirk. He said he couldn't see who her companion was."

"Okay, but why on earth would she be sneaking around if she was meeting a woman? I mean, if it was anyone associated with the pageant, why not just meet them in the hallway of the hotel? It makes no sense to sneak out to the beach."

Dana bit her lip. "Okay, fine. It was *probably* a man."

"Ohemgee, we have a Murderous Midnight Mystery Man on our hands," Marco said, a gleam of what I could only describe as glee in his eyes.

Before I could rein in his alliterative enthusiasm, I heard my cell trilling out my Madonna "Vogue" ringtone from my purse. I pulled it out and took a look at the screen.

Uh-oh. I recognized that number.

Ramirez.

CHAPTER THREE

———

Is it wrong that I had a moment of hesitation before I actually stabbed the *on* button? Not, mind you, that I normally disliked speaking with my husband. But considering I'd recently given statements to the local police, I had a feeling that this call might not be full of hearts and rainbows.

"Hi, honey," I said into the phone.

"What's going on there?" came his clipped response.

I gulped. No, "Hi, babe." No, "How are you doing?" No, "Gee, I miss you." I knew what this meant. My husband was in cop mode.

"Just hanging out with the girls, having a couple of drinks." Notice I was being completely truthful.

I heard a sigh and what was possibly a grunt on the other end of my connection.

"According to the *L.A. Informer's* website, 'Beauty Queen murdered in Paradise, Los Angeles fashion designer Maddison Springer questioned,'" my husband read off.

"They mentioned I was a fashion designer?" I asked. Hey, all publicity was good publicity, right?

However, clearly my husband did not agree with me, as that grunt was loud and clear this time. "Maddie..."

"Okay, but look, it totally wasn't my fault. I just *happened* to get up a little bit early, and I *happened* to go down to the pool, and I *happened* to find the dead body of a beauty queen, okay?"

Silence greeted me on the other end. I almost preferred the grunting.

"Honey?" I asked.

"Why is it I was hoping you would just *happen* to have an uneventful vacation with your friends and *happen* to not do anything more exciting than get a sunburn on the beach?" My husband's voice dripped with sarcasm.

In Ramirez's defense I did have sort of a habit of finding dead people. I was starting to think of it as my own special talent. Some people could pick winning lottery numbers—other people had an uncanny knack for guessing the weather. It was never actually my fault when I encountered a dead person. I mean, I'd never caused anyone to be dead. I just had a bad habit of finding them that way.

In fact, that was the way I had met my husband, while he was investigating a homicide case. So, if you looked at it that way, my special talent wasn't *all* bad.

Though the way my husband was back to grunting *and* sighing on the other end, that was kind of debatable right now.

"I am not involved," I said very pointedly. "Yes, the police questioned me. But that's all. They just wanted to know what I'd seen."

The memory of the scene must have sneaked into my voice, as it cracked on the last word.

"Are you okay?" Ramirez said quickly.

See why I loved the big lug? In two seconds flat he could go from Bad Cop to Concerned Husband.

Honestly, the quick switch took me off guard, and I felt unshed tears back up behind my eyes. Just because this wasn't the first dead body I'd ever seen didn't mean I ever got used to it. Maybe someday I'd figure out how to do that detached thing like a medical examiner might, but today was clearly not that day.

"Yeah, I'm okay," I lied, sniffing back those tears. I turned my head away from my friends, heading out of the Lost Aloha Shack and back toward the hotel. Even with the tears mostly unshed, I was going to need to do a mascara reapply before I was fit for human eyes again.

"Did you know her?" Ramirez asked, his tone softening.

I shook my head, even though I knew he couldn't see me, as the tropical breeze blew my hair side to side. "Not really. But I'd seen her practicing. Everyone seemed to agree she was the front-runner of the contest."

"You think that's why someone killed her?" my husband asked, always the homicide detective.

"I don't know. It's possible, I suppose." I didn't mention that was one of Marco's current theories. The last thing that would reassure my husband as to my noninvolvement was to mention Fablock Holmes.

"Well, I'm sure that the local detective in charge of the case will figure it out."

I could read between the lines as well as any Rhodes Scholar. Ramirez didn't want me to get involved. Which was fine. I had no intention of getting involved. Okay, yes, I asked a few questions with Marco, but I was sure that Detective Whatshisname was perfectly capable of figuring out who had killed Jennifer. And I wasn't involved. I was just asking a couple of questions.

Questions any person who might've *happened* to find a dead body would want answered.

"Maddie..." I heard Ramirez's voice through the phone. "Please tell me you will leave the investigating to the professionals."

"Fine," I agreed. I made my way up the front pathway to the lobby doors of the Royal Waikiki. Just outside, this time well within the twenty-foot radius security had given her, the same protester from yesterday was flashing a sign that read: *Fashion Is Death*. On any other day, I might think that was a little extreme—I mean, I'd *suffered* for fashion, and sometimes, if the heels where high enough, fashion did *hurt*—but I'd never seen it kill anyone.

Until today.

"So, I have your promise that you will not get involved, right?" Ramirez pressed on the other end of the line.

I rolled my eyes. "I'm not getting involved, *warden*."

"I'm serious."

"Yeah, I got that."

"Maddie, repeat after me: I, Maddison Louise Springer—"

I rolled my eyes so far I could see my blonde roots "You're joking."

"Do I need to get on a plane and fly out there?" Ramirez asked

While he was being ridiculous, I could clearly picture his face right now. Black eyebrows drawn down, lips pinched together, that vein bulging in the side of his neck. In a way it was touching that he cared so much about my well-being. And I knew it was probably killing him that he was an entire ocean away, and there was nothing he could do to personally ensure my safety.

So I let the Neanderthal act go and played along.

For now.

"Fine. I, Maddison Louise Springer..."

"Promise not to get involved."

"Promise not to get involved," I repeated. The fact that I was crossing my fingers behind my back was something Ramirez did not need to know.

Ramirez let out a sigh that could only be interpreted via cell phone as relief. "Good. So, where are you off to now?" he asked

"Well, everything having to do with the pageant has been put on hold," I said glancing around the lobby and spying at least two plainclothes officers still milling around, talking to employees. "Honestly I'm not sure if it's even going to go on as scheduled or not. We're sort of in limbo, waiting to see what the police tell us."

"Well, just remember, while you're in limbo—"

"I know, I know. I won't get involved. Geez, I'm stubborn, not deaf."

I could feel Ramirez's grin through the phone. "All right, kid, just stay out of trouble, okay? Go relax. Get a pedicure or something, huh?"

I was just about to protest that a pedicure seemed a little frivolous in light of the murder investigation going on around us, when I spied a familiar face crossing the lobby. It was Ruth Marie Masters, judge number two, and the former Miss Hawaiian Paradise 1962. Not that it was odd she should be crossing the lobby, but what piqued my interest was the fact she was going into the Hula Hibiscus Day Spa, just off the lobby.

"You know, a pedicure doesn't seem like a terrible idea," I slowly agreed.

There was more relieved sighing on the other end, and I almost felt the teeny tiniest bit guilty.

Almost.

"Kiss the babies for me, and I'll give you a call later tonight, okay?" I said, detouring toward the spa.

"Will do. Miss you, babe. Be careful."

"Always," I promised before hanging up.

Then I made a beeline for the Hula Hibiscus.

* * *

A woman with long black hair and almond eyes greeted me at the front desk and informed me that, luckily, they did have an opening for a pedicure right then. She led me to a large, luxurious chair seated right next to Ruth Marie Masters, who was just sticking a pair of pale, boney bare feet into a bubble bath of hot soapy water.

After choosing a nail polish from their rotating display, I took my pumps off and slipped my own toes into what, if my nostrils did not deceive me, was a piña colada scented bath.

"You're with the pageant too, aren'tcha?" Ruth Marie asked, cocking her head my way.

I nodded. "Maddie Springer," I offered. "I'm doing the footwear for the contestants."

Ruth Marie nodded in recognition. "Right, right, right. Laforge said he got some big-name designer from L.A. this year to do the shoes."

I couldn't help a little surge of pride at anyone applying the term "big-name" to me.

"Laforge said he picked out some real fancy-schmancy stuff." Ruth Marie paused, glancing down at my simple pumps.

"I didn't design those," I quickly told her. While they were nice, even I had to admit they were totally off the rack and not exactly "big-name fancy-schmancy."

"Sure," Ruth Marie continued. "Anyway, who knows if we'll even have a pageant this year now."

That was just the sort of opening I was looking for to *not* get involved.

"Tragic business," I said, echoing Dana's sentiments from earlier.

Ruth Marie shook her head. "Young girls these days get themselves into all kinds of trouble. Knocked up, naked pictures on Twitter, getting themselves murdered."

I bit my lip. I wasn't entirely sure that it was Miss Montana's fault she'd been killed.

But Ruth Marie continued on, undeterred, as a slim woman in a floral printed dress sat down and started working on her bunions.

"Back when I was on the circuit, mind you, none of that sort of thing was tolerated. We didn't have any young men coming up to see us at all hours of the night."

"There have been men coming up to see the contestants?" I asked, jumping on the phrase.

"Well, now, I can't say I actually *seen* any men with my own eyes," she conceded. "But I heard them girls talking. Boys this, boys that. Think they were a bunch of cats in heat the way they get on."

I covered an unladylike snort with my hand. While warm and fuzzy was the last way anyone would describe Ruth Marie, I had to say there was something refreshing about her bluntness.

"I don't suppose you heard anything in particular from Miss Montana?"

Ruth Marie shrugged her bony shoulders again. "They're all the same. All these girls, year in, year out, all they think about is boys."

"How many years have you been judging the pageant?"

"Seven," she told me without skipping a beat. "Before me they had Thelma Bishop on the judging panel. She was Miss Hawaiian Paradise 1959, you know?"

I didn't, but I nodded for her to continue anyway.

"Well, Thelma had a stroke a while back. After that she couldn't keep one side of her face from drooping down like eighty-year-old bazongas without a brassiere. Didn't play well on television, I'll tell you that much."

"I can imagine," I replied, trying to erase that unpleasant picture from my mind. "What about the other judges?"

"Well, Dana Dashel's brand-new this year, but you knew that."

I nodded. "And the third judge?"

"Jay Jeffries. He's been with the pageant, oh, what, three or four years now? He started the year that his daytime soap started filming out here on the island. You've heard of it, right? *Island of Dreams.*" She rolled her eyes. "Schmaltzy stuff, I tell ya."

I had to admit that with young twins and a budding career as a fashion designer, I had little time for daytime television. I'd heard of *Island of Dreams,* but I'd never actually seen it myself.

"What about Miss Montana?" I asked as a woman in a matching floral dress sat down in front of me and motioned for me to remove my right foot from the tub for her inspection. "Have you seen her before, or was she new to this pageant?"

"Oh, we get a new crop of girls every year," Ruth Marie told me. "But I never get personally involved with any of them. I just sit back, watch them strut across the stage, and write down my scores."

"I take it Miss Montana's scores were likely to be good?" I pushed

Ruth Marie snorted, the sound something between a smokers' hack and a hungry piglet. "Was there any doubt? Look, I know we're supposed to reserve judgment until the end, yada, yada, yada. But, honey, I've been doing this long enough to know who the winners are and *aren't* in the first five minutes. I grew up in pageants, been doing them since I was this big," she said, hovering her hand down near the top of her pedi tub. "I can spot a winner a mile away. It's in the grace, in the poise, the way they carry themselves. Mark my words, if she hadn't gone to the great crowning ceremony in the sky, Miss Montana would've wiped the floor with these other clowns."

That had basically been my assessment, even though the entirety of my beauty pageant experience came from watching TLC.

"It's a shame she didn't make it to the crowning," I commented, almost more to myself than my companion.

Ruth Marie did the snort-slash-hack again. "Maybe a shame for her, but it's damned good luck for someone else, right?"

I leaned in close. "You think one of the other contestants killed Miss Montana just to get ahead in the competition?"

"Oh, honey, you're new to pageants aren't you?" Her drawn-in eyebrows puckered in sympathy.

"Yes," I said honestly.

"A girl would eat her own young to win a crown like Miss Hawaiian Paradise. You don't even want to know what I had to do to become Miss 1962."

The way those drawn-in eyebrows waggled up and down, she was right. I really didn't.

"Forgive me, but I don't get it. It's just a crown."

"Just a crown! Ha!" Ruth Marie cackled so loudly that she made the woman diligently working on her calloused feet jump. "You're cute, doll."

I opened my mouth to protest, but Ruth Marie ran right over me, leaning in close enough that I could smell the Mahi tuna brunch on her breath.

"Look, all the hoopla may be about a shiny crown, but the reality is whoever gets crowned Miss Hawaiian Paradise is gonna be sittin' pretty. For starters, she's the spokeswoman for the Hawaiian Paradise sunscreen line. And let me tell you, honey, even back in my day that job came with a pile of cash. Then there's the paid speaking engagements, the charity endorsements, the parade and award show appearances." She ticked off items on her fingers, so close to my face that I could tell she was sorely in need of a mani to go with her pedi. "Heck, look at me!" She threw her arms wide. "Fifty years later, I'm still milking it for cash." She finished with a wink before sitting back in her seat.

I had to admit maybe it wasn't such a far-fetched idea that one of the other contestants could have gone so far as to kill off the competition. Maybe Dirk had been mistaken, and the figure he'd seen on the beach with Jennifer wasn't a man she'd been meeting for some clandestine interlude, but one of the other contestants who'd lured Jennifer to her death? Which begged the question…who was the competition's front-runner now?

* * *

I left the spa with Papaya Pleasure toes (which were a color somewhere between pink and orange that was just bright enough to feel tropical) and made my way toward the elevators, fully intending to see if Dana was in her room and to strong-arm her into telling me just who might be taking Jennifer's place as top contender.

Only as I exited the spa and crossed the lobby, a commotion at the check-in desk caught my attention.

A tall man with dark blond hair and a pair of nylon suitcases at his feet was waving his hands at the chubby guy behind the desk.

"I don't care how full you are—this is an emergency, and I want a room!" he shouted loudly enough that his voice carried across the lobby, causing multiple heads to turn his direction.

The clerk behind the desk glanced nervously from side to side, as if looking for backup. "I'm sorry, sir," I heard him say. "We are fully booked. We're hosting an insurance conference and the Miss Hawaiian Paradise Pageant this week—"

"I know all about the damned pageant," the man shouted. "That's why I'm here."

I saw the shoulders of the guy behind the counter visibly relax. "Oh, well, in that case, we have a block of rooms reserved specifically for those associated with the pageant. If you could just give me your name and your affiliation—"

"I am *not* affiliated with that sham of a competition," the man cut him off again.

"Oh, sorry I thought you said you were—"

"I'm here to sue the pants off the Hawaiian Paradise Corporation, this hotel, and anyone else responsible for my girlfriend's death."

I paused. Could this be the boyfriend Jennifer had been so smitten with? I couldn't help myself. Instead of going toward the elevators I quietly rounded the registration desk, trying my best to get a good look at the man.

The man behind the desk visibly paled at the boyfriend's words, his round cheeks going a shade pinker as he stuttered, trying to come up with an appropriately sympathetic response.

"Um, I'm sure that, er, in light of the current situation, we can find something to accommodate you. Name?" The poor man furiously typed on his keyboard, presumably looking for an open room.

"Xander Newport. And make it fast, would you? It's been a long flight, and I'm tired," the guy said, narrowing his eyes at the clerk.

Eyes that had me sucking in a breath.

While this may very well have been Jennifer's boyfriend, he definitely was *not* the guy who had given Jennifer her so coveted, emerald promise ring that matched her beloved's eyes.

For one thing, this boyfriend's eyes were brown.

CHAPTER FOUR

———

Unfortunately, Dana was not in her room once I got upstairs. I texted her, and she replied that she was going over her preliminary score sheets. In seclusion. I had a feeling my friend was taking her judging duties much more seriously than anyone else involved with this pageant.

She promised, however, to meet up with me for dinner at the luau. I tried texting Marco, who responded that he was catching some rays by the pool, which had been cleared for public use by the crime scene techs. He invited me to join him, but I responded that the pool was the last place he would find me on this vacation. I shuddered just thinking about it.

Instead, I dodged the myriad of long legged, giggling girls going back and forth between each other's rooms in the east wing, swapping different colors of nail polish, lipstick, and varying scented lotions, and made for my own room. I booted up my laptop, taking the downtime as an opportunity to go back over the photos of the contestants' outfits that the pageant director had emailed me when I'd originally been booked to do the show. While I had painstakingly picked out just the right pair of heels to go with each contestant's outfit, in each portion of the program, I had shipped several alternate pairs, just in case. You never knew when a contestant might not be used to walking in five- inch stilettos and might need a simple pair of kitten heels instead. Assuming the pageant continued, this was a huge opportunity for my brand. Having my designs on sale in exclusive boutiques throughout the trendy L.A. and Orange County shopping districts was coveted real estate that held a certain amount of prestige. However, I knew that the real money would only start flowing once my designs were picked up by a national chain.

I spent the next few hours double checking each pair of shoes I had chosen to go with each contestant's eveningwear, swimsuits, and talent outfit. By the time I was satisfied, I could already hear the strains of the luau music from down the beach filtering in through my windows. I closed my laptop and took a quick shower, trying to re-energize enough to get my schedule turned around to Hawaiian time.

I did a quick blow dry and mousse thing with my hair, not totally hating the extra volume that the humidity gave me. Then I slipped into an off-the-shoulder, white dress with a fit-and-flare skirt and a pair of silver slingbacks with purple accents that offset my peachy pedicure.

By the time I caught up with Dana and Marco, they were already seated at a table near the edge of the outdoor dining area, sipping happy hour cocktails.

As I ordered one myself from Surfer Dirk, I quickly filled them in on my afternoon, chatting with Ruth Marie and running into the boyfriend at the registration desk.

"Wait—" Marco said, holding up a hand. "So you're saying that Miss Montana's boyfriend isn't really her boyfriend?" His eyes blinked at me beneath his heavy eyeliner. A smoky gray this evening, to complement his all-black ensemble. Skintight black leather pants, a black tank top in a formfitting silk, and black high-heeled boots that added at least four inches to his slight frame. He looked like Dominatrix Barbie, minus the flowing locks.

"What I'm saying is that he may have *thought* he was her boyfriend, but Jennifer was seeing someone on the side."

"Someone serious if he gave her a promise ring," Dana added, twirling her own ring again.

I nodded. If what the other queens had told us was true, and Miss Montana really was going on and on about her emerald ring matching the eyes of the man who had given it to her, that man definitely was *not* her hometown boyfriend.

"Maybe he's wearing contacts?" Marco offered, taking a sip of his piña colada through a bright pink colored straw.

I shrugged. "It's possible I suppose, but how many people do you know who cover up bright emerald eyes with brown contacts?"

"Good point," Marco conceded.

"So who do we think Miss Montana was seeing?" Dana asked.

I shrugged. "I suppose it could be anybody," I said as my eyes wandered around the tables.

"My money is on someone connected with the pageant," Marco decided. "You know how much time these girls put into getting ready for these things? I would be highly surprised if she had time for anything else."

Dana nodded beside me. "I hate to say it, but it makes sense. I'm surprised she had time for one boyfriend, let alone two." She paused. "Ohmigod, you don't think that her secret lover is the one who killed her, do you?"

"Maybe," I mused. "What if the secret lover was worried that Montana was talking about him just a little too much to the other beauty queens? What if he was worried he wouldn't be so secret anymore?"

"Or," Marco piped up stabbing a slice of pineapple in the air for emphasis, "what if the boyfriend found out about the secret lover, and *he* killed Miss Montana in a jealous rage."

"But he only just arrived on the island," I pointed out.

Marco pursed his lips together. "Do we know that for sure?"

"Well, no," I admitted. "But I still think our undercover-lover is still more likely."

The three of us looked over the assembled crowd. While the dining area was dominated by the insurance conventioneers, all dressed in slacks and matching polo shirts with their faithful duck mascot embroidered on the back, I recognized a fair number of people associated with the Miss Hawaiian Paradise Pageant as well. A few coaches seemed to be occupying a large table near the stage, where a group of women in short skirts wearing flower leis were moving their hips like rhythmic ocean waves. Some of the behind-the-scenes production crew were occupying the bar. A group of beauty queens danced near the stage to the Hawaiian music, their movements a cross between something you'd see in a Vegas club and an attempt at a hula of sorts. They were giggling and laughing despite the events that had gone on earlier that day, clearly enjoying their last couple of hours before curfew. I spied Ruth Marie bending Laforge's ear about something at a table in the center of the room by a large potted palm tree and the pageant's third judge, Jay Jeffries, sipping a martini loaded with onions and olives by himself at a table that seemed to have the perfect view of the beauty queens dancing near the stage.

"One signature Babbling Mermaid," Dirk said, setting a glass on the table in front me full of something fruity topped with a pineapple slice.

"Thanks," I told him taking a grateful sip. Mmm. Tasty.

"Hey, Dirk," Marco said. "Did Miss Montana attend any of the luaus?"

Dirk nodded. "Sure. A lot of the girls started arriving last week, wanting to be certain they'd shaken all the jet lag off and do a little sightseeing before the competition started. I recognized her as one of the first ones to arrive. She and her friends have been in here every night." He nodded to the girls dancing next to the stage. "Of course, I make sure to shoo them out before curfew." He gave me a wink.

"You wouldn't happen to have noticed if she had any *particular* friends?" Marco asked coyly.

Dirk scrunched up his forehead. "Particular?"

"Male," I interpreted. "We're wondering if you noticed any men paying extra attention to her."

"Not that I can think of. Why?" he asked

"Just curious," I quickly covered. "We heard she might have had a close friend here."

My explanation seemed good enough for Bartender Dude, as he shrugged. "Yeah, sorry. Wish I could help you."

I felt my shoulders droop. Then again if Jennifer had been having a secret affair with someone, chances were she would be trying to keep it *secret*.

"But," Dirk added, "you know if I had to put my money on someone..."

"Yes?" Marco and I leaned in closer as one.

"I'd bet on that dude, right there." Dirk narrowed his eyes and pointed toward the lone drinker at the table near the ladies.

"Jay Jeffries?" I asked.

Dirk nodded. "That dude has totally been hitting on every woman who's come through here in the last week. Thinks he some sort of Don Juan 'cause he's on that soap."

"But he's one of the judges!" Dana protested. "It's expressly forbidden for judges to have private personal contact with any of the contestants before the pageant is over."

Dirk shrugged. "I don't know about all that, but I know this dude has had a lot of contact with those beauty pageant chicas. In fact, there were even rumors that he slept with one of the contestants a couple of years ago."

Dana gasped beside me. "It can't be true. The pageant never would've asked him back."

Dirk just shrugged again. "Hey, all I know is what I heard."

As Dirk walked away, I turned to take a closer look at Jeffries. He'd been joined at his table by a tall blonde, who I recognized as Miss California. We were too far away to hear what they were saying over the ukulele music, but the body language was very telling. Jeffries: leaning both elbows on the table toward her, talking rapidly, eyebrows moving up and down in a suggestive pose. Miss California: leaning back, eyes darting for an escape, arms crossed over her chest in a protective pose. Clearly Jeffries was trying to make a move, and clearly the blonde was trying to make a move *away* from Jeffries.

"Check out the eyes," Marco said, his gaze honed in on the same scene as mine. "Green."

"Lots of people have green eyes," I pointed out.

"I just can't believe a judge would be involved with the contestant," Dana said, still shaking her head. "Talk about impropriety."

I watched as the blonde pulled out her cell, pointed to it, then got up and walked away, the look of relief unmistakable on her face. I had to giggle a little to myself. Back in my single days, there were times when I too had used the my-friend-just-sent-an-emergency-text excuse to get away from a smarmy guy in a bar.

Only today I wanted an excuse to talk to the smarmy guy.

"I'm going to talk to him," I said.

Marco's face lit up like Christmas. "What are you going to say?"

I shrugged. "I guess I'll just introduce myself. We haven't officially met yet."

"Just be sure not to mention anything about our theory of Miss Montana having been the front-runner," Dana cautioned. "He still needs to be an impartial judge."

I held up two fingers. "Scouts honor."

I grabbed my Babbling Mermaid drink and threaded my way through the tables to Jeffries' lonely one. As I approached, he gave me a full head-to-toe once-over. I immediately felt like I needed a shower.

"Jay Jeffries, right?" I asked, putting on my biggest, brightest smile.

He nodded, his eyes resting on the fruits of my push-up bra.

"That's right. It's Dr. Calvin Drake in the flesh."

I blinked at him. "Huh?"

Jeffries cleared his throat, a small flash of insecurity darting through his eyes. "From *Island of Dreams*. You are a fan, right?"

"Oh, yeah. Right."

The insecurity vanished, and Jeffries' smile widened again as he leaned back in his chair to get a better look at me. Or at least my breasts. "I know, it's a little intimidating meeting a famous television star in person. But I assure you, I'm just like any other guy."

"That's great," I said, trying really hard to keep that bright smile on my face. "I'm Maddie Springer." I held out a hand.

He grabbed it and shook, hanging onto it just a little too long for my comfort. Was it possible to get hand cooties?

"Care to join me, Maddie Springer?" he offered. I noticed as he gestured to the seat beside him that his balance in his chair was wobbly. Along with his bloodshot eyes, it was a clue that the drink in front of him was not his first of the evening.

Awesome. Liquor loosened lips faster than a jar of Vaseline on a beauty queen.

"Thanks," I said settling into the chair beside him.

"You know something, young lady, you are in luck today," he said, his voice dripping with innuendos I couldn't—or didn't want to!—put my finger on.

"I am?"

"Yes you are, honey," he said, still holding onto my hand. (Ick!)

"Because I just happen to have one autographed picture left tonight, and I'm going to personalize it just for you." He gave me a wink and finally let go of my hand, reaching into a small black case at his feet. He emerged with a 4 x 6 postcard sporting a glossy photo of himself as his alter ego soap star doctor. Though, if I had to guess, the picture was at least a few years old and had undergone extensive Photoshopping. Jeffries pulled a pen from his case as well and began scrolling something across the bottom of the picture.

"Wow, that's very generous of you," I said trying to sound appropriately enthused.

Jeffries finished, slid the autograph across to me, and gave me another wink.

I looked down. He had written his name, cell number, and room number at the resort, followed by the phrase *Let's play doctor*. Ew.

I was still trying to get my gag reflex under control as Jeffries addressed me over the rim of his olive and onion martini. "So what brings you to the paradise of the islands, Miss Springer?"

"Actually, I'm with the pageant," I told him, attempting that bright smile again.

"Not a contestant?" Jeffries scoffed.

My smile dialed down about twenty watts at the disbelief in his voice.

"No," I ground out through what I feared was quickly becoming a grimace, "I'm providing the footwear for the contestants. I'm a shoe designer."

"Oh, right. Wonderful to have you on board, Miss Springer."

"Actually it's *Mrs.* Springer," I enunciated very clearly, pointing to the wedding band on my left hand.

Jeffries nodded but waved his hand as if glossing over the fact. I had a feeling something as simple as a little wedding band had never stopped him in the past.

"Did you just arrive on the island?" he asked, signaling to our friend behind the bar for another drink.

I nodded. "Yesterday. In fact I was just starting to settle in when I found..." I paused, trailing off for effect.

It took Jeffries' vodka-soaked brain a moment to catch up. "Oh, God, you're the one who found Jennifer, right?"

Again I nodded, this time casting my eyes downwards. I didn't have to fake the emotion backing up behind them. Miss Montana's body was a sight I would not soon forget.

"Tragic incident." Jeffries shook his head, clucking between his teeth. "Of course my character, Dr. Calvin Drake, is around death all the time. But I suppose that's not exactly the same, is it?"

"Not exactly." In fact it wasn't the same at all. "Did you know her well?" I asked. "Miss Montana?"

"Of course," he said, pausing to take a sip of his new martini as it arrived. "I make it a point to get to personally know every one of the contestants. I believe that the winner of a beauty pageant should be just as much about personality as it is about her outer beauty, don't you think?"

I nodded, though I was pretty sure he was full of more baloney than the Spam lunch buffet. "I'm so sorry," I said. "Were you two close?"

"Well, you know, as close as any judge can get to a contestant. I mean we're not really supposed to *fraternize* with the girls." He paused. "But the professionals involved in behind-the-scenes, say, *dressing* those girls, well that's a different story, now isn't it Miss Springer?"

"*Mrs.*," I said again.

This time he completely ignored me. This was getting old. Time to go in with the big guns.

"Do you have any ideas who might have wanted to see Miss Montana dead?"

Jeffries' head snapped up. "What you mean? Are you saying you think she was murdered?"

I didn't think I had to point out to him that most healthy, twenty-year-old girls didn't just drop dead of natural causes in a chaise lounge by a pool in the middle of the night. "I think it's very likely."

Jeffries shook his head. "No, there's no way. Jennifer was such a sweet girl. So...well, she was perfect. She wouldn't hurt a soul."

That seemed to be the consensus. Of course somebody didn't think she was such a fantastic girl, or she wouldn't have been poolside getting the sunburn of her life. I decided to take the same road that Miss New Mexico had pointed out. "I find it hard to believe somebody can be so active in the pageant circuit without making a few enemies?"

"Look, you want to talk enemies—then you should take a look at that Laforge."

"Laforge?" I asked, my ears perking up. "Why is that?"

"Because that man is singing his swansong as director of this pageant."

"Meaning he's leaving the Miss Hawaiian Paradise Pageant?"

Jeffries snorted. "Meaning he's being *replaced*."

While I hadn't personally seen anything amiss with Laforge's direction of the pageant, except possibly the heavy hand when it came to scolding the less coordinated contestants, I was having a hard time connecting the dots. "And you think this has something to do with Miss Montana's death?"

"I didn't say that," Jeffries said, throwing both hands up in an innocent surrender gesture. Though I noticed neither hand was very steady. The man was quickly going from inebriated to totally sauced. "I just said if anybody had a grudge against Jennifer's camp, it would be Laforge."

"Because...?" I asked.

"Because guess who is replacing our dear director?"

I shrugged, waiting.

"Ashton Dempsy."

It must've been the blank look on my face that caused Jeffries to continue with a, "Jennifer's pageant coach."

I raised one eyebrow his way. "So you think Laforge had it in for Miss Montana, in order to keep her coach from taking over his job?"

Jeffries gave me a condescending smile. "Honey, Hawaiian Paradise is a *family* corporation," he said, slurring his words together. "You can bet that the bad publicity of having a pageant contestant die on their watch is just about killing them. There is nothing on God's green earth that's going to make them put said contestant's coach on national television now, donchathink?"

While it was clear that Jeffries was half in the tank at this point, he might have also had half a point. The entire purpose of the pageant was to put a bright, shiny face on the Hawaiian Paradise sunscreen brand. If it was true that Miss Montana's coach had been about to replace Laforge, I was sure the corporation was giving serious pause to that decision now.

I glanced over at Laforge, who was still deep in conversation with Ruth Marie. Though in all honesty, it looked like Ruth Marie was doing most of the talking. After my earlier conversation with the aging judge, I knew how much was at stake for the contestants in the pageant. I wondered just how much was at stake for the director. And just what he might do to continue being the director.

* * *

After filling Dana and Marco in on my conversation with Jeffries over a plate of teriyaki and one more Babbling Mermaid, I decided to call it a night. I was definitely feeling the effects being in the middle of my own *CSI, Hawaiian Paradise* episode. I left Dana and Marco debating the merits of piña coladas versus mai tais and headed for my hotel room. I swapped my linen pants and wrap top for a pair of pink pajamas with cute little boy-short bottoms and made a quick call home to update Ramirez on my day of getting a pedicure, having drinks at the Lost Aloha tiki bar, and matching shoes with pageant outfits. All true. All carefully avoiding any actions that might possibly be construed as sticking my nose into anyone's investigations. Then

I grabbed my tablet and pulled up a relaxing book as I went to sleep.

I was just getting into a fun beach read by one of my favorite authors when my tablet started making pinging noises and a window popped up signaling a Skype call was coming in. I didn't recognize the avatar of a grumpy looking cat, but the name next to it said *Mom*.

I raised an eyebrow. As far as I knew, my mom had only recently mastered the ability to initiate a phone call via Bluetooth in her car. (And even then, she had accidentally dialed me while singing song lyrics to her radio more often than on purpose.) Generally Mom and technology went together like peanut butter and dill pickles, but I hit the "accept" button anyway. Immediately her face filled my screen, her baby blue eye shadow circa 1985 and hot pink lipstick clashing in 252 pixels per inch brilliant color. Love my mother as I did, her sense of style had paused somewhere in the mid-eighties like a broken Betamax player.

"I don't think she's in there," I could hear Mom saying. "Maddie? Maddie, pick up the computer. It's your mother," she shouted.

I grinned. "Hi, Mom."

"Oh my word, I think I heard her. Maddie, is that you? I don't see anything." She squinted at the computer, her features contorting as they moved in toward her webcam.

"Mom, I'm here. Click the video icon," I told her.

"Did you get Maddie to pick up the computer?" I heard my stepfather's voice in the background.

"I don't know, Ralph. I can hear her, but my screen is still showing Candy Crush."

"Maybe you got her voicemail. Can you leave a voicemail?"

I rolled my eyes. No need not to. Apparently they couldn't see me.

"Mom, it's me. It's not a voicemail. Click the video icon. It looks like a little movie projector."

But no one was paying attention to me.

"Do we need to be plugged into the phone line, Ralph?" Mom asked. "Where's the modem line?"

"Try adjusting the screen," my stepfather yelled. "Maybe you need to zoom in."

I suddenly got an up-close-and-personal view of my stepfather's nasal hairs as he moved in.

"Don't zoom!" I pleaded. "I can see you fine."

"I don't see myself," said Mom.

"You don't need to see yourself. I see you. You see me."

"Maybe we should turn the monitor around, Ralph," Mom suggested.

Good grief.

"Did you call for a reason, Mom?"

"Maddie, we're worried about you. Are. You. Okay?" My Mom shouted as if actually trying to get me to hear her from an ocean away. "We just heard on the news about that poor girl from your pageant."

Oh, boy. I don't know why I had hoped that the death of a beauty queen would remain local news. I should've known it would be inevitable that it would get back to my family on the mainland.

"I'm fine, Mom."

"Are you sure, honey? I don't think that hotel is safe. They said on the news that someone is killing beauty queens."

"Singular. One beauty queen died."

"Honey, I think maybe you should come home. Does the hotel have adequate security? I saw on *20/20* that traveling to foreign places is not safe right now."

"Hawaii is not a foreign country, Mother."

"You know what I mean. Some of those places just don't have the modern security we do here."

I glanced up from my tablet at the flat screen television, minibar filled with imported bottled water, and high-speed Internet access in my luxury hotel room. "It's pretty modern here. I think I'm fine."

"I think I've almost got it!" I heard my stepfather say. "It's got to be this cable. I think maybe we need to put it in the monitor. Do we need to hook the monitor up to the phone? I think maybe if we just hook this cable up like this—"

My screen went suddenly blank. Then Skype told me I had lost the call.

Thank God for small favors.

I closed Skype and went back to my book.

Several chapters later, my lids finally started to feel heavy again, and I shut my tablet off, laying my head down on the soft feather pillows. I was just starting to drift off to dreamland when I heard a noise outside in the hall.

I opened my eyes and glanced at my bedside clock. 12:43. Way past curfew for any of the pageant contestants in this wing.

Despite the drowsiness settling in, I couldn't help my curiosity winning out. I tiptoed to my door and opened it a crack.

Just in time to see the back of a beauty queen, scarf tied over her head and wearing a long, black coat, slip into the elevators before the doors slid closed behind her.

CHAPTER FIVE

———

Thanks to an exhausting day, I was happy to say that the next morning I awoke perfectly acclimated to Hawaii time. I showered and blow-dried my hair, then did a mascara and lip gloss thing, adding a little extra concealer under my eyes as a concession to said exhausting day. I threw on a pair of white capri pants, hot pink strappy sandals with a mid-rise heel, and a flowing, sleeveless top in a pink floral print that was very on trend for spring. Then I quickly made my way downstairs toward the Tropical Tryst breakfast buffet.

As the elevator opened onto the lobby I could see that just outside the front doors our friendly neighborhood fashion protester was already hard at work. She was wearing dingy gray Birkenstocks, gray linen pants at least one size too large, and a black T-shirt that looked like it had seen one too many washings. She was holding up a big sign that read *I Am Not A Slave To Fashion.*

I hated to tell her, but in that outfit, the sign was redundant.

I made my way across the lobby to the Tropical Tryst where a long counter filled with pastries and tropical fruits took up one wall. Along another, a buffet table was filled with chafing dishes of sausage, bacon, pancakes, eggs, and other types of traditional American breakfast foods simultaneously calling my name. I spotted Marco at the made-to-order omelet station and joined him, plate in hand.

"Good morning, dahling," he said, giving me a big bright smile as he waited for his egg white omelet.

"So far it's better than yesterday," I agreed. "Spinach?" I asked, gesturing to the pile of greens being stirred into his omelet mixture.

"Kale," he corrected me. "It's a superfood."

I blinked at him. "It's finally happened. Dana's converted you to the healthy side, hasn't she?"

Marco grinned. "Hardly. I just read an article in *Cosmo* about how it's supposed to take five years off your skin's appearance." He winked at me. "It may taste like rabbit pellets, but a boy's gotta do what a boy's gotta do to look this hot."

I covered a very unladylike snort. "Point taken."

Marco was dressed today in a pair of white pleather Bermuda shorts, white loafers with no socks, and screaming neon turquoise baby-doll T-shirt that read: Queen. While I recognized it as one of the Miss Hawaiian Paradise promotional shirts, I was pretty sure Marco was enjoying the double entendre.

I gave my order of a Denver omelet, complete with ham (Aren't diet gurus always tell you to eat more protein?), cheese (What woman doesn't need more calcium, right?), and green peppers (Vegetables! I'm sure these were *almost* as good for the skin as kale.). My mouth was beginning to water from the heavenly scents as I heard a familiar voice behind me.

"Good morning, Maddie."

I turned to find Laforge striding up to the omelet station. In all honesty, I was a little surprised he remembered my name from our brief introduction when I'd first arrived on the island.

"Good morning," I said, mustering up my most cheerful voice for my boss-for-a-week.

"I trust there were no more incidents this morning?" While the words were benign enough, the tone in his voice sounded almost as if he blamed *me* for *finding* Miss Montana.

"Not so far," I said, punctuating it with a smile.

"Hmm." Laforge pursed his lips together. Clearly he did not appreciate my attempt at levity.

As with yesterday Laforge was dressed in a pair of skintight pants that I could easily see helping him sweat away an extra ten pounds by the time the afternoon humidity hit. He'd topped it off with a pale pink button-up shirt, un-buttoned one too low for my taste, reminding me of a '70s disco king. An image that was further reinforced by the large gold medallion hanging around his neck and the pair of expensive sunglasses perched on his nose, almost completely obscuring his eyes from view. I wondered if they were for fashion or if Laforge was nursing a hangover.

"I'd like you to meet my good friend, Marco," I said, tactfully changing the subject as I turned to my companion.

Laforge gave Marco a quick up and down. "I see you're enjoying our promotional T-shirts," he said, just that hint of West Hollywood style bitchiness in his voice.

"I feel like a diva in it," Marco answered cheerfully.

"You *look* like a diva in it," Laforge said, though I wasn't sure it was exactly a compliment.

I could tell Marco caught the tone in his voice as well, as he squared his shoulders, narrowed his eyes, and pasted on a smile more fake than Miss Arkansas's breasts. "It takes a diva to appreciate one, doesn't it, *dahling*?" Marco asked, gesturing to Laforge's conspicuous sunglasses. "Indoor shades. Very drama."

"Hmm," Laforge mumbled through a smile that matched Marco's insincerity. "I'd say *Prada* is always appropriate, isn't it?"

"Practically timeless," Marco retorted. "You know, unless they're from *last* year's collection."

Laforge's eyes narrowed. Marco's smile grew bigger and sassier.

I could quickly see this turning into a fashion face-off and decided to intervene before my friend diva-ed me right out of a job.

"Any word yet on whether or not the pageant will go on as scheduled?" I asked, again using my brilliant subject-changing skills.

Laforge let out a deep sigh. "Sadly, no. I'm meeting with the detective in charge of the case later this morning, and hopefully they will give me something I can take to the corporate powers-that-be."

"It would be such a pity if they shut it down. You know, it being *your last year* here and all," Marco said. He just had to get that last jab in, didn't he?

Laforge's head snapped up from his perusal of the omelet bar. "What do you mean my 'last year?'"

"Oh, I'm sorry. Maybe I was misinformed. I thought I heard you were leaving the pageant?" Marco blinked innocently.

Laforge's jaw tensed, though his eyes were still obscured behind last year's Prada shades. "I don't know what you think you heard, but, trust me, I'm not going anywhere."

I raised an eyebrow and silently wondered if Miss Montana's death had anything to do with Laforge's current confidence that he would be staying on as pageant director next year.

"Who told you I was leaving?" Laforge demanded.

Marco looked to me.

"Uhh..." I paused, not sure I wanted to rat out Jeffries. While he was definitely bar-slime, I wasn't sure I wanted to make an enemy of the soap star. Especially if he was Miss Montana's secret-lover-slash-killer.

"It was Dempsey, wasn't it?" Laforge's eyes searched the room, as if expecting to see Dempsey pop up at one of the tables. "That up-start hack has been gunning for a director's position ever since Jennifer's first pageant win."

"Hack?" I asked, jumping on the word.

"Listen, Jennifer was winning because Jennifer was good. It had absolutely nothing to do with Dempsey's coaching." He paused, a sneer curling his lips. "Just ask Dempsey how many winners he's coached in the past. Trust me the zero he gives you will be fatter than his bloated gut."

With that, Laforge turned on heel and stomped out of the room, sans breakfast.

"Geez, someone's panties are in a bunch this morning," Marco mumbled.

"Yeah, well, at the risk of them bunching me right out of a job, keep your Prada comments to yourself, Joan Ranger."

Marco blinked innocently at me. "Who, *moi*?"

* * *

While Marco and I indulged in our omelets, Dana joined us with a plate of fresh fruit, plain yogurt, and organic granola with little bits of what looked like birdseed in it.

"Any word on the pageant yet?" she asked, voicing what was clearly on everyone's minds morning.

I shook my head. "Still up in the air."

"At least according to La Director La Passé," Marco added.

Dana arched a questioning eyebrow.

"Don't ask," I told her. "Marco met Laforge earlier." I quickly filled her in on Laforge's insistence that he was staying on as pageant director and the information he'd divulged about Jennifer being Dempsey's meal ticket.

"Hmm," Dana said, chewing on this development as her jaw worked on her crunchy granola. "If that's true, Dempsey definitely wouldn't have any reason to want Jennifer out of the way."

"But Laforge might," Marco pointed out. "Like Jeffries said, if Laforge wanted to tarnish Dempsey's reputation, killing his only successful client might go a long way toward that end."

"But we only have Jeffries' word for the fact that Dempsey was even in the running for director," I pointed out. "And who knows if Jeffries was just trying to divert suspicion from himself? I still think he's the most likely candidate for Jennifer's lover on the lowdown."

Dana shook her head. "Honestly, I just cannot believe that a judge would be sleeping with a contestant," she said, doing more crunching.

"I have to ask—are you eating birdseed?"

Dana pursed her brow at me. "What?"

"The little brown flecks in your granola. Birdseed?"

"Flax seed. It's super high in omega-3 oil," she said around another crunchy bite.

"It's also stuck in your teeth," Marco kindly told her, gesturing between his own two front teeth with a perfectly manicured pointer finger.

I was about to point out that the kale hadn't been terrifically kind to Marco's own Pearly Whites, when my cell started Vogue-ing from my pocket. I pulled it out to find a new text from Mom.

15 a miracle cans were killed overstays list beer
I blinked at the text. I had no clue.
What? I reluctantly texted back.
A couple of seconds later I got: *sorry. Auto type not twerking write.*

I stifled a snort. *You mean "not working right?"*

There was a pause, then: *Right.*

Try turning autotype off I suggested.

A few minutes later a new text pinged in. *15 Americans were killed overseas last year*

I barely stifled an eye roll.

I'm not overseas I texted back. *I'm just by the sea* I added, looking out the window at the beautiful blue waves crashing on the white sandy shores outside the resort.

Despite the fact that a girl had died here just yesterday, I had to admit that the scene was the farthest from sinister you could get. To my right sat a family with two adorable young boys and a teenager in a pair of shades and a straw hat, the two boys giggling as they threw pieces of pineapple at each other. To the left I could see Miss California, Miss New Mexico, and Miss Arkansas giggling over breakfast smoothies together. And near the buffet a long line of men in slacks with duck-emblazoned shirts was starting to form. In every way it seemed like your average vacation hub. Except somewhere among its vacationers, a murderer lurked.

I don't think you're safe! do u have pprspry?

I stared at the text my mother responded with, mentally sounding out the last word with a myriad of different vowels. Finally I gave up.

What?

A few seconds later her response came in *PEPPER SPRAY*

I rolled my eyes with abandon this time. Hey, she couldn't see me, right? *Not allowed on the plane.*

what??!! ur unarmed?!!

Easy on the exclamation points. you don't wanna hurt yourself

There was a pause, then *r u tryin to be funny?*

I smirked. *did it work?*

ur stepfather is not laughing

How she could type out the entire word of "stepfather" but couldn't type out "pepper spray," I had no idea. Trying to decipher how my mother texted was like trying to decipher Kesha's dress code.

i'm safe, luv u, gotta go, I typed, then I strategically set my phone to silent.

* * *

After breakfast Dana, Marco, and I wandered around the gift shop, took a leisurely walk through the gardens on the grounds, and generally meandered about, not quite sure what to do with ourselves. Finally we found ourselves back at the Lost Aloha Tiki Shack. While it was a little early in the day for imbibing, the three of us ordered pineapple Mango smoothies and sipped them as we strolled down the beach.

Again I was struck by the dichotomy of the tragedy that had occurred at the resort the day before and the seemingly serene landscape before me. The beach was clean white sand stretching as far as the eye could see, broken only by rock formations covered in various tropical foliage at random intervals. The ocean was a perfect crystal blue like some sort of painting. And not a cloud dared mar the sky above us as the warm sun beat down on my bare shoulders.

About halfway down the beach Marco grabbed my arm in a vice grip, shaking me out of my admiration for the tropical landscape.

"There he is!" Marco stage-whispered to me.

"Who?" I asked, scanning the beach. A smattering of tourists filled it, both patrons of the resort and locals from the looks of them.

"There!" Marco pointed an arm straight ahead to where a large, rotund man lay sunning himself on a beach chair, his ample shoulders pinking under the sun as they peeked out of a white tank top straining against his beach-ball-sized belly. "Isn't that Dempsey?"

I had to admit, I'd only caught a glimpse of him before. I honestly couldn't be sure.

However it seemed Dana could. "That is definitely Dempsey." She frowned. "How can he be sitting out here enjoying the beach when his client was just killed?" she asked.

I shrugged. Though I supposed there was no law against mourning in the sunshine.

"Let's go interrogate him about the director position," Marco said.

My turn to grab his arm. "Whoa there Fablock. You almost interrogated me right out of a job at breakfast. I say we let the poor man enjoy his day in peace."

Marco looked at me as if I'd grown two heads. "You're joking, right? What if he knows something about who killed Jennifer?"

"Then he would've told the police."

Again with the two-headed look.

"Okay, fine," I gave up, throwing my hands in the air. "We can go offer our condolences."

"And interrogate him!" Marco said.

"And *talk* to him," I amended.

"You're no fun," Marco mumbled.

Dana wisely kept quiet during the exchange, sipping at her smoothie as the three of us made our way over to Dempsey.

It wasn't until we were blocking his sun that he opened his eyes and squinted in our direction.

"May I help you?" he asked. Up close I could see that Dempsey's hair was a dyed black and he almost looked as though he were wearing a layer of makeup over his face. (A face which held a pair of eyes that were brown, I noted, not emerald green.)

"I'm so sorry to bother you," I started. "But I wanted to offer my condolences. Maddie Springer." I stuck my hand out toward him. "I'm doing the footwear for the pageant."

"Oh. Right." Dempsey struggled to a sitting position while he reached one sweaty hand out to shake mine. "Right, I recognize you. And you're Dana, right? One of the judges?"

She nodded, sipping at her smoothie. "I'm so very sorry about your client. She was a very talented competitor."

Dempsey's jaw clacked shut, though I didn't know him well enough to say whether it was due to grief, guilt, or coveting that smoothie as he sweated in the sunshine.

"Thank you. It's true, Jennifer was very talented."

"Do the police have any leads on what happened to her?" I asked.

He shook his head, his jowls wavering with aftershocks. "None that they're sharing with me. Though, who am I? Just the person she spent twenty-four seven with for weeks leading up to every competition," he said, heavy on the sarcasm.

I jumped on the opening. "It sounds like you probably knew Jennifer as well as anyone."

"I should say so."

"I don't suppose you know if she'd made any enemies? Why anyone would've wanted to hurt her?" I fished.

I half expected him to deny it and talk about how *perfect* Jennifer had been like everyone else, but instead he shrugged. "Well clearly somebody wanted to hurt her, didn't they?"

"There's a rumor running around that you might be the next director of the Miss Hawaiian Paradise competition," Marco jumped in.

Dempsey grinned, showing off what a great set of veneers could do. "It's a lovely rumor."

"How long were you Jennifer's coach?" I asked.

His smile immediately faded, his expressions sagging in a way that added ten years to his age. "Two years," he said. "Ever since she started going for the national titles."

"How long had she been doing pageants?"

"Oh, honey, she'd been in pageants her entire life. Started off as one of those tiny-tot things before she moved on to bigger and bigger titles. They were paying her way through nursing school."

"I hadn't realized she was going to school." I guess I sort of pictured all of these girls as professional pageant women.

Dempsey nodded. "She had big dreams." The catch in his voice was unmistakable. If Dempsey was faking grief, he was doing a darn good job of it. He cleared his throat. "Most of the girls are in school, though they sometimes take a semester off here and there for a really big pageant like this one. It's worth it to most of them. Pageants are for the young. They all know that at some point they will be aging out of the competitions where there's any real money to be had."

"But Jennifer was a long way from that, wasn't she?" Marco jumped in.

Dempsey paused. "She was twenty. She had a couple of good years left."

"Wow, I didn't realized 'aging out' happened so young," I mused.

Dempsey nodded. "Like I said, it's a young woman's game. The end comes quickly."

I bit my lip, mental wheels turning. "Were any of the other contestants closing in on that end?"

Dempsey shrugged. "Sure. I can think of a couple who have been circling the drain, so to speak, for at least a couple of years."

I cringed at his metaphor. "Who?"

"Well," Dempsey hedged. "Whitney Lexington for one."

"Miss Delaware."

He nodded, a slow smirk spreading across his face. "She's been competing in the eighteen-to-twenty-five category for at least eight years now."

I raised an eyebrow, doing the math. "That would make her twenty-six. I thought the cut off for this pageant was twenty-five?"

"That's what I thought too," Dempsey said with a knowing nod.

Dana did a strangled little gasp beside me. "But don't pageant officials check to make sure the contestants fall within the age range?" she asked

Dempsey shrugged. "Sure, but there's always a way around that. Fake a birth certificate, bribe the judge..." He trailed off.

Dana gasped again, and I caught Marco elbowing her out of the corner of my eye

"Is that what Whitney did?" I asked.

Dempsey put his hands up in a surrender motion. "I'm not pointing any fingers at anyone. I'm just saying that some of these older girls are desperate to hit that big title while they still can. *Desperate.*"

I pursed my lips together. If I didn't know better, I'd say that Dempsey was pretty pointedly *not* pointing any fingers. I wondered if it was because he truly thought Whitney had something to do with Jennifer's death, or if he was trying to deflect attention from someone else.

"I have to ask...you don't know if Jennifer was seeing anyone, do you?"

He raised one eyebrow. "Her boyfriend just came in from Montana."

I sucked in my cheeks, trying to find a way to put this delicately. "I saw him arrive yesterday. I was wondering if maybe Jennifer was close with anyone else? Possibly associated with the pageant...?" I left the question hanging there like last season's mullet-cut dress on a clearance rack.

Dempsey's eyebrows drew together as he tried to read between my lines. "Like who?" he finally asked.

"Well..." I said drawing out the word. Quite frankly Dempsey himself was in an excellent position to be Mystery Boyfriend. Who spent more time with a contestant than her coach? However I had a hard time putting him in the role of leading man. I knew young girls often had a thing for older men, but Dempsey was hardly the distinguished rolling-in-dough type. In fact if I had to categorize him, I would say he was the midsection-looks-like-dough type. Besides, Dempsey's eyes were brown.

"What about Jeffries?" Marco spat out. "We know he has a bit of a reputation with the ladies."

But Dempsey shook his head violently from side to side. "No, you've got it all wrong. Jennifer played by the rules. There is no way she would've been seeing a judge. Fraternization between contestants and judges is strictly prohibited."

Dana shot me an I-told-you-look.

I bit my lip, remembering the scene I'd witnessed last night with Miss California at Jeffries table. While I wouldn't exactly call their interaction inappropriate, it did border on the fraternizing.

"We have a witness who says she saw Jennifer sneaking out the night she was murdered," I told him, figuring it couldn't hurt to come clean.

Dempsey paused, his eyes narrowing. "Who said they saw this?"

"We're not at liberty to say," Marco jumped in, sounding like he'd just watched an entire season of *The Good Wife*.

"Well, whoever it is must be mistaken. Like I said, winning meant everything to Jennifer. She knew that violating curfew was against the rules. And nothing would've made Jennifer jeopardize her title." He shut his mouth with a click, signaling that he'd said his last word on the topic.

"Did Jennifer seem distressed about anything to you?" I asked, feeling distinctly like we were losing him. "Anything in particular on her mind?"

But Dempsey shook his head. "I'm sorry. Jennifer was as happy as could be at this pageant. Everything was going her way. In fact, I believe she was even in the running for Miss Congeniality."

I opened my mouth to follow up on that, however I never got the chance as Dana's phone started singing from her purse.

"Sorry," she said pulling it out and sliding her finger along the smart screen. She glanced at the readout. "It's a text from Laforge."

Before she could say more I heard a vibration going off in Dempsey's pocket as well. He looked at the readout and said, "He's calling an all hands meeting in the auditorium."

We all silently looked at each other, knowing what this meant. The final verdict on whether or not there would be a Miss Hawaiian Paradise Pageant this year.

CHAPTER SIX

———

Marco and I followed Dana down the set of escalators to the lower level where the auditorium was located. Clearly Laforge had sent out a widespread text, as contestants and members of the pageant crew alike filed down the escalators beside us. Everyone wore the same expression of tightly contained nerves. While I was pretty sure the majority of us were hoping Laforge would say the pageant would continue as planned, none of us were exactly sure that we *should* want the pageant to continue as planned. Did that make us insensitive to the dead girl?

The house lights were up in the auditorium, giving it an overly cheery feel for the jittery mumbles of the crowd. Dana walked to the front row, where she took a spot behind a small table that was clearly reserved for judges, carefully sequestered away from contestants. Marco and I filled in two seats near the front on the aisle. I could see Laforge shuffling papers just to the side of the stage. Beside him stood Detective Whatshisname. His head tilted toward Laforge as he mumbled something into his ear, but I noticed his eyes were on the crowd. I wondered if he was looking for anything in particular. Or anyone. Had the detective uncovered some evidence pointing to someone in the auditorium as Jennifer's killer? I couldn't help my eyes wandering over the assembled crowd as the questions pinged back and forth in my brain.

Everyone I had talked to so far had described Jennifer as perfection. She followed the rules, was kind to everyone, and I had a feeling that if she started singing, little Disney characters might have even flocked to her in droves. So why had she taken the risk to sneak out on the night of her death? And who could have hated the possible Miss Congeniality enough to want her dead?

"May I have everyone's attention, please?"

My eyes jumped up to the stage where Laforge was standing, a wireless microphone in his hand. "I apologize for calling you all here on such short notice," he started. His voice was missing that commanding tone I'd heard from him at rehearsals. "However with our live telecast only five days away, time is of the essence."

A wave of murmurs washed through the auditorium at this statement, questioning eyes turning to one another.

"Yes," Laforge said into his microphone, answering the silent question. "The pageant will continue as scheduled." He paused, waiting for another round of murmurs to pass before demanding our attention again. "After discussions with the local authorities—" Laforge nodded to Detective Whatshisname, standing just offstage. "—and sponsors of our pageant at the Hawaiian Paradise Corporation, we have decided it is safe and appropriate to continue forward and dedicate this pageant to the memory of Jennifer Oliver, our Miss Montana." He paused again, and when he spoke his voice was lower, switching from announcer mode to something much more human and filled with emotion. "We feel it is what Jennifer would have wanted."

Another soft murmur went through the crowd.

Laforge took a deep breath and cleared his throat, pulling himself back into presenter mode. Whether the pause for emotion had been intentionally theatric or genuine, it was hard to tell. "I know that this terrible tragedy has taken a toll on all of us. However we will continue rehearsals today. New schedules are posted backstage. We'll break now for a brief recess then meet back here for the dress rehearsal of our opening number in twenty minutes. Thank you." Laforge nodded toward the audience before his thick heels click-clacked offstage to join the homicide detective again.

* * *

After checking the newly posted schedules, I saw that my fitting wasn't until later that afternoon, so Marco and I parted ways with Dana outside the auditorium. She said she wanted to call Ricky with the update on the pageant then grab a cup of coffee to keep her mind sharp as she jumped back into the judging duties. (Of course, in Dana's world a cup of "coffee" meant a nonfat, decaf, soy latte with stevia. Shudder.)

It looked as though Marco and I were on our own for a few hours. Normally we might have spent it lounging by the pool, but he already knew my particular thoughts on that vacation activity. Instead, we decided to do a little bit of souvenir shopping in the village. The area of Hawaii we were staying in consisted of a main village area where locals and tourists alike hung out at various bars, restaurants, and boutiques. There were also open-air shopping malls that catered specifically to tourists up and down the main highway. Our hotel was conveniently located in the center, well within walking distance of it all.

Marco and I paused only long enough to go to our respective rooms and change into our very best tourist garb. I put on a purple and turquoise wrap skirt in a large floral print that practically screamed tropical. I paired it with some strappy slingbacks in a summery white and a matching white tank blouse. The outfit was comfortable, carefree, and cool enough to keep me from having unsightly sweat stains in the humidity. Not, I realized, a concern for Marco as I met up with him outside his hotel room ten minutes later. Marco had gone with a pair of tight denim shorts flirting with the top of his kneecap (sporting perfectly waxed legs beneath that I was slightly jealous of, by the way), a skintight white leather top, and a pair of hot pink espadrilles. He had slung a pink crossbody bag over one shoulder to complete the outfit, and topped it all off with a pair of oversized purple sunglasses. I had to admit he looked beyond fabulous. He also looked like he'd be sweating like a pig at a luau in ten minutes flat.

"Honey, don't you think that outfit is a little hot?" I asked.

"That's what I was counting on, dahling," Marco said, lowering his sunglasses and giving me a wink.

I rolled my eyes. "I meant the temperature. It's like eighty degrees plus humidity outside."

Marco waved me off with a tanned hand. "No worries. I've got that covered." He reached into his pink bag and pulled out a personal-sized, battery-powered fan, flipping it on and holding it in front of his face.

"See? I can look like I'm an '80s video vixen *and* stay cool in the humidity."

I couldn't help a giggle. Marco really did think of everything where fashion was concerned.

Fifteen minutes later we were walking along the main boulevard, happily filling our shopping bags with goodies to take home. I'd found an adorable little puka shell elastic bracelet for Livvie and a sailboat made out of abalone shells for Max. I was having a little bit harder time finding something for my husband. Big bad homicide detectives usually didn't enjoy cute little clamshells with googly eyes glued onto them. Marco on the other hand was going for full-on island fashion, pulling Hawaiian shirts in a variety of different styles. Though instead of the usual loose casual look he was getting them all in a women's size extra small. I prayed for their teeny tiny buttons.

We were just coming out of the Waikiki Wonders gift shop and searching for something akin to a Starbucks, when I spotted a familiar face in the crowd just across the courtyard. He was sitting by a fountain where small children were throwing coins in exchange for wishes. Jennifer's boyfriend. Or at least the public boyfriend, Xander Newport, the one who had flown in from Montana the day before. Apparently he *had* found the Starbucks as he had a paper coffee cup in his hand. He leaned against the back of a park bench, staring off into space. Part of me felt incredibly sorry for the guy. Not only had his girlfriend been cheating on him, a condition to which he had apparently been oblivious, but now she was also deceased.

Of course there was always the possibility he *hadn't* been oblivious. It's just possible that he knew Jennifer was cheating on him. Maybe he had traveled to Hawaii not to mourn the death of his beloved girlfriend but to cause it. I know, I had an imaginative streak. What can I say? Life with a homicide detective had colored my view of the world.

"Who is that?" Marco asked, gesturing to the guy.

"Who?"

"The guy you were staring at."

Was I staring? Oops.

I quickly filled him in.

"Ooo...let's go talk to him," Marco said, forging ahead before I could stop him. While I agreed it would be interesting to hear his take on his girlfriend's death, I wasn't quite sure how to tactfully approach a grieving boyfriend

Apparently Marco didn't have any such compunction. "Xander Newport, right?" he asked

The guy snapped out of his vacant stare, his eyes going straight to Marco and widening slightly. In his defense anyone's eyes would widen slightly if Marco was approaching them.

"Yes?" he asked, searching Marco for any sign of recognition.

Marco shot a hand out toward him. "My name's Marco. I'm with the pageant."

Which was a slight stretch. However he was *with* the pageant even if he had nothing to do with it.

"Oh, right. Of course," Xander said, absently shaking Marco's hand. "I should have guessed."

While he mumbled the last part, it didn't escape Marco's radar. Fortunately, he took it as a compliment. "It's the shoes, right? I thought they screamed pageant diva."

Xander gave him a wan smile.

"We wanted to offer our condolences," I jumped in.

Xander's eyes shot to me. "And you are?"

"Maddie Springer." I offered my hand as well. "Nice to meet you."

Xander shook my hand but didn't return the greeting. He had the dark, brooding thing down to a tee. However, I had to concede that it looked good on him. While I had no idea who Jennifer's secret lover had been, part of me was surprised that she would take a second lover at all. Xander was what you would call classically handsome. Dark blond hair curled in waves off his head, hanging just a little long in the back, enough to be fashionable but not so much as to look like he was lacking in the grooming department. He had the sort of big brown eyes and wide smile that reminded me of a Ryan Seacrest. Tanned skin, white teeth, outfit right out of a J.Crew catalog. Everything about him looked perfectly put together but somehow appropriately casual at the same time. All in all, he looked like the absolute perfect match to a beauty queen.

"I'm so sorry for your loss," I said.

His brown eyes immediately went down to his coffee cup which he twirled in his hands, fidgeting. "Thank you I—I can scarcely believe she's gone."

"Terrible to be visiting paradise under such circumstances," Marco said clucking his tongue. "When did you say you got in?"

"I didn't." His eyes narrowed.

"Uh, what he means is I'm sure you must still be in shock over the whole thing." I shot Marco a pointed look.

Marco nodded. "Right. Shock. So sudden."

Xander's eyes went back to his cup. "Very sudden."

"I can't imagine who could have hurt Jennifer. Everyone seemed to like her," I said.

"Of course they did," Xander shot back defensively.

"When was the last time you talked to her?" Marco cut in.

Xander took a deep breath, as if drawing the memory out. "Night before she died."

"And how did she seem?"

"What do you mean?" His sandy brows drew together.

"Did she seem agitated? Upset? Scared?" Marco probed.

Xander started to shake his head then paused and shrugged his shoulders instead. "I don't know. She seemed the way she always did. She talked about the pageant, the girls. That was it."

"Did she mention any of the girls in particular?" I asked. If one of the other pageant contestants *had* been gunning for her, maybe Jennifer had had an inkling of who.

Xander shook his head, looking down into his coffee cup again as if trying to recall. "I don't know. I wasn't paying close attention to be honest. Maybe Britney?"

"Whitney?" I asked, immediately thinking of Miss Delaware.

He nodded. "That sounds right."

"What did she say about Whitney?"

Xander shook his head again. "I don't know. Like I said, I wasn't really paying close attention. She talked about how hard they were working on the routines, how excited she was to be here."

This wasn't exactly front-page news. Nor was it scandalous. I was dying to ask if he knew that his girlfriend had been seeing someone else, but I knew that even if he did know, he was unlikely to tell me, a.k.a. a stranger. And if he didn't know, I certainly wasn't going to be the one to break the news to this poor grieving GQ.

"Did she know any of the girls from previous pageants?" Marco asked. "Did she have a history with any of them?"

Oh, good question. I leaned in to hear the answer.

"Sure," Xander said. "I mean, all these girls kind of travel on the same circuits, you know? There are only so many national level pageants. Once they make it to this level, they're seeing a lot of the same faces over and over."

"Like Whitney?" I pressed

But Xander shrugged again. "Look, I'm sorry. But I didn't really know her pageant friends. When she was at home she spent time with me. When she was competing, she spent time with her pageant friends. The two worlds didn't really collide."

Until now. Clearly someone from her pageant world had spilled over into her personal life. And I was dying to know who that was.

No pun intended.

* * *

On the way back to the hotel Marco and I contemplated Whitney aging out of the competition—and possibly even lying about her age. I also filled him in on the mysterious girl I'd seen leaving after curfew last night.

"You think it was Whitney?" Marco asked

"Honestly, it was too dark to tell. She was tall and slim...but that could apply to just about any one of the fifty-one girls here." I paused, correcting myself. "I mean fifty."

"Do you think the girl who left last night was the same person Jennifer was meeting on the beach the night she died?"

"Or," I said, "did the same person who lured Jennifer out after curfew also lure last night's girl out as well?"

"Hmmm," Marco pondered. "But last night's girl came back alive. We would've heard if one of the contestants wasn't accounted for."

"Good point." I had to admit I felt like I was going around in circles. It was possible Whitney'd had it in for Miss Montana, and it was also just as possible that her boyfriend or secret lover had done her in. The fact was we had lots of suspects, and lots of theories, but absolutely zero evidence.

"I'd really like to know who that girl was I saw last night," I mused aloud. I paused trying to think of who might know if someone had been sneaking around the hotel. As we approached the building I suddenly thought of one person who saw all the comings and goings from this hotel.

Our friendly neighborhood fashion protester.

Today she was standing outside the doors, holding a new sign that read *Beauty is Skin Deep*. I tried not to dwell on the irony that it looked like her skin was quickly getting burned in the afternoon sun.

"Do we have to?" Marco wined. I could tell that in his current outfit he was feeling a little bit scared of Ms. Protester. Especially since it looked like she had a bucket of red paint at the ready should anybody walk in wearing fur. And Marco's pleather did look rather authentic.

"Buck up, sister," I told him playfully. "She can't be that bad."

Marco shot a look toward her all-grey ensemble, shuddering a little when he got to her Birks. "Are you sure..."

I grabbed him by the crook of the arm and steered him toward our girl. As we approached I heard her shouting at a pair of insurance salesman leaving the hotel.

"Don't let our daughters become slaves! We're prisoners of our own body image!"

"Excuse me," I said coming up behind her.

She spun around, her stringy brown hair flapping behind her. "What do you want?"

Marco yipped and jumped back a step at her combative tone.

"Hi, I'm Maddie Springer," I said, holding my hand out to her.

She looked at it as if it was a snake. Or maybe just a fabulous snakeskin pump.

"And? Look I'm totally within my right to peacefully protest here, so if you don't like it—"

"Actually, I was wondering if I could ask you a couple of questions."

"Are you with the pageant?" she asked, eyes narrowed.

"I am a bit of a consultant," I said, being completely truthful. Of course I left out the part that my consultations were providing some of the fashions for the event.

She snorted. "That ridiculous farce. You know what those women go through just to parade around like cattle on that stage?"

Actually, I kinda did, being the one who was providing the footwear for said parade.

"Right, well, I was wondering if I could ask you—"

"And who are you?" she said cutting me off and turning on Marco.

He yipped again. "Marco. Not in the pageant."

"Hmph," she snorted again. "Don."

"Excuse me?"

"I'm Don," she introduced herself. "Spelled *D O N*."

I raised an eyebrow.

"Short for Donatella."

I blinked at her.

"As in Donatella Versace?" Marco asked. I could hear the barely contained giggle in his voice at the irony.

Don narrowed her eyes at him again. "Look, I can't help it if my mother was deluded and named me after some Botoxed, spray tanned, crazy Italian fashion mogul."

"Right. Of course. Makes perfect sense," I said quickly moving on. "I noticed that you're keeping a very vigilant post here." I motioned to the front doors of the lobby.

"Well, as long as they continue to poison the minds of our young girls, I'll be here."

"Uh-huh," I said. "I bet you have a clear view of anyone coming or going from the hotel from here, don't you?"

"Nobody gets by me!" she said proudly, her chin lifting. I noticed it could use a good plucking along with her eyebrows. Eek.

"I wonder...did you happen to see anyone leaving here last night? Late?"

Don rolled her eyes at me. "Only about a hundred people. It's a hotel."

I hated to admit that the sarcastic fashion victim had a point.

"It would've been around twelve forty-five?"

Don shook her head. "I was gone by then. After that one girl died, the police have been total jerks about me sticking to the times on my permit. 11 PM is when I have to leave."

Bummer. That meant I was back to square one with the slippery girl from last night. However since Don had opened the door to talking about the dead girl...

"Were you here at the front doors the night that she died?"

Don nodded. "Yeah, and I saw her leaving. I already told all of this to the police. Trust me, they grilled me like crazy. Like they thought I had something to do with it!"

I looked down at her *Death to Fashion Slaves* T-shirt and couldn't imagine what had given them that idea.

"But they can't make me leave. It's my First Amendment right to free speech, you know!" Don shouted, getting worked up now.

"Anyway back to Jennifer," I said. "Did you see where she went?"

"Yeah, she took off toward the beach. But that's the last I saw of her."

"You didn't see her coming back?"

Don shook her head *no*. "But the police say she was found at the pool right? That's at the back of the hotel. She would've gone around to the side entrance if she was meeting someone there."

"You think she was meeting someone?" I asked

Don rolled her eyes at me. "She didn't kill herself, now did she?"

Okay, this was getting me nowhere.

"Did you happen to see anyone else leave the hotel that night?" I asked.

Don opened her mouth to answer, but I held up a hand to stop her.

"Specifically anyone else involved in the pageant? Any of the other girls?"

She shook her head *no* again. "You know those pageant girls—they have a curfew, right? Like little children. So sexist. You don't see any of the men involved in the pageant with a curfew. They are free to come and go into the wee hours of the morning."

"Are you saying you saw one of the men associated with the pageant leave the hotel that night?" I asked, honing in on her wording.

Again with the eye rolling. "Duh!"

I took a mental deep breath. "Who?"

"Well there was that soap star, Jeffries. That bit of chauvinistic slime was heading toward the bar. Shocker," she added. "And then there was the pageant director."

"Laforge?"

She nodded. "He was out there with Dempsey."

"Wait—" I held up a hand. "You saw Laforge heading to the bar *with* Dempsey?"

"Yeah. So?"

I bit my lip. If Dempsey and Laforge were really so at each other's throats, what were they doing sharing a drink the night Jennifer had died?

"You know," Marco said taking a tentative step toward Don, "I have an eyebrow threading kit up in my hotel room. If you just gave me half an hour—"

I elbowed him in the ribs.

"What are you trying to say?" Don asked, putting her hands on her hips

"Nothing! My friend here has nothing to say." I shot him a pointed look

"What? I was just offering my expertise as a salon employee."

I was just dragging Marco away before Don decided to use her bucket of red paint after all, when I felt my phone vibrating from my purse.

I quickly told Marco I'd meet him upstairs and pulled my cell from my pocket.

I looked at the readout, saw Mom's smiling face staring back at me, and swiped my finger across the screen.

"Hello?" I asked.

"Maddie, honey it's your mom," my mother yelled, loudly enough to momentarily stun me.

"I know, Mom. Your name came up on my phone."

"You're on speakerphone!" she shouted into the phone.

"Mom, you don't need to yell. I can hear you fine."

"What? Can you hear me now?!"

I held the phone away from my ear. I was going to be deaf by the end of this call. "Loud and clear," I mumbled.

"I'm here with Mrs. Rosenblatt!" she screamed.

"Hiya, Bubbee!" Mrs. Rosenblatt yelled in the background.

Mrs. Rosenblatt was a three-hundred pound Jewish psychic who spoke to the dead. She was also my mother's best friend. While they made an unlikely duo, the truth was that Mrs. Rosenblatt had been through two husbands since meeting my mom, proving that their bond had what it took to last.

"Maddie!" Mom yelled. "Mrs. Rosenblatt has been talking to Albert, and he's concerned about you!"

"Albert?" I asked searching my memory banks for info associated with that name. While I knew Mrs. Rosenblatt had been married multiple times, I didn't recall any of them being Alberts.

"I give up. Who is Albert?"

"Her spirit guide!"

Mental forehead thunk.

"Tell Albert not to worry," I assured her. "I'm fine."

"Bubbee, is that you?!" Mrs. Rosenblatt screeched. "Hold on, let me get closer so you can hear me."

"No! You don't need to get any closer. I can hear you fine—" I started.

"MADDIE!" Mrs. Rosenblatt's voice came in a distorted rumble right next to the microphone.

I jumped, a ringing instantly spreading through my eardrum.

"Maddie, Albert says there's some bad mojo going on there."

Well, I couldn't argue with the spirit guide there.

"I'll look out for mojo, Mrs. Rosenblatt," I assured her

"Hawaii is famous for bad mojo. You remember that Brady Bunch episode where Bobby found that cursed tiki idol?"

"Was that mojo or juju?" I heard mom asking in the background.

Good grief.

"I'm sure my mojo *and* my juju are fine," I said.

But no one was listening to me.

"Albert wants to know if you have come in contact with any tikis lately?"

"Tikis?"

"Yes. Enchanted ones specifically?"

"Enchanted tikis?"

"Wikipedia says it's juju. That's bad luck!" Mom shouted.

"So did Bobby have tiki juju?" Mrs. Rosenblatt asked.

"Gee, you know, I'm so busy I've really got to go—" I started.

"Maddie, I've got the episode up on my YouTube," I heard Mom shout in the background. "It was definitely juju that Bobby Brady had. Maddie, can you hear me?" Mom yelled, her voice moving closer to the telephone again. "It's juju, honey."

"Thanks, Mom," I mumbled, a headache brewing between my eyes.

"When Bobby found that tiki at the construction site, Greg almost died surfing, and all the terrible things happened to the kids. You need to get rid of the tiki, Maddie."

"I don't have a tiki," I reassured them.

"I think you need a cleansing, Maddie," Mrs. Rosenblatt offered. "I know a witch doctor who could conjure one up real good. She's online now. She even takes PayPal!"

"I'm fine," I tried to tell her.

"Do you need help? Should we come down there? I could do a cleansing in person. Of course, I've never done a Hawaiian tiki juju cleansing, but I'm always up for challenge," Mrs. Rosenblatt said.

"No!" I said, my volume almost matching theirs. "I'm fine!"

"Maddie—"

"You know what, Mom, I can barely hear you. Your voice is so far away. Must be a bad connection. I'll try calling you later from a landline..." I trailed off, quickly hanging up.

I know it was mean to lie to my mother. I blamed it on the bad juju.

CHAPTER SEVEN

———

After grabbing a quick bite at the lunch buffet, I was scheduled to do a fitting with Miss New Mexico for the stilettos to go with her eveningwear look. And considering she'd been the only person so far to talk ill of the dead girl, I was planning to make the most of my time with her.

I made my way to the auditorium, and as soon as I walked in I saw that the girls were still working out the kinks in the dance numbers. God bless her, poor Miss Arkansas was still tripping over her feet. It would be a wonder if the stage dressing survived her version of dancing. I saw Dana's face pinch as she watched her, my friend obviously trying to see the best in each contestant. The other two judges just looked bored, as if they'd already made up their minds who their top picks were.

I quickly made my way down the right aisle and slipped into the backstage area. In contrast to the craziness going on out front, the backstage was actually quiet at this time of day—most of the contestants either on stage or sitting in quiet pairs with their coaches, going over their giant binders of sample interview questions for the dreaded preliminary interview judging, which was scheduled to begin momentarily.

"Maddie, I was wondering when you'd arrive," Laforge said, casting an eye toward the large bejeweled watch on his left wrist. Even though I was five minutes early, according to my cell. I noticed that he was still wearing his oversized, last-season shades from earlier today, making me wonder if that hangover was still hounding him or if they really were an indoor fashion statement. "Desi will be meeting you in Dressing Room A for her fitting any moment." He gestured to a short hallway leading off from the backstage area, along which I could see several marked doors. "We've had to schedule extra fittings today.

Losing an entire day in our already tight schedule is just something we were not prepared for."

"No problem," I told him, mentally calculating how much time I could spend with each girl.

"Thank you, Maddie I—"

Before he could finish we both heard a loud crashing sound from the stage. Laforge turned his head toward the commotion, just visible from our spot in the wings. "Oh, for the love of heaven, Arkansas. How many times have you crashed into that same column?" He didn't wait for the unfortunate contestant's answer, rushing onto the stage and leaving me on my own.

I quickly made my way toward the dressing room he'd indicated, feeling bad for Miss Arkansas but glad that I was out of his sights.

There were four different dressing rooms, marked A, B, C, and D. Over the door to Dressing Room B, someone had taped a sign indicating it was reserved for the show's host, a TV personality from the E! Channel. C and D were labeled with the word Crew, and Dressing Room A held one word on its door: *Shoes*.

I pushed through and found that all of the footwear designs I had picked out at home for the contestants and had shipped ahead of time to the hotel were stacked in neat rows of shoeboxes along the walls. I grabbed my tablet and did a quick inventory, making sure that no shoe had been left behind. I was just finishing up and satisfied that everyone's footwear had arrived in good condition when the door opened, and Miss New Mexico poked her head in.

"Hi. I'm supposed to do a shoe fitting in here?" she said. Today she had on a pair of skinny white jeans that would have shown every teeny ripple of fat, if she'd had any. She'd topped it with a simple, pale yellow tank blouse that highlighted her unnatural tan. (Which was a little on the orange side for me, making her look like a sunburst.) Her hair was teased into a large coiffed brunette helmet, and she had more makeup on than the clown at my children's last birthday party.

"You're in the right place," I told her.

"Maddie, right?" she asked, coming into the room. "I remember you from yesterday."

I nodded. "It looks like we're fitting you for your eveningwear, swimsuit, and the commercial-break dance numbers, correct?"

"I guess so. Laforge just told me to come in here and try on shoes," she said.

"Right, well let's get started with your eveningwear. This is your gown?" I asked, using my tablet to pull up the photos I'd been emailed of her dress. It was a stunning off the shoulder red number with a long sequined train. When she nodded, I grabbed her shoebox containing the black satin four-inch pumps I'd chosen to complement the dress. Though, at the time, I'd had no idea how tall New Mexico was, let alone her hair. I hoped that the extra inches the heels gave her didn't count against her in the judging.

New Mexico slipped the shoes on and tried walking around in them. I had to say she was a total high heels pro. She looked as if she'd been born in stilettos.

"These are super cute," New Mexico said, checking herself out in the full-length mirrors mounted to the wall behind the door.

"Thanks," I said, unable to keep the beam of pride out of my voice. "I'm glad you like them."

"Well, honestly, I'm just glad I'm going to get to wear them on stage at all! I can't believe the competition was almost canceled. As it is, now we're having to double up on rehearsals. Talk about Jennifer screwing us over even in death!"

Clearly New Mexico had not been a fan of the dead girl. It made me wonder...had Desi had something personal against Miss Montana?

"From what I've been hearing, Jennifer was well liked by everyone." I paused, gauging New Mexico's reaction.

She grinned, a slow thing that was anything but friendly. "Well...let's just say that not *everyone* loved Miss Montana."

"Oh?" I asked, raising one eyebrow in her direction as I grabbed another shoebox from the stack, this one containing the sapphire blue stilettos to match her swimwear outfit.

"Sure, Jennifer was sweet and kind and yada, yada, yada."

"But?" I prompted.

"It became crystal clear, to me at least, on the first day we arrived in Hawaii that someone had it in for her."

"How so?" I asked.

"Well, we were all getting our costumes together on our racks in the main dressing room...you know, the one set up in the green room?"

I nodded. While I'd seen the few private dressing rooms off the backstage area, it was clear there certainly weren't fifty-one of them. The girls each had one small luggage rack assigned to them in the green room and one vanity in which to do their hair and makeup.

"Go on," I prompted.

"Well, Jennifer couldn't find her bikini top. She said it was missing."

"Did she misplace it?"

"Ha!" New Mexico barked out. "You really didn't know Jennifer. Jennifer did *not* misplace her pageant costumes. Everybody knows that. Heck, even Maxine wouldn't misplace her costume. It's like the cardinal rule."

"So...it was stolen?" I asked.

"Well, I don't know if I would say 'stolen'..."

"But somebody did take it?"

New Mexico looked over her shoulder, as if making sure no one was listening. Which, since we were in a closed dressing room, nobody was. "All I know is that Jennifer's coach, Dempsey, was carrying on about how it was a clear case of sabotage against his client. But Jennifer said that maybe it just slipped out somewhere or got lost in the luggage."

"Always Miss Congeniality," I mumbled.

"Seriously!" New Mexico said. "I mean, what a big fat phony."

As soon as the words popped out of her mouth, her hands reached up and covered her lips. "That was going a little too far, wasn't it?"

I shook my head. "Don't worry. I know what you meant." What she meant was she hated Jennifer. I stored that tidbit away for later.

"Anyway, we all felt bad for her, you know? I mean swimsuit is a huge portion of our overall score. You don't have your costume, you're screwed."

"So what did Jennifer do?"

"Well, luckily there are, like, a million bathing suit shops here. So Dempsey ran out and picked up a couple of different bikinis. Jennifer luckily found one she liked."

She was lucky. She'd had a perfect sample size body. Anything would have looked good on her.

"So if you had to guess, who sabotaged Jennifer's wardrobe?"

New Mexico's eyes went big and round. "Gosh, I don't know," she said. "But I do know that Whitney has come in second place in the last two competitions we've all competed together in." She did a big wide innocent smile that was anything but.

If I didn't know better, I would say that Miss New Mexico was throwing Whitney under the bus. From everything I'd learned about Whitney, she was doing well in the competition, and she was desperate to win before she aged out— if she wasn't already lying about her age now. She *did* have an easy access to Jennifer's room. Jennifer and Desi's room was two down from mine and directly across the hall from the one shared by Whitney and Maxine, Miss Arkansas. It would have been fairly easy for Whitney to slip into the room unnoticed and steal Jennifer's top. And with girls going in and out, arriving and changing at the rapid pace I'd seen yesterday, doors were always opening and closing, girls slipping into each other's rooms.

Which begged the question: where had Whitney been the night of the murder?

There was one person who I was sure knew of Whitney's nighttime activities: her roommate, Maxine, Miss Arkansas.

As soon as I finished with Desi, there was a parade of a dozen more contestants coming in and out for their fittings. By the time I finally had a moment to slip back into the auditorium, the interview questions were in full swing. Miss Arkansas was standing on the stage next to Laforge, being read her interview questions for the preliminary round of judging.

While on the televised version the judges only had to hear the top three finalists give their answers, in the pre-televised portion of the competition all of the contestants participated in a question-and-answer round on which they were scored. I wasn't sure how many the judges had to see today, but by the looks on their faces it was one too many. Ruth Marie looked half-asleep, her elbow resting on the judges' table, her chin in her hand. I'd be hard-pressed to tell you whether her eyes were open or closed, as the wrinkles and extra skin on her face were smooshed up toward her eyelids.

Jeffries was staring at the contestant on the stage, his eyes glazing over as if he were sleeping with them open.

Only Dana seemed to be paying attention, though I could tell that the day had taken its toll on her as well. Her usually perfectly styled strawberry blonde hair was pulled back into a loose messy knot secured with a pen. The lipstick had been chewed off her lower lip, and there were traces of eye makeup along her cheek as if she'd been rubbing at her eyes.

"This is our last interview contestant of the day," Laforge told the assembled judges. "We'll conclude with Miss Arkansas."

Arkansas did a big smile toward the judges as Laforge pulled her question from a fish bowl filled with scraps of paper. "And our question for Miss Arkansas is..." he started

Maxine's smile froze on her face, and I could see fear in her eyes.

"What are your feelings on euthanasia?"

Miss Arkansas blinked her false eyelashes up and down a few times before she began her carefully modulated response. "I was raised with the belief that people the world over deserve the same respect, care, and consideration as people in the United States. We are all one big family of humans, no matter where we hail from. As such, I believe we must respect and care and give consideration to the youth everywhere, including the youth in Asia."

From the judges' table I heard Jeffries snort, Ruth Marie stifle a hacking cackle, and Dana do a small groan. Me? I bit my lip to keep from laughing out loud.

I watched Arkansas walked off the stage, the bright smile still on her face even as her eyebrows formed a *V* of confusion. I think she was still trying to figure out the question. I jogged to catch up with her just as she slipped backstage.

"Maxine?" I called

Her blonde head whipped around, her eyes blinking a couple of times before recognition set in. "Oh, Maddie, right? Shoes?" she said

Even while her bulb wasn't the brightest, her smile was somewhat contagious.

"Yes," I said, smiling back at her. "I'm providing the shoes for the pageant. I was wondering if I could talk to you for a moment."

"Sure. What's up?" she asked, twirling a lock of hair in her index finger.

"I had a couple of questions for you about your roommate."

"Whitney?"

"Yes. I was just curious how well you know her?"

"Just the last few days you know? I've heard of her and seen her on the pageant circuit before, but we've never competed in the same categories." Arkansas paused, sucking in her lower lip, causing a void in her pink lipstick. "Truth is, this is my first time competing at a national level pageant." She sent me that bright-eyed smile again.

"Well, I'm sure you'll do very well." I think I was at my white lie quota for the day. "Anyway, I was wondering...the night that Jennifer died, did you hear anything or see anything odd?"

Arkansas shook her head back and forth, her blonde locks whooshing against her cheeks. "No. The police asked me this too. I had no idea Jennifer snuck out. At least not that night."

"Not *that* night?" I asked jumping on the wording. "Had she snuck out before?"

"No," Arkansas started, then that lip got sucked back into her mouth again.

"Look, I'm not one of the pageant directors," I told her, trying to ease her concern. "You don't need to worry about me telling anyone or getting the other girls in trouble."

"Well," she said, "there was that one night. It was when we first got here. I did hear somebody out in the hall. After curfew. I heard a door opening and then closing. And then footsteps in the hallway. I guess they were leading to the elevator."

"But you didn't see who went out?"

Arkansas shook her head again. "No, sorry. I honestly didn't really think anything of it. I thought maybe one of the girls was having trouble with her room and had to go back down to the front desk or something."

"In that case you would have heard them coming right back, wouldn't you?"

Arkansas nodded. "I guess. But I didn't. For like an hour."

I raised an eyebrow.

"I have kind of insomnia," she admitted. "Sometimes I have a really hard time sleeping. That night the sound of the door opening woke me up. I tried to get back to sleep for about an hour before I finally took a sleeping pill. It was just starting to kick in when I heard a door click shut again. I'm assuming it was the girl coming back."

My turn to chew on my lip. So one of the girls had disappeared for an hour. Had it been Jennifer? And if so, where had she gone? Had she been meeting someone on the beach that night too? The same someone who'd ultimately killed her?

"What about the night that Jennifer died?" I asked. "Did you hear anyone else leaving?"

She shook her head. "No, not that night. I had trouble sleeping that night too, so I took a sleeping pill early. I was out like a light."

"So I guess you wouldn't have known it if, say, your roommate had slept through the night or not?"

"Whitney? Well, I don't know. I mean I guess she..." She trailed off, her eyes suddenly going big. "Oh my gosh, you don't think Whitney could have had anything to do with Jennifer's death, do you?"

"Do you?" I asked

"No way." Arkansas' head swung back and forth again. If she wasn't careful that sucker was gonna twist right off of her shoulders. "Look, Whitney is driven, I'll give you that. But she is a total professional. You should see her stuff in our room. It's completely tidy, all lined up with, like, military precision in her makeup drawer. There's no way Whitney would do anything like this."

"Okay," I said reassuring her. However I noted Arkansas had just admitted she hadn't known Whitney more than a few days.

I spent the rest of the afternoon fitting other various girls for their shoes and trying to make up for all of the time lost the day before. Getting ready for a live production like this was hectic enough, but doing it a day behind schedule was beyond hectic. Laforge ordered boxed dinners in for everyone involved, and by 10 o'clock that night I was ready to drop and was seeing high heels even when I closed my eyes. Laforge finally called it a night, sending everyone off to their rooms with a promise that we would be heading out at a bright and early 6 AM the next morning for an on-location shoot at Iolani Palace, which would air during the televised pageant's opening credits.

I groaned, wondering why someone hadn't taken *him* out instead.

I trudged up to my room, changed into a pair of capri-pant sleepers and a hot pink tank top, and pulled up Ramirez's cell number on my phone.

Two rings and he picked up. Considering the time difference, he must have been waiting up for my call. A thought that filled me with warm fuzzies.

"Hey, babe," he answered.

The tension in my shoulders immediately eased at the familiar sound of his voice.

"Hey, yourself."

"How's my favorite girl doing?" he asked.

I couldn't help smiling. "Good. But busy."

"With...?" I could hear the suspicion loud and clear.

"You don't trust me, do you?" I asked.

Ramirez chuckled on the other end. "Honey, I'm not that naïve."

If I hadn't been lying to him I might've felt insulted. As it was, I felt more warm fuzzies that he knew me so well. And loved me anyway.

"Laforge has us working double time," I said, being 100% truthful now. "We lost a lot of time yesterday, so we worked straight through dinner."

"Geez, how long does it take to put some shoes on?"

My turn to laugh. "Oh, honey, you know as much about designing shoes as I do about the Stanley Cup."

"I'm impressed," Ramirez said. "You can name a cup."

"I'm learning," I said, stifling a yawn.

"Am I boring you?" Ramirez asked.

"Sorry, it's just been a long day," I said.

"I understand. Hey, get some sleep, babe. We'll talk tomorrow."

"Kiss Livvie and Max for me?"

"Will do," Ramirez promised. "Love you. Miss you." And then he blew kisses into the phone. Very not-alpha cop. Very endearing. I couldn't help the smile taking over my face and wishing just a tiny bit that I wasn't here in paradise but back home in his arms...which, in truth, was its own kind of paradise.

"Miss you, too," I said as I hung up.

I set my phone on the nightstand beside the bed. I leaned over and turned off the lights and was just snuggling into my pillow thinking warm happy thoughts about my husband when I heard it.

A noise out in the hallway. The tell-tale sound of a large, fireproof, hotel room door opening.

My eyes popped open, and I glanced at my bedside clock. Just past midnight. I quickly ran to the door of my own room and opened it a crack, peeking out. I was just in time to see the elevator doors closing on a woman in black slingback flats and a little black dress.

I paused just long enough to grab flip-flops and a sweatshirt, shoving my room key and phone into the pockets, before I slipped of out of my room after her.

This time I was going to catch that beauty queen in the act.

CHAPTER EIGHT

———

I ran to the elevators and stabbed the down button. There were three separate sets of elevator doors. I'd seen the girl go down in the center one. I stood nervously tapping my foot in my last minute flip-flops as I willed the doors in carriages number one and three to open. Finally number one did, and I ran inside pushing the L for the lobby. I crossed my fingers hoping that nobody on the floors below me needed a ride down. It was going to be a miracle if I could catch up with the woman in the little black dress in the lobby as it was. If I had to stop for three or four flights of tourists, I was sunk.

Luckily the gods of following queens were with me as my elevator shot straight to the bottom floor, opening off the lobby with a subdued *bing*. I jumped out of the carriage, my eyes whipping back and forth for any sign of the LBD. Unfortunately at this time of night, the lobby was far from empty, as vacationers arriving after their red-eye flights mingled with guests dressed to the nines went for a night on the town. I was sorely out of place in my pajamas and clutched my sweatshirt closer around my middle, hoping no one associated with the pageant saw me.

I was just about to give up when I saw a woman dressed almost as out of place as I was. It was the little black dress and black slingbacks I'd seen disappearing. However she also had a large black hat, black sunglasses, and a pale gray scarf that was tied over her head. As far as disguises went it was excellent. I could tell she was female, but which one of our female competitors I'd be hard-pressed to come up with. She quickly strode out of the hotel doors, down the paved pathway toward the Lost Aloha bar. I ran after her, doing a stop-start-stop-start thing as I ducked behind a palm, then behind a rather portly man heading toward the doors, and again behind a luggage rack once I got outside. I wasn't sure I was doing a great job of surveillance. If LBD woman turned around she had a pretty good chance of spotting me. Fortunately for me she seemed to have a one-track mind, and she made purposeful strides forward. But instead of continuing on her path toward the Lost Aloha, she veered left off the path and toward the beach.

I have to say I was pretty darn impressed with her ability to walk on the sand in her slingbacks. I saw now why she opted for flats even though they completely clashed with the outfit. Luckily my flip-flops did the job as well. I waited until she was a few paces ahead of me, and then I followed as closely as I could, trying to keep to the lush tropical plants bordering the beach rather than the wide open sand dunes. She went several yards down, and the farther she got from the resort, the harder it was to see her. There was just the tiniest sliver of moon in the sky, providing precious little light. I could still see the lights of the tiki bar and the resort in the distance, but they did little to illuminate LBD Woman.

Thankfully, they also did little to illuminate me as I crept along the bushes, praying that I didn't encounter any local animals nesting there. Did they have rats in Hawaii?

Luckily before we got completely away from civilization, LBD Woman abruptly stopped. It took my eyes a few moments of adjusting to the darkness before I realized why.

There was another figure on the beach.

I crept a little closer, trying to distinguish if this one was male or female. Unfortunately they stood with their backs toward me, facing the ocean, so I had zero chance of seeing faces. I could just barely make out voices over the roar of the tide. The woman in the dress's voice was high and almost frantic. The other was deep and low. If I had to guess, I'd say the second figure was male.

I hoped the sound of the ocean also masked any rustling sounds I made as I crept closer, ducking down behind the foliage, straining to hear any part of their conversation.

"That was our deal," I heard the female voice say.

I couldn't quite make out the man's response, but his words came quickly in a sort of growl. Whatever he said, he wasn't happy

"Don't think I won't do it," the woman threatened, her voice louder this time.

"You can do whatever the hell you want. But you'd better keep your mouth shut."

I raised an eyebrow. Now this was getting interesting. A particularly large wave crashing on the beach swallowed the first part of the woman's response, but I caught the tail end.

"...again with Jennifer."

My ears perked up. Whoever they were, they were talking about the dead girl. Suddenly I wondered if I was looking at Jennifer's killer...Or killers? I tried to lean in a little bit closer and caught part of the man's response.

"No one better know about this."

"What they know is up to you, but I can promise you this," the woman said. Unfortunately the rest of her statement was again swallowed by a wave coming up on the shore.

Dammit. I had to get a little bit closer. Just getting snippets of their conversation, my imagination running wild to fill in the blanks. I took a step closer toward the couple...

And heard the sound of Madonna's "Vogue."

I quickly stuck my hand in my pocket and fumbled around for the off button on my phone.

"What was that?" the woman asked, whipping around.

I dove into a naupaka bush, making myself as small as possible. Hoping they thought I was a rat. (Oh, God, let there be no real rats in this bush!)

"What was what?" the man shouted back

"I heard something. I heard Madonna music."

"Probably just some kids back at the resort."

"Look, I have to go," the woman told him. Then I heard rustling, which I presumed was her walking away. As much as I was dying to know her identity I didn't dare pop up from my hiding place now. I waited a three-count, and then I peeked my head over the bushes to make sure they were both gone.

The beach was empty.

I slowly untangled myself from the naupaka then sprinted back to the resort. My only hope of finding out the identity of the mysterious couple was to get back up to our floor before my missing queen could reach her room. I ran around the back of the hotel, through the poolside entrance instead of the front. I practically slammed into the bank of elevators, timing on my side as they were just opening to let off a group of men in duck shirts. I jumped in, hit the button for the twelfth floor, and did an antsy foot-to-foot dance as I watched the numbers of the floors light up.

We finally hit the twelfth, and the elevator doors slid open.

Just as a door down the hall slammed shut.

I quickly moved toward it. Room 614. And since one of its occupants was currently deceased, I knew exactly who had been sneaking out of it tonight.

Desi, Miss New Mexico, was the woman in the little black dress.

* * *

I slipped back into my room, my mind reeling with new theories. Had Desi killed Jennifer? And, if so, who was the man she'd been meeting on the beach? If Desi had wanted Jennifer dead, it seemed like it would've been a lot easier to kill her in the privacy of their shared room than to lure her outside. Or, for that matter, to walk downstairs with her under the guise of friendship. And how did the mystery man on the beach fit into it?

I took my sweatshirt off as I got back into bed, pulling my phone out of my pocket as I did. I looked down at the readout to see who the offending caller had been who had almost blown my cover.

Mom.

She'd not only called, but sent a text when she hadn't been able to get through. I swiped my finger across the screen to see her message.

Cleverly ornery, will salve you, juju classing fort Cummings

What the...? I shook my head. I was too exhausted to try to decipher what Mom's auto text was trying to say. Whatever it was, I was sure she'd call me about it in the morning.

* * *

The next day started way too early. The late-night excursion onto the beach coupled with Laforge's 6 AM call-time had me doing a zombie impression. Somehow I stumbled downstairs to the Tropical Tryst and downed about a gallon of coffee before finding my way to the front of the hotel where we were to meet before being bussed to our location shoot.

Sitting outside of the hotel lobby doors at the curb were two large luxury tour buses. Beside them stood a line of beauty queens, each toting a rolling suitcase that I knew contained their arsenal of makeup, hair products, and emergency changes of clothing. At the head of the line stood Laforge, a tablet in his hands, his fingers gliding over the screen in rapid succession as he checked contestants in.

He was dressed in another pair of skintight pants (I was beginning to wonder if he had stock in them), though today he had chosen a bright yellow color that reminded me of SpongeBob. He'd paired them with a silk, polo style shirt in bright red with turquoise hibiscus flowers in a large, retina-burning print. He was again wearing his signature oversized sunglasses, and today he was adorned in a straw panama hat in a sparkling white that matched his white loafers sans socks. I would say this for him: at least he wouldn't be easy to lose on our field trip.

I could see the judges already seated on one bus and Marco standing in the line, sucking down the last of his coffee from a paper cup. I quickly joined him.

"Good God, doll, what happened to you?" he asked when he spied me.

"Good morning to you, too, Marco." I paused. "Is it that bad?"

"Honey those bags under your eyes are definitely over the airline weight limit."

"I had a long night."

I filled Marco in on what I'd seen last night and Desi's late-night escapades on the beach.

By the time I was done Marco's face was stuck in a perpetual shut-the-front-door expression of disbelief, and we were at the front of the line, stepping onto the bus.

"Who do you think she was meeting?" he whispered, his eye shooting around the bus's occupants as if the answer lay there.

Which, honestly, it very well could.

"I don't know," I whispered back, doing the same as my eyes settled on Desi's brunette head. She was seated halfway down the bus next to Miss Delaware. "But as soon as I have a chance to get Desi alone, I intend to find out."

"Excuse me," Laforge said as he approached us, tablet in hand. "Are you planning to accompany us on this official pageant personnel excursion?" He gave Marco a pointed look, starting at the top of his spiked pink hair and slowly moving down his frame to take in today's outfit. He had on a pair of hot pink booty shorts in a cropped length normally only seen on MTV. Above that he was wearing one of the Hawaiian printed shirts he'd picked up on our shopping excursion earlier, a pink and baby blue printed top that was tight enough to have been painted on him. (If I had to guess, I'd say it had been made for 10-year-old girls.) The entire outfit ended in a pair of vintage 1980s hot pink jellies, which encased his pink painted toenails.

"Are you saying I shouldn't?" Marco asked putting his hands on his hips. His eyes narrowed at Laforge.

"I'm just saying that you are not on my list." And the tone in his voice didn't sound the least bit upset about it.

"Ah, Marco is actually my assistant," I said quickly jumping in before Marco could respond.

While I couldn't actually see Laforge's eyes behind his oversized sunglasses, I could almost feel them narrowing in his posture. "I'm sorry, but the pageant does not have it in its budget to pay for an assistant for you, Maddie."

I shook my head. "No need to pay for him. He's a volunteer assistant."

Laforge looked from Marco to me and back again. Luckily he had a bus full of giggling, easily distracted beauty queens and an airtight shooting schedule to keep, and finally he nodded. "Fine," he huffed then turned on his heel and walked off the bus doing a final check of his tablet.

I grabbed Marco by the arm and pulled him into two empty seats near the back of the bus.

"I bet it was Laforge on the beach last night," Marco grumbled.

I turned on him. "Why would you say that?"

Marco shrugged. "Well doesn't he look a little worse for the wear this morning? I mean, did you see that hideous outfit? Talk about loud."

Considering Marco's clothes were practically screaming, I wasn't sure I should comment on that.

* * *

The Iolani Palace was once the home to the United States' only royalty, King Kalakaua. Now a national historic landmark, it played host to tourists from around the world who visited the restored first and second floors, each decorated in colorful themes, took in the collections of historical Hawaiian artifacts, and strolled the lush landscaping of the grounds. Probably the most not-to-be-missed part of the palace, at least according to the travel website Marco pulled up on his phone as we rode into downtown Honolulu, was the famous statue of King Kamehameha I, erected just in front of the palace. As our buses pulled up, I could see a camera crew had set up on the grounds near the outdoor Coronation Pavilion, a large domed structure sporting ornate Roman columns and official crests.

We quickly filed out of the buses amidst Laforge barking orders, and the queens wasted no time in pulling out their powder compacts, lipstick, and hairspray, putting their last-minute touches on before going on camera. Dana and the other judges were ushered over to a trio of seats under a large tree in the shade to watch the proceedings. Boom microphones, bright lights, large white reflectors, and a slew of cameras descended on the Coronation Pavilion.

Under Laforge's direction, each of the remaining fifty contestants had her moment in front of the camera, giving a short intro of herself and her state. Then all fifty girls stood in a semicircle around the Pavilion doing a choreographed dance number. Which would have gone easily, had Miss Arkansas not been in the mix.

After an hour and a half, Marco finally wandered toward the palace to look for the gift shop, and I took a spot on a bench in the shade, fanning myself with a printout of the day's schedule to combat the muggy heat. I had my eye on Desi, watching her do her dance steps, but unfortunately there was no way to get her alone in this crowd, let alone with cameras on her. I was sure I would have a chance soon.

"Hot one, isn't it?"

I looked up to see Dempsey's large frame beside me. If I was hot, he was melting. I could see his artfully applied makeup running down his face in the beads of tan colored sweat.

"Sweltering," I agreed. "I can't imagine how their hair doesn't frizz in this humidity," I said, pointing toward the queens.

Dempsey chuckled, taking a seat beside me. "I'll tell you a little secret."

I leaned in close.

"Vinegar." He grinned

"Vinegar? Like, they drink it?"

He shook his head, his jowls wobbling with him. "After shampooing, if you comb in vinegar, then rinse with cold water, it will make your hair appear thicker, sleeker, and frizz resistant."

"Good to know," I said locking that away for future reference. I paused. "I'm surprised you're still staying on with the pageant," I told him.

Dempsey raised both eyebrows at me.

"I mean, considering you don't have a contestant in it anymore." I was doing my best to be delicate, but on little sleep, lots of caffeine, and 90% humidity, I was in no mood to play cat and mouse.

"Actually I do," he informed me.

My turn to be surprised. "Really?"

Dempsey nodded at Maxine. "Miss Arkansas over there."

He must have seen the shocked look on my face as he smiled and added, "The poor kid needed some help. I've got no delusions of winning, but I figured I could step in temporarily for her at least."

"It's nice of you to try to help her," I said.

He nodded. "Well, I'm here and able, and she arrived without a coach. Can you imagine?" He clucked his tongue. "And that egomaniac Laforge keeps putting poor Maxine right up in the front, knowing she doesn't have the world's best rhythm. It's like he was setting her up to fail. Like he's trying to sabotage her or something."

Sabotage was an interesting word. One I'd heard a few times lately.

"Like someone was sabotaging Jennifer?" I asked.

Dempsey paused, and then he nodded slowly. "You heard about that, did you?"

"Queens do talk."

"Well, it's true. Look, Jennifer didn't misplace things. That missing bathing suit top was no accident."

"So you do think someone stole it on purpose?"

"I *know* someone did. It was just our good luck we found something that fit in time. I mean, you must now how difficult it is to find a bathing suit that fits properly."

I tried not to take that personally. "Was there any investigation into the theft?"

Dempsey shook his head. "Jennifer didn't want to pursue it. Look, she was no dummy. She knew it was the other contestants who voted on Miss Congeniality, and she wanted that title along with taking the entire competition. So, she said she just wanted to put it behind her and move on."

"Just out of curiosity, what did the stolen top look like?"

"It was a white, bandeau style, with a seashell embellishment on the front. Very beachy, and very appropriate for this competition. Jennifer spent weeks searching for just the right style. So when she had to throw something on last minute, well, I'm sure she lost some points with the judges there."

"And you think that was someone's intention in the first place?"

"Oh, I know it was."

"You have any guesses who?" I asked.

Dempsey mashed his lips into a thin line, his eyes going out over the contestants crowded into the Pavilion, trying not to dance on top of one another. His eyes narrowed as he honed in on one in particular, right at the front of the line, next to poor stumbling Maxine.

Whitney.

"If I had to guess, I'd put my money on that filly right there."

CHAPTER NINE

———

Things were starting to look bad for Whitney. And for Miss Arkansas, after another less than dazzling dance number at the Coronation Pavilion. But I couldn't worry about her. Clumsiness hadn't killed Miss Montana. I wished I could be as certain that Miss Delaware hadn't.

As soon as the contestants finished the taping, Laforge herded them onto the bus to head off to the local television station to film a promotional spot, while the rest of us were dismissed to return to the hotel. I was happy for the break. While Dana headed off to change and catch a couple of minutes at the pool, I thought Marco and I could put our time to better use. I wanted to talk to Don, the protester, again. I wanted to be sure I had her story straight and that I'd get the same story twice in a row.

She wasn't hard to find. She was back outside the lobby with her sign du jour, this one reading *Break the Fashion Plate*, which was an interesting perspective since she'd clearly done that years ago. No bucket of red paint in sight, which was a relief.

She seemed less than enthusiastic to see us again, lowering her sign with a loud sigh. "You're back."

"And as fabulous as ever," Marco said.

I shot him a look that I intended to say *not helpful*. "I was hoping I could ask you a few more questions," I told her.

She rolled her eyes. "Is it about the same thing as before? Because I already told you everything I saw. You *and* the police," she added pointedly.

I pretended not to notice the attitude. "You said you saw some of the pageant people around the grounds a few nights ago."

"When that girl was killed." She gave one sharp nod. "That's what I said."

"You saw Jay Jeffries at the bar," I prompted.

"I saw him heading *to* the bar," she corrected me. "I didn't see him *at* the bar."

I conceded the point with a shrug. "And you saw Ashton Dempsey and the pageant director, Simon Laforge, at the bar, too?"

"Not *too*. I just told you—"

"Did you see them *going* to the bar?" I cut in.

She drew back a little. "I said that I did. So what?"

"You're sure you saw the two of them?" I asked. "Together?"

Her fist went to her hip. "You want it carved in stone? I know what I saw. Are you trying to call me a liar?"

Marco's eyes widened and shifted my way.

"Absolutely not," I said quickly. "I just wanted to be sure I heard you right, that's all."

"You heard me right," she snapped. "Now, unless you two want to pick up signs and join me, why don't you let me get back to something more important?" She glared down at Marco's hot pink jellies. "Nice shoes."

I bit my lip to keep from laughing. Marco might never wear those shoes again now that they'd gotten Miss Crocs' endorsement, even if it was drenched in snarkiness.

He didn't have quite the same reaction.

"Oh, honey," he said on a dramatic sigh, "there's hope for you yet."

Her eyes narrowed into slits. "What's that supposed to mean?"

"Well, let's be real," he told her. "Birkenstocks? Positively tragic. I see you in a kitten heel. Maybe an Ann Taylor metallic." He held a finger to his chin, assessing. "And this?" He did an arm sweep that encompassed her moss-green pants and mud brown Runway Slave T-shirt. "Have you ever considered wearing an actual color? I think a nice dusty rose would really flatter your skin tone." His eyes drifted upward to her mousy brown hair, but he wisely kept his opinion to himself.

Don looked at me. "Is he serious?"

"He does have a way with style," I said.

We both looked at Marco's screaming Hawaiian shirt and hot pink booty shorts.

"Usually," I added.

Don was not amused. "Well, save your advice for the talking mannequins," she told him. "I'm not interested."

Marco shrugged. "Suit yourself. Honestly, it's exhausting to talk to some people."

"Thanks for your time," I said to Don.

"Whatever," she mumbled at me.

Marco was right. She was exhausting. But she was also helpful, whether she intended to be or not. She'd given me a lot to think about as we left her to her hostility and threaded our way along the path toward the hotel. Why would Dempsey and Laforge meet for drinks? From what I knew, they weren't exactly besties. I'd barely seen them look at each other. And was it possible Jay Jeffries had joined them for some reason? Or did he have his own agenda, maybe one wearing a bikini and holding a bottle of Hawaiian Paradise sunscreen?

Marco blotted his forehead with the back of his hand. "This humidity is a killer, isn't it? I think I hear a piña colada calling my name. Want to come along?"

I shook my head. "You go on. I'll catch up with you later."

He gave me a little wave over his shoulder as he headed toward the Lost Aloha Shack and Surfer Dirk. "Don't do anything I wouldn't do!" he called out.

There wasn't much chance of that.

* * *

Ever since I'd found Miss Montana's body, I'd been going out of my way to avoid the pool area. The image of Jennifer lying there was still too close to the surface for comfort. But things were always less foreboding in the daylight, and I couldn't avoid the pool for the rest of the trip, so I decided to change into my swimsuit and join Dana for a few hours of leisure before pageant activities picked up again. My hope was that my friend's company would help blur the sharp edges of the lingering memory. I hurried up to my room to change and grab some sunscreen and a hat.

I found Dana on a chaise lounge on the far end of the pool, but she wasn't alone. Her fellow judge, Ruth Marie, was sitting with her, and Ruth Marie seemed to have a lot to say (as usual), punctuating her sentences with hand gestures. And from the frown marring Dana's features, she didn't seem to like what she was hearing. As I got closer, Ruth Marie abruptly got up and hurried away, leaving Dana staring after her with an expression of concern.

I sat down beside her. "Everything alright?"

She gave a start. "Oh, Maddie. I didn't notice you." She threw another glance at Ruth Marie's back and gave a little head shake. "Can you believe this?" she muttered.

"What was that all about?" I asked.

"I should've known better," Dana said, turning her attention back to me. But she sounded more like she was talking to herself than to me. "I work in Hollywood, for God's sake. You'd think that nothing would surprise me anymore."

The poolside waiter appeared with a smile. I ordered a mimosa, Dana ordered another daiquiri, and we were silent until he moved on. "So, what was that all about?" I asked her, gesturing in the direction of Ruth Marie's retreat.

Dana turned to face me. "Tell me something," she said. "Was I naïve for thinking I was actually being asked to judge a beauty pageant? I mean, I know there's a lot on the line here. The Hawaiian Paradise Corporation wants the right girl, and the winner has to fit their marketing plans. I get that. We're talking about a huge amount of money." She sighed. "But I thought I was judging these girls on their merits, not just passing out undeserved scores."

I was confused. "Did Ruth Marie ask you to pass out undeserved scores?"

Dana shook her head. "No, not exactly. Well, yes, but I don't think it was her idea. I think she was just relaying the request."

"She asked you to *cheat*?" Maybe we were both naïve, but the idea shocked me.

Dana let out a long sigh. "You could call it that."

I couldn't think of anything else to call it. "How are you supposed to do that without losing your credibility?"

"All three judges are being *encouraged* to crown a certain beauty queen, at least according to Ruth Marie. I'm expected to do my part." She took a sip of daiquiri, looking glum. "Or so I've been told."

I silently contemplated this. I'd assumed beauty pageants weren't necessarily all about beauty, but I'd had no idea this many strings got pulled to ensure a particular winner. "Encouraged by whom?"

Dana shrugged. "Someone up high at corporate, I guess. After all, this is about their money."

The waiter came back with our drinks, set them on a small glass table between our chairs, collected Dana's empty glass, and left us again.

"So who's the lucky girl?" I asked, fully expecting to hear Miss Deleware's name.

Dana sighed and took another long sip of her fresh daiquiri. "Desi. I'm supposed to pad her interview score by ten points."

I felt my eyebrows rise at this. An extra ten points could very well make Desi the front-runner in the pageant instead of Whitney. Which would put Desi in line for a whole lot of endorsement money. And maybe that gave her a whole lot of reasons to want Miss Montana out of the way. I sipped my mimosa, thinking that Desi's stroll on the beach the night before no longer seemed to involve any possibility of an innocent romance. It might have had everything to do with her buying her way into first place. But who was doing the selling? Was it Laforge? He was certainly in a position to make it happen for her. Or maybe she'd gone directly to the top and was conspiring with someone from the Hawaiian Paradise Corporation. If only I knew who she'd been meeting with, it could answer a lot of questions.

"What are you going to do?" I asked Dana.

She stared off across the pool. "Well, I'm a judge," she mumbled, again more to herself than to me. And she took another sip of daiquiri. Her glass was already half empty. Her gaze shifted and fell on an adorable set of little blond-haired twins wearing matching floaties, splashing in the shallow end of the pool, but she seemed to hardly notice them.

I could see that she needed time to process what had just happened and her role in it. I relaxed back into the chaise and closed my eyes, but my mind was whirling. The implications of Ruth Marie's request were huge, and they were ugly.

And Miss New Mexico was right in the middle of them.

* * *

We passed the rest of the afternoon peacefully by the pool, with no further sign of Ruth Marie or the pageant contestants or even Marco. The twins eventually left with their parents, replaced by a group of giggling teenaged girls who spent much of their time at the edge of the pool with their heads bent over cell phones. I didn't press Dana for any more details, and she seemed lost in her own thoughts.

Around five, we headed back to our respective rooms to shower and dress for dinner. I lingered in the hot spray, letting it massage out the few knots that hadn't melted in the sun's warmth, before slipping into a pale green halter dress that complemented my developing tan. I paired it with silver slingbacks and a chunky silver cuff bracelet with silver dangly earrings.

At six thirty, I headed out to meet Dana at the Lost Aloha Shack for drinks before dinner. The bar wasn't overly crowded, and I could see she wasn't there yet, which gave me the chance to talk to Desi. I hoped to ask her about sneaking out the night before and maybe her knowledge of or involvement in the new campaign to crown her Miss Hawaiian Paradise. If I could figure out how to do that gracefully, though I had my doubts about that. It wasn't easy to ask someone if they were cheating their way to the top.

Except I didn't see Desi, either. Instead, I found Whitney, Maxine, and a few of the other contestants at the bar, dressed to the nines with full makeup and perfect hair, looking every bit the beauty queens they were despite a day spent in the sun and humidity. As I approached, I asked them if they'd seen Desi.

"Not since we got back from filming the promo spot," Whitney told me. "Maybe she's still in her room."

"Why don't you join us for a drink?" Maxine added. She swept her hand out like a game show hostess and promptly knocked over her empty glass.

"Thanks," I said, helping her pick it up, "but I'm meeting a friend." I glanced around again for Dana...only my eyes fell on another familiar figure. Xander Newport, sitting alone at the bar. His head hung low, his shoulders were slumped, and his hair was spiky and uncombed. He looked defeated. "Excuse me," I said to the girls.

My cell phone rang as I was making my way toward him.

"Hey, Mads." It was Dana. "I hope you don't mind, but I think I'm going to skip dinner tonight."

"Of course I don't mind," I told her. "Are you alright?"

"Yeah, I just want to take some time to go over my notes and...scores." She hesitated. "I've got a lot of thinking to do."

"You'll do the right thing," I said. "You always do. Call me if you need to talk."

"I'll catch up with you tomorrow," she said, and disconnected.

Seconds later, I slid onto the stool beside Xander. "Mind if I join you for a few minutes?"

He lifted his dark eyes to mine, and I felt a stab of sympathy when I saw the despair in them. "Suit yourself," he said. "But I'm not very good company."

"I understand," I told him. "I'm sure this is very hard for you."

I noticed Surfer Dirk heading our way, bobbing his shaggy head in time to the music being piped out of speakers mounted throughout the bar area. "Hey, chica!" he greeted me. "You're looking sun-kissed. You must've caught some tasty waves today."

I couldn't help but smile. "Sorry, no tasty waves. I spent the afternoon by the pool."

"That's cool. Not very rad, but cool." He slapped a napkin down in front of me. "What'll you have?"

"Bay Breeze, please," I told him.

He raised his eyebrows in Xander's direction. Xander shook his head, and Dirk bopped off to mix my drink.

"You're with that pageant, aren't you?" Xander asked.

I nodded. "But I'm a shoe designer. Not a contestant."

"Yeah. I figured."

I frowned at him.

"You knew Jen?" he asked me.

"I saw her," I admitted. "I didn't get to know her." I hesitated. "She seemed very—"

"She was," he said, not letting me finish. I looked down at his glass, wondering how many drinks he'd had. "She was everything," he continued. "That's why I just couldn't lose her, you know?"

My Spidey senses tingled. "Lose her?" I repeated.

He nodded. "I couldn't just let that other guy take her away. I mean, she was perfect."

"So, you knew Jennifer was seeing someone else?" I asked slowly, watching his reaction.

He nodded, his shoulders slumping, any fight I'd seen in him before completely drained.

"That's why I'm here. Because I didn't want to lose her. I was making some—what do you women call it?—grand romantic gesture." He snorted into his near-empty glass. "You like that, right? Flowers and all that? Yeah. Didn't work out so well, did it?"

I hardly knew what to say. It was all so tragic and horribly sad. "Do you have any idea who she was seeing?" I asked carefully.

"She wouldn't say." His shoulders lifted and fell in a deep sigh. "It didn't really matter. She told me it was over between us, and she was ending it. And I thought I could change her mind if I just showed up here. Like I could sweep her off her feet or something." His voice caught. "Maybe I could have, if I hadn't shown up too late."

"You can't blame yourself," I told him firmly. "No one could have seen this coming."

"Yeah."

"When did Jennifer break it off with you?" I asked.

He sighed again. "As soon as she got to Hawaii. She called and said it was over. Nice Dear John, huh?" He drained his glass without waiting for an answer, got up and wandered off, a heartbreaking picture of solitude among the happy, oblivious tourists.

Dirk arrived with my drink, and I sat with it quietly, considering what Xander had told me. Wondering if whoever Jennifer had been seeing had been the last person to see her alive, maybe even the person who had caused her death. Wondering who might know who that person was. Wondering what that commotion was I was hearing down the beach.

I cocked my head, listening to voices that seemed familiar, seemed like—

Oh, no. No way.

Before I had time to fully comprehend it, my mother and Mrs. Rosenblatt came rushing into sight on the beach. They turned together toward the Lost Aloha Shack, both of them carrying brightly striped beach bags that bulged with tabloid newspapers, books, rolled-up beach towels, and who knew what else. The bags were the only subtle thing about them. Mrs. Rosenblatt was wearing a neon peach muumuu that flowed behind her like a riptide in the ocean breeze. In comparison, Mom had a toned down wardrobe of pale pink capris and a loose-fitting sleeveless top and sandals, but what she lacked in sartorial splendor she made up for in cosmetic overload. Her eye shadow color pretty much matched my new pedicure, and her lipstick was a frosted bubblegum pink. Cyndi Lauper would have been jealous.

They spotted me right away at the end of the bar and broke into matching huge smiles as they lumbered over in a cloud of coconut scented suntan oil.

"What in the world are you doing here?" I asked after we'd exchanged hugs. Surfer Dirk drifted by and took their order for "something pretty with extra umbrellas." Surprisingly, this request didn't seem to confuse him in the least.

"We came to help you out," Mrs. Rosenblatt announced, lowering herself carefully onto a stool. "Sounded like your juju needs a good cleaning."

Seemed to me like my juju was my business, but okay.

"I told you we were coming," Mom said. She perched on the stool Xander had just abandoned, using his discarded napkin to wipe the bar. "Didn't you get my text last night?"

I frowned, trying to remember. "I don't think so."

Mom pulled out her cell phone and sifted through her sent text messages. "Here it is!" she said. "Oh. Well. Maybe that wasn't very clear." She held it out, and I read *Cleverly ornery, will salve you, juju classing fort Cummings*. "It's the darned voice recognition," she said by way of explanation. "It's not trustworthy."

"You should see some of the nonsense I've gotten," Mrs. Rosenblatt agreed. "Whatever happened to using a phone to make an actual phone call, anyway?"

That's what I'd like to know. I'd gotten that text at the worst possible time, while I'd been hiding in the bushes on the beach trying to spy on Desi and her mystery man.

"What this thing should have said," Mom explained with great patience, "is *Cavalry on the way, we'll save you, juju cleaning forthcoming*. See? That's not so complicated." She beamed at me. "And here we are!"

"Here you are," I said, fighting the urge to roll my eyes. "But how did you get a room? Between the pageant and the convention, the hotel seems pretty full."

"It's booked solid," Mrs. Rosenblatt said cheerfully.

"We've got that all figured out," Mom added. "We'll just bunk with you, dear. We won't bother you a bit, will we, Dorothy?"

"Not a bit," Mrs. Rosenblatt agreed. "Well, there is that matter of forgetting my breathing strips, but with any luck, my little snoring problem won't be any issue at all."

Snoring problem?

"And I need to be near an outlet," Mom said. "I can't sleep a wink without my heating pad."

"A heating pad?" I blinked. "But it's over ninety degrees."

"I don't argue with the arthritis, dear," Mom said. "If my bones want heat, I give them heat."

"And tomorrow we'll get that juju cleaned right up," Mrs. Rosenblatt said. "Of course, we'll have to pick up a few things first. But we'll take care of that. Nothing for you to worry about."

Too late. I was already worried.

"Here we are," Dirk announced, swooping in to hand over two rainbow-colored drinks. "Something pretty for the major chicas."

"Aren't you sweet," Mom told him. She nudged me with an elbow and whispered, "What's a chica?"

"It's a good thing," I whispered back.

"Oh, Betty, look at this." Mrs. Rosenblatt held up a glass of bright blue something or other topped with half a dozen little umbrellas. "It's just the color of my Ollie's eyes."

I don't know how she remembered the color of her Ollie's eyes, considering he'd been the first in a string of five husbands, but I liked her sense of romance.

"Cheers!" she added.

We'd just see about that.

CHAPTER TEN

———

Cheer might have been overstating my mood the next morning, thanks to Mrs. Rosenblatt's little snoring problem, which practically made the drapes shimmy off the rod. I was definitely not cheerful while I spent much of the night staring at the ceiling, my hands crossed on my stomach, fingers laced together, my legs straight and rigid. My mother, on the other hand, had curled herself around her heating pad like a fetus in the womb, drifted off into blissful unconsciousness, and didn't move for the rest of the night.

I really had to see about a heating pad.

Bleary-eyed after about three hours of sleep, I headed down to the Tropical Tryst buffet while I reluctantly filled my two well-rested roommates in on what I knew so far about Jennifer's death.

Ruth Marie was in the buffet line when stepped in behind her. Immediately I started to think about her instruction to Dana to pad Miss New Mexico's interview score. I wondered if she knew who had issued the instructions, or if she'd just been passing along the message. Maybe Ruth Marie had even gotten the message wrong, and the pageant wasn't as crooked as it now appeared. I hoped that was the case, for Dana's sake.

And that led me to wonder about Dana. There was still no sight of her, and I decided to check on her after breakfast. It wasn't like her to drop out of sight for too long.

Mom elbowed me in the waist. "Is that who I think it is?" She pointed her chin toward Ruth Marie's back.

I put my finger to my lips in a *hush* gesture. "It's Ruth Marie Masters. She's one of the judges."

Mom did a little squeal. "It is not!"

I smiled. "You've heard of her?"

"Have I *heard* of her? Miss Hawaiian Paradise of 1962? Who *hasn't* heard of her?" Mom grinned at me. "I bet she's a fountain of information."

My smile disappeared. "Wait a minute—"

Mom reached over, tapping like a woodpecker on Ruth Marie's shoulder. "Excuse me, aren't you Ruth Marie Masters?"

Ruth Marie turned with a put-upon sigh. "Please, if you don't mind, I'd like to just—" She stopped when she saw me and morphed instantly into pageant mode with a dazzling smile. "Maddie, how nice to see you."

I willed a smile back into place. "Ruth Marie, I'd like you to meet—"

"I'm Betty Springer," Mom said, thrusting her hand forward. "I'm such a huge fan. I watched you win the Miss Hawaiian Paradise crown way back in 1962. Those were the days." She rolled her eyes heavenward, reminiscing. "Such glamour and excitement. Nothing like today's pageants."

Ruth Marie brightened. "You're so right. I'm sorry, what was your name again?"

"This is my mother, Betty Springer," I said. "And this—"

Mrs. Rosenblatt grabbed hold of Ruth Marie's hand and gave it several vigorous pumps. "Dorothy Rosenblatt." She narrowed her eyes. "You have a confused aura."

Ruth Marie took back her hand and rubbed it a little. "Confused...?"

"Aura," Mrs. Rosenblatt repeated. "It's brown. Brown means confused. I can fix that for you."

"Oh." Ruth Marie gave me an uncertain look. I did a tiny shrug. "Well, I suppose that would be fine."

Mom gave a dismissive little wave. "We're not here to fix auras, Dorothy. This isn't a business trip. We're just here for some girls' time with my Maddie, remember?" She did an exaggerated wink, and I rolled my eyes. Nothing subtle about that. "We're very proud of her," she told Ruth Marie. "My little girl, working at the Miss Hawaiian Paradise pageant. Such a prestigious pageant. Well, of course, you know all about that, being one of the winners."

I winced at Mom's heavy handedness, but Ruth Marie seemed to be lapping it up.

"I can still remember the evening gown you wore," Mom went on. "Dior, wasn't it?"

"Yes, it was Dior." Ruth Marie leaned in close to her, just two girlfriends sharing a secret. "Do you know, it took five hours to custom fit that gown?"

"Well, it was just beautiful, and you were beautiful in it." Mom linked her arm into Ruth Marie's elbow. "You must join us for breakfast. I'd love to hear all about your pageant days. You look like you could still compete. Isn't she gorgeous, Dorothy?"

"Gorgeous," Mrs. Rosenblatt agreed, but she was looking at the omelet bar.

"Thank you for the offer, but I have so much to do." Ruth Marie tried to slide her arm free, but she was like a fish on a hook. Mom wasn't losing this one.

"Nonsense," Mom said. "Everyone has to eat." She took a look around the seating area and pointed. "Dorothy, why don't you go claim that table. It's right next to the fountain. It'll be like dining al fresco."

My eyes followed the direction of her point, and I noticed Jay Jeffries across the room, sitting alone with a plate of fresh fruit and a cup of coffee in front of him. He seemed deep in thought, paying no attention to the activity flowing around his table. As I watched him, I couldn't shake the feeling that he seemed the most likely candidate to have been the mystery man Jennifer had been seeing. He wasn't my idea of a stud—as far as I was concerned, Ramirez pretty much had that category locked up—but maybe Jennifer had gone for the pushy, womanizing type. There was no accounting for taste where men were concerned.

"...dear?" Mom was asking.

I dragged my attention back to the buffet. "I'm sorry?"

"I said, aren't you going to join us?"

I glanced back at Jeffries. "Sure. I just want to say hello to someone first."

"Don't be long," Mom said. "We haven't got much time."

"We don't want to miss that hula lesson at ten," Mrs. Rosenblatt added.

Her remark didn't hit me until I was halfway across the room toward Jeffries, and when it did, the visual of Mrs. Rosenblatt in a grass skirt almost stopped me in my tracks. Hopefully that comment had been strictly for Ruth Marie's benefit. The alternative was too much for me to wrap my head around.

As I expected, Jeffries readily invited me to sit down. "Would you like a cup of coffee?"

I was going to need something to keep me awake, but I wasn't having it with him. "No, thanks." I leaned forward, keeping my voice low enough to avoid being overheard. I'd already decided that the direct approach was best with someone like Jeffries. Especially since I probably had a limited amount of time before he reached for my knee under the table. "I hope you don't mind my asking, but as a judge, have you been told to pad Desi's scores to push her into first place?"

Jeffries didn't hesitate. "Yes, of course." He bit off a piece of mango. "In fact," he said while he chewed, "I relayed the message to Ruth Marie. And I believe she spoke to Dana. So we're all on the same page."

I was taken aback by his blasé attitude. "Who told you to do that?"

"I...I don't remember." Jeffries swallowed and patted his lips with his napkin. He didn't look at me. He remembered, alright. He just clearly didn't want to say.

"Was it someone from Hawaiian Paradise?" I pressed. "I can understand why a request from corporate would be hard to refuse."

"I really don't remember. I'm sorry." He reached for his coffee, his eyes darting to a point somewhere behind me and lingering there.

I glanced over my shoulder. Laforge was at the buffet, piling fruit on his plate and...was he striking poses? I blinked and took another look, along with every other diner within a ten foot radius of the buffet. He was hard to miss in impossibly tight white shorts and a peach fishnet top offering peek-a-boo glimpses of his faux tanned and hairless torso. His giant sunglasses were firmly in place, his hair gelled and immovable above them. And he was definitely making moves better suited to a photo shoot than a breakfast buffet. Even if he did have good legs.

"It was Laforge," I said, turning back to Jeffries. "Wasn't it?"

"I already told you, I don't remember." His tone had grown irritated. He looked past me again, as if seeking guidance from Laforge. He wasn't going to get it. It was clear that all of Laforge's attention was focused on the yogurt bar, where Marco was now doing his own supermodel thing in blazing yellow booty shorts and an emerald green crop top. The hair was spiked, the eyeliner was thick, and the pink jellies had made a return appearance. I had to admit, he had a pretty smooth routine down as he moved along the yogurt bar. He somehow managed to get his breakfast together while at the same time doing the over-the-shoulder, hand to the waist, leg stretched to the side thing like a red carpet diva. He repeatedly glanced over at Laforge. Watching them, I couldn't help but roll my eyes. Men will be boys.

I thought fast. The direct approach was getting me nowhere with Jeffries. Maybe it was time for the tactless approach. "Were you in a relationship with Jennifer?" I asked bluntly.

That got his attention. He dragged his gaze away from Laforge and widened his eyes in a pantomime of surprise. "What? No, of course not. Why would you even suggest such a thing?"

I lifted an eyebrow and said nothing.

"Okay." He held up his hands in surrender. "Alright. I admit it, I did try to hit on her. Who can blame me? The girl was gorgeous. But I'm sorry to say I didn't get anywhere. She just kept pointing to that damned promise ring, like it actually meant something." He shook his head. "Can you imagine?"

"She turned you down," I said.

His mouth twisted as if it pained him to admit it. "Yes, she turned me down. That has *never* happened before, believe me." He ran a hand over his hair, barely touching it, but I could still see the oily sheen left on his palm. Ick.

"Women don't turn me down," he added. "I'm Jay Jeffries."

That would be reason enough for me, but I opted for the kind route since I believed he was actually being honest with me for once. "I'm sure it's only because she was in a relationship already," I told him.

He snorted. "You think?"

I had no idea. "I'm sure of it," I told him.

"You know," he said, eyes straying to my ringed left hand, "being in a relationship doesn't have to mean you can't have any fun." He punctuated that statement with a wink.

"Oh, gee, would you look at the time? I've got a fitting..." I trailed off as I quickly got up from the table and made a bee-line for the door. Without coffee. Apparently being totally squicked out had a great wake-up factor.

* * *

It turned out that Mom and Mrs. Rosenblatt actually had been scheduled for a hula lesson at ten o'clock, but because an all-out search had to be undertaken to find a grass skirt of sufficient size to fit Mrs. Rosenblatt, they'd been offered a private lesson at a future date. Which fit right into their plan to go into town to find some anti-tiki potions to ward off the island's bad juju instead. Oh boy.

After they'd gone off on the hotel shuttle, I joined the pageant personnel gathered in the auditorium for a dress rehearsal of one of the dance numbers. Everyone, that is, except for Desi, who was nowhere in sight. I tried to ignore the apprehension that tingled up my spine at her absence. A contestant wouldn't miss a rehearsal unless it was for a very good reason. Or a very bad one. Desi was looking guiltier and guiltier by the second.

I took a seat a few rows back and watched Laforge stomp around, clearly in a snit about having to wait for Miss New Mexico. Or maybe because Marco had outdone him at the breakfast buffet fashion showdown. The contestants milled about near the stage, chatting in small groups while keeping anxious watch on Laforge.

"Ladies, your attention!" he called out after a reasonable three minute wait. "We're going to get started now. Places, please."

"But Desi isn't here," Whitney said.

"She knew the call time," he snapped. "Now, places, please."

The contestants scurried to take their assigned places. This dance number was designed to begin not on the stage but on the floor, moving down the aisles between seating sections, before each contestant ascended to the stage in turn for the big finale. It would be a real crowd pleaser, assuming Miss Arkansas didn't fall on her way up the steps.

"And, Jackie, music, if you would," Laforge called out.

I watched as the girls broke into motion, their symmetry clearly broken by Desi's absence as they shimmied and high-kicked their way toward the stage stairs. Whitney navigated the steps flawlessly, not breaking rhythm, and on the other side of the stage, Maxine missed only one or two beats before beginning her jazz walk toward center stage. Except she hadn't taken more than two steps when she pitched forward and fell flat on her face.

And let out a bloodcurdling scream that had Laforge waving his arms and yelling, "Stop the music!" He stormed toward the stage. "What in the name of—" He stopped midsentence, and even from the audience I could see his complexion go white.

I jumped out of my seat for a better look, and I felt the blood rush out of my own face.

This time Maxine hadn't fallen over her own feet.

She'd fallen over Desi, lying dead on the stage.

CHAPTER ELEVEN

Within a half hour, the auditorium was a churning sea of police officers and crime scene techs, each following their own specific choreography. The pageant personnel were corralled into the rear seating area, far from the stage, and one by one called to the front to give statements and hair samples. I waited my turn, trying not to look at Desi's crumpled form up on the stage, a pool of blood beside her head as she lay just inside the wings where she'd been shadowed until Maxine's unfortunate discovery. My mind whirled with the new and horrifying possibility that Jennifer had never been a specific target at all. Was someone out to get the pageant girls in general? As far as I knew, Jennifer and Desi's only link beyond the pageant itself was that they'd met with someone on the beach and, shortly after, been found murdered. But who would possibly want to kill beauty queens?

I let my gaze slide over the group and fall on Whitney, sitting silently beside her roommate, Maxine. Both looked pale and unnerved. Whether or not that reaction was genuine, I couldn't say, since this turn of events held a silver lining for Miss Delaware. After all, now that Desi was out of the picture, Whitney would vault right back to the front-runner position. I wondered if she had known of the judges' directive to pad Desi's scores. Did this competition mean enough to Whitney to kill off her competition one by one?

Laforge left his seat to follow Detective Whatshisname to the front of the auditorium, and my eyes followed them. It was easier to believe that Laforge would harbor a grudge about possibly being edged out and seek revenge of some sort against the Hawaiian Paradise organization. It was clear he had a mean streak. But did he have a homicidal one?

I settled back, chewing on my lip while watching Laforge talk to the police detective. His arms were crossed in a defensive posture, but he looked unsettled, and he ran the backs of his hands across his eyes a few times as he spoke. I was no body language expert, but he seemed genuinely upset to me. Whether that was because of Desi's murder or because his last chance pageant was evaporating in front of him was another question.

Then it occurred to me. Maybe I'd been looking in the wrong direction. Maybe it was someone not involved in the competition at all, but someone who felt strongly enough against pageants and beauty queens in general that they might try to do away with the whole affair by eliminating its participants. A crazy idea, but was it any crazier than standing outside in a *Fashion Kills* T-shirt looking to douse people with a bucket of red paint like our friendly neighborhood protester, Don? It seemed worthwhile to do some checking into her background, and I decided with the pageant once again looking like it was on hold, now might be the perfect time.

"Maddison Springer." Detective Whatshisname stood at the end of my row, notebook in hand, Bic at the ready. "Follow me, please."

I left my seat and followed a respectful distance behind, even though I'll admit I was curious to see what he'd written in his notebook after speaking to the others. While a crime scene tech went about taking my hair sample, the detective assessed me with tired eyes. The lines on his face seemed more pronounced, as if etched more deeply by worry. I was sure the two dead beauty queens were weighing as heavily on him as on the rest of us.

"Tell me what you know about the deceased," he said.

"She's Desi—Desiree DeMarco," I said. "Miss New Mexico. But you already knew that, right?"

He didn't say anything. He just looked at me in that inscrutable way that cops had. I'd seen that look from Ramirez more times than I cared to remember.

"She was Jennifer's roommate," I added. "Miss Montana. The first..." My voice trailed off.

"Victim," the detective finished for me.

I nodded, careful to avoid the natural inclination to glance at Desi's lifeless body.

He jotted something in his notebook. "How was Miss DeMarco doing in the competition?"

I considered how to answer that. "I'm not a judge," I said carefully, "but I'd heard rumors that she was doing well." Or would have been, as soon as the padded scores were registered.

"Just like Miss Oliver," he said, but it wasn't a question so I didn't reply. "Did you happen to hear any other rumors?"

I shook my head.

He flipped back through his notes. "And if I remember right, your room is on the twelfth floor, the same floor as the contestants. Did you see or hear anything there you think might be pertinent?"

My first impulse was to say no, since all I saw was Desi's back as she got into the elevator. After all, for all I knew, she might have been going down to the bar for a drink or to the lobby to pick up a message. But in hindsight, I knew better. I knew she'd been going to her mysterious meeting on the beach. So while I wasn't ready to admit to lurking in the bushes in an unsuccessful attempt to eavesdrop, my conscience wouldn't allow me to withhold any more than that.

"I heard a door close," I told him, "and when I got up to look, I saw Desi getting into the elevator at the end of the hall."

"Was she alone?"

"As far as I could tell," I said. "I didn't see anyone else."

"And what time was this?"

"Just past midnight. I was just going to sleep, and the sound woke me up." I shrugged. "They're heavy doors."

He studied me for a moment. "Can you think of anything else you want to tell me?"

The thought crossed my mind to suggest he look into the source of Protestor Don's hostility, but it didn't feel right to drag her into the investigation without real cause. Not when I could drag her into it myself. "Not right now," I hedged. "Is it okay if I go back to my room?"

He closed his notebook with a nod. "I'm sure I don't have to tell you to watch your back."

He sure didn't. After two murders in the span of a week, I planned to watch my back and everyone else's too.

* * *

I meant to go up to my room, but along the way I ran into Dana and Marco sitting in the lobby having cocktails under the shade of the towering palm trees, the fronds dappled with sunlight. Because the contestants had only been rehearsing rather than competing in a scored activity, the judges hadn't been present when Desi had been found. But from the way Dana's hands were shaking, I could tell she'd been in the lobby long enough to see the army of police officers swarm the hotel. If I knew Marco, he was trying to distract her from the grim reality, but I didn't think he was having much luck. He seemed grateful when I sat down.

I filled them in on what had happened.

"This is beyond awful." Dana stared into her drink. "I can't believe this is happening."

"Did you talk to the police?" Marco asked me.

I nodded. "I didn't have much to tell them. But I do have an idea." I shared my plan to talk to Don the protester.

"Dahling, I'm in," Marco said, fanning himself with his hand. "All this R&R is making my brain as sharp as a cotton ball. I *need* to put myself to good use."

"I saw you putting yourself to good use this morning," I told him. "At the yogurt bar."

"Oh, that." He flapped his hand. "It was all in good fun. I *was* fabs though, wasn't I?" He sipped from his drink, batting his impossibly long lashes at me over the rim of the glass.

"I just can't believe it," Dana said. "First Jennifer and now Desi? What's going on around here? Do you really think this Don person could have something to do with it?"

I shrugged. "It's a place to look. I can't stand the thought of doing nothing. Any ideas where to start?"

"We could check the peaceful protest permits that have been issued recently," Dana suggested. "I'm sure they're available to the public."

"We could do that," Marco agreed. "Or we could do this." He put down his cocktail and made a beeline for the front desk. Dana and I exchanged glances and followed him. "I'd like to speak to the manager, please," he told the desk clerk.

The chubby clerk seemed dismayed by the request, as if he'd personally breached the hotel's code of conduct. "Is there anything I can help you with, sir?"

"Let's see," Marco said. "Are you familiar with the tragically ungroomed person who stands on your grounds every day protesting from sunrise to sunset?"

The clerk nodded immediately. "That's Don."

"Right. Don." Marco glanced back at us. We nodded, too, as if this was something new to us. "And Don's last name would be...?" Marco's eyebrows arched in anticipation.

"Oh. Um..." The clerk frowned, thought a moment, turned, and called out, "James, do you know Don's last name?"

Another clerk appeared from the office area, a lanky twenty-something with a Beatles mop of black hair. "Don from Housekeeping?"

"Don with the signs," the clerk said.

"And the unplucked eyebrows," Marco added.

"And the bad attitude," I put in.

"Oh." James nodded. "That's Don Curcio. I think she lives over in Honolulu. Did she harass you or do something to damage your property? Because I can have Security remove her from the grounds."

Having seen her in action, I figured she'd probably harassed everybody, but I didn't want to cause her any undeserved trouble.

"I'm not sure," Marco said. "The stain may come out. In the meantime, I know a complimentary pitcher of daiquiris will soothe my hurt feelings."

Dana and I exchanged a glance, and barely contained eye-rolls.

"Of course, sir. I'll arrange that for you right away." The clerk snatched up a pen. "Your room number?"

Marco turned to Dana and me. "Ladies, where shall we take this little adventure?"

"My room," I said immediately, and gave the clerk the room number.

"I'll have a pitcher sent right up," the clerk assured us. "I'm terribly sorry for the…" He hesitated, probably because he didn't know what he was terribly sorry for.

Marco stepped smoothly into the hesitation. "As long as it doesn't happen again. You've been very helpful." He turned to Dana and me. "Ladies? Shall we head on up to the room?"

"Very nice," I told him on the way to the elevator. "And completely shameless."

"Thank you," he said with a smile.

* * *

"I don't believe it," Marco said a little while later.

"I never would have thought it," Dana said.

"I didn't see *that* coming," I said.

We were in my room, sharing the pitcher of banana daiquiris that the front desk had sent up, staring at a photo of Donatella Curcio we'd found in an Internet search. Not Don, the fashion train wreck, but Donatella, the former beauty queen. Which was surprising in itself. More surprising was that she had actually been gorgeous once upon a time, right down to the shining hair and Vaseline'd smile.

Marco snatched the tablet from me and gaped at it. "This cannot be her," he said. "Look at that hair. Those eyes." He blinked at it. "Those eyebrows. There are *two*."

Dana looked at her own tablet, where she'd pulled up some biographical information. "This says she competed in a half dozen national pageants, although she never won any of them."

"Always the bridesmaid," I mused.

Marco nodded. "I know that might do it for me. I don't handle rejection well." He looked at Don's picture again. "Wonder what the winners looked like."

Dana read further. "Get this. She actually competed in the Miss Hawaiian Paradise competition two years ago!"

Marco squealed. "She did all that damage to herself in only two years?"

"Two years?" I repeated. Jennifer and Desi had each been competing for more than two years. The pageant universe was a small one. They'd probably known Don in her former life, possibly even competed against her. Maybe even beat her. And from what I'd seen so far, Don wouldn't take that gracefully.

"Who won that year?" Marco asked.

Dana's eyes scanned the page. "Huh."

"'Huh' what?" I asked.

"Well, it looks like Don might have had a chance of winning this one. If," she added, "she hadn't been disqualified."

I leaned over her shoulder. "Why? What happened?"

"She was disqualified for trying to gain an unfair competitive advantage." Dana looked up from the screen. The corner of her mouth twitched. "Seems she was known among insiders as the Cupcake Peddler."

That didn't sound so bad. I could think of worse things than cupcakes. "What does *that* mean?"

This time Dana did smile. "It means she made daily trips to the bakery and plied all her competitors with cupcakes in the hopes they'd gain enough weight to make *her* look good."

"Oh, that's dirty," Marco said. "But delicious. Were they red velvet?"

Dana rolled her eyes. "It doesn't say."

"Does it say double fudge chocolate?" he asked.

She gave him a look.

He shrugged. "Just asking. I know if *I* was going to fatten up the competition, I'd go with double fudge chocolate."

"That's hardly the crime of the century," I cut in.

"But still against the rules," Dana pointed out.

"And it did get her disqualified," Marco added. "Voila, a grudge is born."

I nodded slowly, thinking. Marco had a point. First Don had managed to collect a string of pageant losses, then gotten herself disqualified for not playing fair at the granddaddy of all pageants, the Miss Hawaiian Paradise. Even if that had been her own fault, it was enough to give anyone a jumbo sized grudge against the beauty pageant circuit in general and Miss Hawaiian

Paradise in particular. The question was, had she channeled that grudge into peaceful protest or twisted it into something much worse?

"I think it's time to have another talk with our fallen beauty queen," I said. "It's possible—"

Just then the door opened and a slew of shopping bags spilled into the room in front of Mom and Mrs. Rosenblatt. Their cheeks were flushed from the heat and obvious excitement. "Oh, there you are!" Mom dropped her bags onto one of the two queen beds with a sigh of relief. "We were hoping to catch you."

"Ooh, retail therapy!" Marco dove for the shopping bags. "What do we have here?" He hooked a finger over the top of one and peeked inside. His mouth puckered. "Now that demands an explanation."

Mom slapped his hand away. "You'll see when the time comes."

"Honey, the time is *now*," Marco told her. "I don't think I can wait."

"Don't be such a Nosy Nelly," Mrs. Rosenblatt admonished him. She frowned and jabbed her thumb in my direction. "It's supposed to be a surprise. You can help us later."

My instincts suddenly went on red alert. "Help you what?"

"Not important, dear," Mom said. "Don't you want to hear what we found out?"

"Are those daiquiris?" Mrs. Rosenblatt asked, eyeing our glasses.

Marco poured her one and handed it over. Mom accepted the cold glass and rolled it back and forth across her forehead while she perched on the edge of the bed, staying close to the shopping bags. "You know we went to town for some juju potions."

"You're gonna have the best juju on the island," Mrs. Rosenblatt promised. "We're loaded up."

I wondered if maybe they were loaded up on something besides juju potions. Mom was practically giggling with delight.

"While we were in town. We should go back there together, dear," she told me. "It's the quaintest little place. Do you know they had—?"

"You were about to tell us what you found out," Dana prompted.

"Oh. Of course." Mom drank some of her daiquiri. "What I was about to say was we talked to some locals. It's always helpful to get the perspective of the locals."

"You never know what you don't know," Mrs. Rosenblatt added. "Being a tourist and all."

Mom nodded. "Are you ready for this?"

"More than ready," I said.

"Spill it, dahling," Marco told her. His eyes were wide with anticipation.

"It seems Xander Newport was seen in town at the Curling Wave bar having himself quite the time," Mom said. "He was even *flirting* with some of the local girls." She frowned. "Do they still call it flirting? I'm a little out of touch with the dating scene."

Dana and I glanced at each other, and I could see Dana struggling not to smile. "Anyway," Mom went on, "they thought he was just another obnoxious tourist—that's what that darling little brunette girl said, wasn't it, Dorothy? Obnoxious?"

"I think it was the blonde," Mrs. Rosenblatt said.

"Well, anyway, *someone* called him obnoxious. But they didn't think much of it. Until…"

We all leaned forward as one.

"Until Miss Montana was murdered," Mrs. Rosenblatt cut in.

Mom pooched out her lower lip. "I was getting there, Dorothy."

"So get there, already," Mrs. Rosenblatt told her.

"Now they're all wondering if he had something to do with it," Mom finished. She looked at Mrs. Rosenblatt. "There. Happy now?"

"Wait." I put my glass down and stood, suddenly too amped to sit still. "Are you telling us that Xander was already on the island when Miss Montana was murdered?"

Mom nodded. "That's what we heard."

"And from enough people that it has to be right," Mrs. Rosenblatt said. "After all, where there's smoke, there's fire."

"This could change everything," I said. I tried to remember when Xander had claimed to arrive in Hawaii and realized he'd never actually said. It had been my assumption that he'd gotten here following Jennifer's death, since that was when I'd first seen him at the hotel. But now it seemed clear that my assumption was wrong. He'd said that his pursuing her to the island had been a grand romantic gesture, meant to win her back from her new love. But could it really have been an act of revenge for dumping him? Had I misread the grieving Xander at the Lost Aloha bar? Maybe it hadn't been grief he'd had been feeling at all, but guilt.

Was it possible Xander had never planned to reunite with Jennifer at all, as he'd claimed, but had actually come to Hawaii for the sole purpose of killing her?

CHAPTER TWELVE

———

After we'd finished the pitcher of daiquiris, Dana left to go Skype Ricky, and Marco decided to try his luck at a little surfing. (Though I had a feeling there would be more surfer ogling than actual surfing on his part.) Mom and Mrs. Rosenblatt practically shoved me out of the room to ensure I wouldn't nose through their purchases, although the official excuse was that they needed some relaxation time after a hectic morning of shopping.

I didn't mind a little alone time. I decided over a quick Caesar salad lunch that my next course of action would be to follow up on the information I'd learned about Donatella Curcio. While I definitely wanted to ask Xander some questions about his indeterminate arrival time on the island, I wasn't sure I wanted to do it just yet, and I knew that I didn't want to do it alone. I felt reasonably safe talking to Don on my own. So I headed down to the lobby to find her.

Ten minutes later, I had covered every inch of the lobby and adjoining public spaces, even poking my head into the gift shop and dining room. Don was gone. Which was strange, since as far as I could tell, she hadn't missed a day of protest since the pageant personnel had checked into the hotel. Despite the recent events, I didn't want to think something had happened to her. Maybe she'd had a dentist's appointment? Or maybe she'd gone on a shopping trip for some new poster board?

Still, I stood in line behind a young couple at the front desk, waiting to talk to James, the helpful mop-top desk clerk. The couple must have been newlyweds, judging from their shameless public display of affection, and I found myself smiling as I watched them. I also found myself thinking again about Max and Livvie and Ramirez back at home. I wanted to hear the breathless sort of excitement in their voices when they told me about their days. I missed them like crazy, and I missed the daily chaos that was our lives more than I thought I would. I told myself I'd call Ramirez as soon as I could carve out some time alone in the room. It felt like a long time since I'd talked to him.

"Did you enjoy the daiquiris?"

The question pulled me out of my thoughts. The newlyweds were halfway across the lobby, tugging their luggage toward the hotel's porte cochere with one hand, holding hands with the other. James was behind the desk waiting patiently for me.

I assured him that we had and thanked him for the pitcher. "I was hoping to ask Don a few questions," I told him. "But I don't see her anywhere. Has she been here today?"

James rubbed his chin as he thought about it. "Come to think of it, I haven't seen her since the police showed up this morning."

I frowned. "But she *was* around earlier?"

"Oh, yeah." He nodded. "It takes a lot to keep Don away from here."

A lot of police, apparently. I couldn't help but wonder about her aversion to law enforcement. Don certainly wasn't the shy type, nor did she seem easily intimidated. Could it be that she'd been taken away for questioning by the police?

"Of course," James added, "things got a little hectic, so I can't say I paid her much attention."

"Understandable. I'll try again later." I turned to go back to my room when I spotted Ruth Marie emerging from the Hula Hibiscus Day Spa, blowing on her newly manicured fingernails. She kept glancing over her shoulder as she hurried toward the elevators, as if she expected to find someone creeping up behind her. There was a rigid set to her shoulders that spoke to her unease.

I intercepted her before she could step into an open car. "Ruth Marie, could I talk to you?"

She jumped a little, her eyes going wide. "Maddie!" She tried to smile but it dissolved into a nervous laugh. "You startled me something awful. I'm afraid my nerves are on edge lately. I guess I'm jumping at shadows." She held out her hands to show off her iridescent peach nails. "I thought this might help calm me down, but it didn't really do the trick."

"I think everyone's upset right now," I told her. "Would you mind if we sat down for a few minutes?"

Ruth Marie's gaze moved past me to scan the lobby. "Are your mother and her friend going to be joining us?"

There was no way I would admit that they were preparing for a juju cleansing, whatever that meant, so I just smiled. "They're busy going through the spoils of their shopping trip."

"Oh." I thought I heard a little relieved sigh. "Alright, then." She followed me over to one of the conversation areas and settled in, careful not to smudge her polish. People trickled past us, moving through the lobby, but no one glanced our way, and after a few moments, Ruth Marie seemed to relax a little. "I had the most interesting time at breakfast," she said politely.

I could plainly see the years of pageant training kicking in. She sounded like she was under the spotlight answering an interview question, right down to the pasted-on smile and forced sincerity.

"Your mother remembered things even I had forgotten," she added. "Although that didn't stop her from asking me about them." Absently, she blew on her nails. "So many questions," she muttered.

"She's something of a pageant buff," I told her. Or at least she pretended to be. "Mom's a big fan of yours."

"So she told me." Her small practiced smile faltered. "Over and over again."

I grinned. "Thank you for being so gracious. She loved being able to reminisce with you about your pageant experiences." I hesitated. "I remember her mentioning another Miss Hawaiian Paradise contestant who seemed to have an interesting story. Her name was Donatella Curcio. Do you happen to remember her?"

"Donatella...?" Recognition flooded her face. "Oh, yes, the Cupcake Peddler." Her nose wrinkled, and she let out a hacking laugh. "I certainly do remember her. I think everyone on the circuit remembers her."

"For trying to fatten up her competition?" I asked.

"Please." Ruth Marie blew on her fingernails some more. "Those girls were lining up in the hallway for those cupcakes. They were practically placing orders. The way I saw it, Donatella was doing them a favor. Poor anorexic things."

I couldn't help a grin.

"You know what happened, don't you?" she continued.

I shook my head.

"It was the stupidest thing I'd ever seen. One of the girls—it might've been Miss Connecticut. It was usually Miss Connecticut. She acted like Harvard had been built just for her, that one. Well, Miss Connecticut wanted red velvet, and Donatella gave her pumpkin spice. That put her sequins in a snit. Pumpkin spice is a perfectly fine cupcake, but no, she wanted her red velvet. Well, she should've gotten in line sooner is what I say. Miss Pennsylvania got the red velvet. So bingo." She snapped her fingers, then remembered her manicure and quickly checked her nails. "The Cupcake Peddler was born."

"So the unfair advantage accusation came from another contestant?"

Ruth Marie snorted. "Oh, the unfair advantage nonsense was just a convenient excuse to be rid of her. That wasn't why she was ousted."

I sat forward, intrigued. "Really? What was it?"

She shrugged. "I don't really know that I should say."

I fought the urge to roll my eyes. *Now* she was going demure on me? "I won't tell a soul." I crossed my heart. "But I love a good story."

"I don't know if *good* is the word for it," she said. "More like *seedy*." She glanced to either side to be sure no one was within earshot. "She was found in a…well, let's just say a compromising position with one of the pageant judges." She sat back, shaking her head. "It was disgraceful. That never would have happened in my day."

Probably more like it never would have come to light. "Do you remember who the judge was?" I asked. I wasn't sure if his identity would mean anything, but it was better to know than not.

"Of course," she said at once. "It was that cheesy soap opera actor, Jay Jeffries."

It was better to know, alright. I propped my chin on my fist to keep my mouth from dropping open. "Are you sure about that?"

"Quite sure, honey pie. It was the talk of the pageant. No one was sorry to see her go, I can tell you."

I tried to imagine Don hooking up with Jay Jeffries. It was hard enough to imagine Don as a beauty queen, even though I'd seen the photos. And the more I thought about it, the more irritated I became that Don had been disqualified while Jeffries had gone on to continue judging future pageants. Talk about a double standard. Don's bad attitude was starting to make sense. I would have been surprised if she hadn't been upset.

"Of course," Ruth Marie was saying, "the whole sordid mess should have never come to light in the first place. And it wouldn't have, if he'd known the meaning of the word *discretion*."

I blinked in surprise. "Jeffries confessed he'd..." I searched for the most inoffensive word. "...compromised her?"

She snorted again. "Certainly not. That weasel wouldn't confess to getting out of bed in the morning. I'm talking about Donatella's coach."

My eyes went wide. "Her *coach* ratted her out? Why would he do that?"

Ruth Marie shrugged. "He gave some cockamamie story about protecting his contestant, but I think the real reason is he was trying to win some brownie points with the Hawaiian Paradise Corporation. Coaches sometimes turn into pageant directors."

"Wonder whatever happened to him," I mused.

She looked at me with surprise. "I'll tell you what happened to him. He went on to coach Miss Montana. Donatella's coach was Ashton Dempsey." She blew on her fingernails one last time and pushed herself from her seat. "I really do need to take care of some things. Nice chatting with you, Maddie."

I gave her an absent nod and a half smile while I tried to absorb what she'd just said. Ashton Dempsey had caused his own client to be disqualified from presumably the biggest pageant of her life? Try as I might, I just couldn't see the sense in it. It seemed to me he stood to gain more if she remained in the pageant and managed to win it.

But that did chalk up another reason for Don to have a major chip on her shoulder. Enough of a chip to kill Dempsey's new client, Miss Montana, out of revenge or jealousy? Even I could see that was a stretch. It would make more sense for her to kill Dempsey himself. Plus it still wouldn't explain why Desi had wound up dead as well. As far as I knew, she and Dempsey had had no connection.

Although it was painfully clear there was an awful lot I didn't know.

My cell phone alerted me to a text message. I glanced down to see Laforge was calling an immediate all hands meeting in the auditorium. So a decision had been made about the fate of the pageant. I wasn't sure which way I wanted it to go anymore. If contestants kept dropping like flies, I wasn't sure this was really the kind of publicity that would do my shoe line any good after all.

I made my way across the lobby, still lost in thought, and almost walked straight into Mom and Mrs. Rosenblatt heading in the opposite direction. They'd changed into what Mom called resort wear: white walking shorts and a pale blue lightweight sleeveless sweater for her, a yellow and white striped muumuu for Mrs. Rosenblatt that I could have sworn I'd seen once at the beer garden of a county fair.

"You're not going back to the room, are you?" Mom asked.

"There's really no reason to go back there," Mrs. Rosenblatt added. "You'd just be getting in the maid's way. They don't really like that."

"Why don't you come with us," Mom said. "We're just on our way to the Lost Aloha to grab a bite to eat."

"And a drink," Mrs. Rosenblatt added. "They make excellent daiquiris here."

I bit the inside of my cheek to keep from laughing. "You *really* don't want me near those shopping bags, do you?"

Mom and Mrs. Rosenblatt exchanged dismayed glances.

"It's not that we don't trust you, honey," Mom said.

"It's that we don't trust anyone," Mrs. Rosenblatt said. "Some things can be very bad in the wrong hands."

And I'd thought the murders had been alarming.

"Your bags are safe for now," I told them. "We've just been called to a meeting about the pageant." I saw a few sober beauty queens filing through the lobby toward the escalators in the back. Some chatting quietly, others keeping entirely to themselves. Jay Jeffries followed not far behind them, clutching his tablet and looking harried.

"Do you think it's going to go on?" Mom asked.

I pulled my attention back to her. "What's that?"

"The pageant, of course. Do you think the pageant will go on?"

I shrugged. "I wouldn't be surprised. There's a lot at stake, after all."

"A lot of money, you mean," she said. "I think it's awful. They should just call it a day and send everyone home while they're still safe and sound."

At this point, I couldn't disagree with that sentiment. "I have to run, but why don't we all meet for dinner?" I suggested. "I'll arrange for Dana and Marco to come along, say around six-thirty?"

Mom pulled me into a hug. "We'll see you then. Be careful, dear."

After they had left, I hurried into the auditorium, taking a seat a few rows from the front next to a grim-looking Dana. Mercifully, the curtain was closed, prohibiting any view of the stage where Desi had been found just hours earlier. The lights weren't fully on, leaving remnant shadows to fall randomly over faces, accentuating the shared grief. A strained hush lay over the room like a shroud. The contestants were seated together, but there was none of their usual chatter. Instead, they sat somberly waiting to hear what Laforge had to say. It occurred to me that under the circumstances, they must feel especially vulnerable, and I hoped the pageant was taking precautions to ensure their safety as best they could.

Laforge stood on the floor in front of the stage, and even though the lights were low, I could see he was pale and disheveled looking. And although the room was on the cool side, his face glistened with sweat. As pageant director, I guessed the ultimate responsibility for the things that went on would fall squarely on him. It was plain to see he wasn't coping with those things too well.

He clapped his hands. "May I have everyone's attention, please?" He waited a few unnecessary beats for the silence to quiet down. He took a deep breath. "I've spoken with the Hawaiian Paradise Corporation," he began, "and after some discussion, we have agreed that the best way to honor the memories of Miss Montana and Miss New Mexico...Jennifer and Desi..." He paused to gather himself. I heard a sniffle somewhere behind us. "...is to continue with the pageant," he finished.

"Big surprise," Dana mumbled. I threw her a *Sssh* frown.

"But we'll be changing a few things," he went on. He looked out over the room, not focusing on anyone in particular. "We're still working on the specifics, but now that we have fewer contestants and less time to prepare, we'll have to cut out some scenes, maybe even eliminate a portion of the competition to fit the timeline. We'll make it work." I saw his Adam's apple bob as he swallowed. "We have to make it work."

"Wrong," Dana said, her voice low but hostile. "We don't *have* to parade around in swimsuits and evening dresses. We *have* to survive the week. But I guess Hawaiian Paradise doesn't much care about that, as long as they don't lose the money they've put into this thing."

I stared at her. "What's gotten into you?"

Laforge was droning on about adding an In Memoriam segment to the pageant out of respect for the dearly departed. A short one, because they had to fit the timeline.

Dana shrugged. "I guess I just don't see the point anymore."

"Then why don't you quit?"

"Believe me," she said, "I thought about it. I even had the phone in my hand to call in my resignation. But it wouldn't be fair to Ruth Marie and Jay Jeffries. Or to the remaining contestants, really. What if they can't find another judge in time? Then all they've done is for nothing. I'm pretty much stuck." She sighed. "Sorry. The show must go on, right?"

I squeezed her hand and said nothing. But I wondered how many more beauty queens would have to be lost before the show *wouldn't* go on.

* * *

A few hours later, after a dinner of seared mahi-mahi and free-flowing tropical drinks (with extra paper umbrellas for Mom and Mrs. Rosenblatt), the mood had lightened considerably. I wasn't quite ready to take a solitary moonlit walk on the beach, but I was able to shake much of the sense of dread that had been weighing me down since the discovery of Desi's body.

Unfortunately, that sense of dread came crashing right back when the front desk clerk called my name as I passed through the lobby after dinner. I hurried to retrieve the folded message slip he offered, instantly afraid there was some problem at home, quickly checking my cell phone to be sure it was powered on and sufficiently charged.

The message was from Ramirez and thankfully, its content wasn't exactly what I'd feared. No mention of fires or plagues or locusts at home. It was, however, very clear that my husband wasn't at all happy with me. I read the terse message, my chest tightening.

When were you going to tell me about Body Number Two?

Gulp.

I looked up at the clerk. "Do you know when this message came in?"

"No, ma'am." He pointed. "But you can ask the guy for yourself. He's right over there."

"Where—" I spun around.

And looked straight into my husband's dark eyes.

CHAPTER THIRTEEN

———

"Maddie." Ramirez said it as a statement, not a question, his voice a little too loud even in the open-air lobby. A few guests glanced over at us, looking away quickly when they saw his expression. His cop face was firmly in place, and staring at Ramirez's cop face was like staring at a block of granite: unyielding. Dark eyes, hard jaw, all business. He was wearing faded jeans and a royal blue T-shirt that defined his abs and shoulders like an anatomy chart. If I didn't know him, cop face or not, I might risk staring at him. He looked that good.

Even though he was fuming. But, hey, it wasn't like it was my fault another body had been found. I hadn't killed her! And when I'd assured him I wouldn't get involved, it hadn't been a total lie. I wasn't *getting* involved. I was *already* involved. How could I not be, after finding Jennifer's dead body?

I took a deep breath and gave Ramirez a little one finger wave. "Hi, hon."

He crossed the lobby in two quick strides, suddenly so close I could feel the angry heat radiating off his body. "I'm waiting for an answer," he growled. "Body Number Two? Did you just think I wouldn't hear about it?"

I shrugged. "I'd kinda hoped," I squeaked out.

His eyes narrowed, and that vein in his neck started to bulge.

I noticed a security guard stepping out of his office near the front desk to assess the situation. I floated a smile in his direction meant to imply that Ramirez and I were just another happy bickering couple. He stared at me with deep suspicion before retreating back into his office.

I took Ramirez's hand and pulled him toward the elevator bank. "Of course I was planning to tell you," I said. "I just...well things have been so busy...with the pageant stalling and...things..." I trailed off, hoping he thought "things" referred to shoes and not tailing murder victims in the middle of the night. *Please, please, please, don't let him know I've been—*

"Things like interrogating beauty queens?" he asked.

I rolled my eyes upward. *Thanks a lot, universe.* What had been a bunny slope had just become a black diamond trail.

I opened my eyes wide and blinked innocently. "Who me?"

His eyes narrowed again in response. "You can cut the innocent act, Springer, I've already talked to Detective Kalanihankuhihuliha."

I was impressed. While I couldn't be certain, I had a suspicion he'd just pronounced Detective Whatshisname's name correctly.

"He told me," he continued, "that after the second murder both Miss Delaware and Miss Arkansas brought your name up during their interviews."

I bit my lip. "They did?"

He nodded. "Uh-huh."

"Because they liked my shoes so much?" My voice was bordering on Minnie Mouse territory now.

His head shook. "Nuh-uh. Because you'd been questioning them. About the dead girl."

I gulped. "We might have talked a little, you know, just making conversation..."

Luckily for me, the elevator doors dinged open then. I jumped inside, grateful for the break from his Bad Cop stare. If only for a moment.

Ramirez stepped in beside me, his presence suddenly making the small carriage feel claustrophobic. He opened his mouth to continue his tirade, but before he could a life-sized duck jumped into the elevator with us.

I blinked.

Ramirez blinked.

The duck said, "'Sup."

"Uh...hi," I responded.

"Insurance convention," the duck said, addressing my husband's confused stare. "I'm the mascot?"

Ramirez cleared his throat. "Right. I've, uh, seen the commercials."

The duck nodded. "Cool." The duck folded his wings in front of him, patiently waiting as the elevator ascended.

I felt a giggle bubbling in my throat but held it in just long enough for the elevator doors to open at the sixth floor and let out fine feathered friend off.

Luckily the giant water fowl had lightened my husband's mood considerably.

"You know," Ramirez said as soon as we were alone again, "Hawaii does have a police force."

I knew. I'd met most of them. Twice.

"Sorry?" I said. Though it came out more of a question.

He turned around to face me, just enough Bad Cop still in his eyes that I had to fight the urge to fidget.

"Really sorry?"

If I didn't know better, I'd have said I saw the corner of his mouth twitch up like it was fighting a smile.

"Do you know what it took for me to get here? I had to leave our kids with my mom. I hate leaving the kids."

"I know," I said. And I did. I'd been missing my munchkins the entire time I'd been here. "And I know I should have called you the second Desi's body was found. It's just that between Mom and Mrs. Rosenblatt showing up here, and staying in my room I might add, then the uber full pageant schedule, and the idea of a killer on the loose...alone time to call home has been scarce."

Ramirez's eyes softened a little. "These pageant people are running you ragged, huh?"

I shrugged. "Sort of."

He reached out and tucked a stray strand of hair behind my ear. "You okay?"

I fought a lump in my throat. For all his Bad Cop scariness, I knew it was only because he was worried about me. I nodded. "I've missed you," I told him, and I meant it.

"Me too." He leaned down and placed a slow kiss on my lips that warmed me right down to my toes.

When the elevator let us out at the twelfth floor, I slid him a sideways grin. "You know, we probably have another hour or two before Mom and Mrs. R get back to the room."

Ramirez shot me a look. "You're not getting off that easy," he said, but I noticed the corner of his mouth twitch upward again.

Something told me I could get off that easy if I wanted to. And while part of me was dying to continue that kiss in a more private setting, another part was dying to get his perspective on everything that had happened since the start of the pageant. He was, after all, a pretty darn clever homicide detective. It was possible, even likely, that he might recognize an important detail that I'd overlooked.

Then again, it was also possible that the first part of me would win, and I'd tear his shirt off with my teeth the minute I got him alone.

We stepped into the hallway to see Maxine alone, struggling to open the door to her room. She was wearing an orchid-print sarong and high strappy heels, with a flower tucked behind her right ear. She looked up as we approached, her eyes widening slightly when she saw Ramirez, a reaction I totally understood. "Oh, Maddie, thank goodness it's you. I'm having a little trouble getting into my room."

As I made the introductions, I couldn't help but notice that Ramirez didn't once look at Maxine's orchids. Gotta love the guy.

"I have to tell you," she said, "I'm sort of nervous about walking around by myself, but Whitney wanted to stay to watch the dancers, and I have a bit of a headache, so I came back here to lie down. I'm not being dumb, am I? I mean, what could happen between there and here, right?" She gave a nervous little laugh.

"You should probably stay with a buddy," Ramirez told her.

Maxine's eyes got wide. "Oh, I do. Whitney and I have been roomies from the start."

Ramirez looked at me, his eyebrow raised. I gave a little shrug.

Maxine held out her keycard. "Do you think you could help?"

Ramirez took it and two seconds later pushed her door open. She breathed a little sigh of relief. "I must have been trying it backwards. I'm such a goof sometimes. Thank you so much."

He stepped inside and took a quick look around the room before handing her the keycard. "Make sure the door locks behind you," he told her.

We said goodnight, waited until we heard the click of the lock on her door, and a moment later let ourselves into my room. I switched on the lights, noticing immediately that the shopping bags were gone, the beds smoothed to perfection in their absence. There weren't any tikis or odd tchotchkes in sight. Just a new box of breathing strips on the bathroom counter—Mrs. Rosenblatt must have picked it up on her shopping trip. That in itself would go a long way toward juju cleansing, as far as I was concerned.

Ramirez took an approving look around. "Nice digs."

I grinned. "Wait'll you see the view from the balcony."

He stepped through the double glass doors onto the balcony, and I heard him whistle. "Sweet."

"It's beautiful, isn't it?" I called.

After a few minutes, he came back into the room, his hair slightly tousled from the ocean breeze. "I could get used to this," he said, his eyes softer now as they roamed the room. That is, until they landed on a pile of papers sitting on top of the dresser. "What are these?" he asked, taking a step toward them and fingering the one on top.

I leaned forward for a better look. It was the business card that Surfer Dirk had given me.

"Oh, it's just Dirk's phone number in case I wanted a surfing lesson."

He turned very deliberately to face me, one eyebrows raised. "And this?" He held up a signed photo of Jay Jeffries.

"Uh, Jay Jeffries' photo?"

"And room number," he observed, the second eyebrow joining the first at his hairline.

I kicked off my heels and lowered myself onto the edge of the bed, willing myself not to look guilty. Again. "I can explain all that."

"This—" He held up a third scrap of paper, Detective Whatshisname's card. "—I get. This—" He held up Surfer Dirk's again. "—I think I can put two and two together. But *this*—" He held up Jeffries' photo with two fingers like he was afraid of getting cooties from it (which might not have been too farfetched). "—I'd *love* to hear an explanation for." He dropped it and crossed his arms over his chest as he sat down beside me.

"Okay, first, I didn't write that room number," I told him. "Jay Jeffries did. He's one of the judges. And he hits on anything with two legs and a pair of boobs."

"Not making me any happier," Ramirez said.

Was that jealousy I heard in his voice? Cute. "You don't need to worry about him," I said. "He knows where he stands with me. Which is nowhere."

Ramirez gave a noncommittal grunt. "And you kept his room number because...?"

"It's not what you think. It was just in case I needed to question him later about..." I trailed off, realizing he'd just caught me confessing to exactly the kind of investigating he'd been accusing me of. Damn. The man was good.

He gave me a knowing look, but there was definitely a hint of a smile behind it now.

I scrunched my nose up in defeat. "Fine. Guilty as charged!" I held my wrists out in a mock surrender to handcuffs. "I, Maddison Louise Springer, have been investigating a murder. Happy?"

"Hardly," he answered, the smile widening. He stretched out on the bed, leaning on one elbow, and regarded me with an assessing stare. "Okay, lay it on me, Springer. What do we know?"

I pulled my legs up and crossed them beneath me. "We know we have two dead beauty queens, both of whom were seen meeting someone on the beach the night before their bodies were found. We don't know who that someone is, but I'm pretty sure the second one was probably a man. And we know that someone wanted Miss New Mexico to win this competition, so much so that the judges were instructed to inflate her scores."

"And we don't know who that someone is?" Ramirez said.

I shook my head. "Could be someone from corporate. Word is they've sunk a lot of money into this pageant."

"Doesn't seem like it should be hard to find out where that instruction came from," Ramirez said.

I nodded. "None of the judges seem to know. It was just passed down the line. And of course, whoever issued the order wouldn't want to be identified anyway."

Ramirez considered. "Seen by whom?" he asked finally.

"What?"

"The nighttime meetings on the beach. Who saw them?"

Oops. I was ready to tell all, as long as *all* didn't include my traipsing around the hotel grounds alone at night and disguising myself as a bush to get a clearer view. "They're reliable witnesses," I said with deliberate vagueness.

Ramirez's eyes narrowed. "You won't be doing that again, will you?"

"Not a chance," I said immediately.

The muscles in his jaw tightened, hinting that Bad Cop was not pleased. I couldn't really blame him.

"I only saw Desi on the beach," I added. "I didn't see Jennifer. Miss Delaware, that's Whitney, saw Jennifer from her hotel window." I thought some more. "But no one has a bad thing to say about Jennifer. With the exception of Miss New Mexico, everyone seemed to like her. I can't figure why anyone would want her dead."

He scrubbed one hand across his face and sighed. "So who's the front-runner now that Desi's out?"

"Whitney. And she stands to make a small fortune as Miss Hawaiian Paradise. Which is kind of a shame, because there's a distinct possibility that Whitney is actually too old for this competition." I hesitated. "But it's not just the contestants. There's a woman with a very bad attitude named Donatella Curcio who's been on the hotel grounds since day one protesting all things fashion and beauty, and it turns out *she* was disqualified from this very same pageant two years ago under false pretenses."

"Meaning what?"

"She passed out cupcakes to her fellow contestants," I said. "The official word was she was trying to gain an unfair competitive advantage. Think the fatted calf."

Ramirez frowned. "I don't get it."

"That's because you've never dieted to fit into a dress," I told him. "But that whole thing wasn't what it seemed to be, either."

"As in?"

"As in she was actually sleeping with one of the judges."

"Let me guess," Ramirez said. "Dr. Pretty Boy?" He gestured to Jeffries' photo.

"Bingo."

"So his moves do work on some women," Ramirez said.

I looked at him. Definitely a touch of jealousy there. "But, get this: Don's coach, Ashton Dempsey, was the one who discovered the affair, and he threw his own client under the bus."

"What a prince."

"That's not all," I said. "Dempsey's a bit of a common denominator. He was also coaching our first victim, Miss Montana. Plus he was spotted at the Lost Aloha bar recently with Simon Laforge, the pageant director. That doesn't seem all that unusual, except the two are definitely not BFFs. Dempsey's gunning for Laforge's job as director. Laforge is under a lot of pressure with so much money on the line, so who knows what that conversation was about. He's something of a character himself, wants things done his way, on his timeline, which is usually *right now*. Word is he's getting the corporate boot after this pageant. I can believe it, after what's gone on here."

Ramirez shook his head. "I need a scorecard here."

"Wait," I told him. "That's not all. Then there's the boyfriend." I filled him in on Xander Newport, his shady arrival time, status as new ex-boyfriend, and now-you-see-it-now-you-don't grief.

When I was done, Ramirez remained quiet for a while, considering. I chewed on my lower lip and waited, knowing the cop in him was at work.

Finally, he said, "I'll go talk with the local police in the morning and see what they have so far. Hopefully an autopsy report will be in by now on the first victim. Maybe there will be something concrete in it linking the two homicides."

"That's a good idea," I agreed. It was energizing to have Ramirez in on the investigation. "I'll try again to talk to Donatella Curcio and see if I can fill in some blanks about why her coach would rat her out."

Ramirez shot me a look.

But this time I stood my ground. "Do you really expect me to sit back and do nothing just because the cavalry has arrived in town?"

He sighed. "I'd kinda hoped."

I grinned and gave him a peck on his stubbled cheek. "I'll be careful. I promise. I'm just going to have a little chat in broad daylight. Scout's honor."

"You were never a girl scout, were you?"

I shrugged. "I could have been."

His eyes narrowed at me, though his smile punctuated a dimple in his left cheek. "You know, part of me thinks I should just put you on the first plane home."

I smiled back. "What does the other part want?"

His eyes went warm and wicked. "The other part wants to make the most of an impromptu Hawaiian vacation." And he pulled me down alongside him, his arm heavy and reassuring around me. The lingering scent of his aftershave was a subtle, musky blend that seemed uniquely him. The blackness of his eyes and the darkness of his stubbled jaw line lent him a sort of dangerous look that was hard to resist.

"I like that part," I told him. "But we've been up here for an hour already."

"Am I on a timer?" he asked, nuzzling my hair. "Because I work well under pressure."

Didn't I know it. "My roommates will be back any second," I said reluctantly.

Ramirez drew back to look me in the eye. "That's a lot of pressure." He pushed himself upright with a groan and ran his hands through his hair. "Fine, I'll go bunk with Marco. Does he have any roommates?"

I laughed. "Not as far as I know."

"Then I'll see you in the morning." He bent over to give me a kiss. "Stay in your room." And another more lingering kiss punctuated with a sigh. "Can't we let your mom and Mrs. R room with Marco?"

"We could," I said, "but none of them would ever be the same again."

* * *

I slept better than I had in days, thanks in part to Mrs. Rosenblatt's use of her new breathing strips as well as the knowledge that I was no longer muddling through the investigation alone. It pained me to think of it as muddling, but to be honest, I wasn't making much headway. Hopefully Ramirez's participation would change all that.

By the time I woke up at eight the next morning, both Mrs. Rosenblatt and my mother were gone, with no sign of a note left behind. I didn't really mind. I was just happy that they seemed to be having a good time occupying themselves. I didn't dare think about what they were occupying themselves with.

I unplugged my cell phone from its charger and found Ramirez had left me a voicemail. He was also up and out early, on his way to the police department as planned, leaving me on my own for the time being. Since the contestants were busy with the preliminary swimsuit judging all morning, I wasn't scheduled for any fittings until later that afternoon. I decided to splurge and order a room service breakfast which I ate out on the balcony, basking in the morning sun. I could feel the tension of the past few days unwinding, and I knew that my husband was the reason. If I could have had Max and Livvie with me, too, it would have been the perfect setting.

Except, of course, that it wasn't the perfect setting. It was the place where two women had been killed, and others could very well be in danger. I looked out over the ocean, admiring the gradient shades of blue and turquoise while I thought. I still planned to find Don at some point, but it occurred to me that although Don's history with the pageant and Ashton Dempsey was significant, it was Whitney who had benefited the most from the deaths of both Jennifer and Desi. Following each murder, Whitney had been bumped from second place to first. Given her age, this pageant was in all probability Whitney's last, and last pageant meant last chance. Last chance meant desperation.

That seemed like reason enough to put Don temporarily on hold and talk to Whitney instead. I dressed quickly, pulled my hair into a French braid, and headed for her room. Hopefully I could catch her there, before she began her pageant activities for the day.

Maxine opened the door to my knock, but it was a different Maxine than the polished beauty queen who'd been unable to keycard herself into her room the night before. This morning, she was wearing no makeup to conceal the dark shadows under her eyes. Her hair was pulled back into a scruffy ponytail. She was dressed in a pink cami and green shorts pajama set, with her feet stuffed into fuzzy white slippers. A hot pink bikini top dangled from her fingers, like I'd caught her about to dress for today's competition. Her eyes darted up and down the hallway before she pulled me into the room, sliding the deadbolt in place the second the door closed behind me.

"Are you alright?" I asked her, concerned.

"I didn't sleep a wink last night," she told me, although I'd already guessed that by her shadowed eyes. "I wanted to prop a chair against the door, but Whitney said to stop being ridiculous. Do you think it's ridiculous?"

I didn't think it was ridiculous at all. In fact, I might have done just that if I'd been a contestant. But I didn't want to add to her anxiety by admitting I thought that was a good idea. I also didn't want to lie to her by telling her she had nothing to worry about. So I said, "I don't think it's ridiculous to do whatever makes you feel safer." I glanced toward the bathroom. There was no sign of Whitney, and the door stood open.

"I don't know what happened." She sank down onto the bed. "I thought I was handling all of this okay. I mean, last night I came up here by myself and everything, right? But then all of a sudden, it just hit me, someone's killing off the contestants who do well in the pageant, and any of us could be next!" She looked up at me with horror in her eyes. "I could be next!"

I didn't have the heart to tell her she didn't have much to worry about in that department. I sat down beside her. "I think you're doing all that you can do. You're making sure your door is locked. You're not taking unnecessary chances. Just try not to be alone if that makes you uneasy." I glanced out the sliding doors. No Whitney on the balcony. "Whitney's at the auditorium already?"

Maxine shrugged. "Whitney was gone when I woke up. I didn't even hear her leave."

"I'm surprised to hear that," I said, "after she was out late last night."

"Oh, she always obeys curfew," Maxine said quickly. "She's really good about that."

"Does she go out at night a lot?" I asked, wondering how far I could push this before Maxine caught wind of my intent.

"Some. Not always with me, of course. She likes to go dancing." Another tiny shrug. "I'm not really a good dancer."

No revelation there. "Who does she go dancing with?"

"I don't really know," she said. "The other girls, maybe. I'm just her roomie. It's not like she tells me everything. I mean, considering we hardly know each other, that'd be kinda weird, don't you think?"

Weird, but helpful. I tried another tack. "How about two nights ago? Did she go out then?"

"Two nights ago?" Maxine rolled her eyes toward the ceiling, thinking. "No," she said, dragging the word out, "I don't think so."

I wasn't convinced. "How can you be sure?"

With one finger, she traced the faint paisley pattern on her shorts. "Well, I was sleeping, and I'm sure that Whitney was too."

I looked at her, not quite sure what to do with that. "You're sure she was sleeping?" I repeated.

Maxine seemed surprised. "Well, sure. What with the curfew and all."

Right. I stood, turning toward the door. "Just be careful, okay?" I gave her a quick smile before I left, wishing I could have a do-over on the last ten minutes. Maxine's naïveté was charming on one level and dangerous on another. To her. Maybe her high level of anxiety was her best protection.

My cell phone alerted me to a text message as I was leaving Maxine's room. I took a look at the screen. *Como mark zoom sap.*

I paused and narrowed my eyes at it, hoping it would morph into something that made sense. No such luck. But I was pretty sure who had sent it. I dialed Mom's number.

"Good morning, dear! Did you sleep well?"

"Very well," I said.

"She slept very well," Mom repeated to someone.

I heard Mrs. Rosenblatt bellow in the background, "It's the breathing strips!"

I grimaced. "You and Mrs. Rosenblatt were out early today."

"Yes, we...uh..." I heard a fumbling sound as if she was covering her cell phone with her hand, and then I heard her yell, "I think she knows!" There was a voice in the background, and Mom yelled, "She *knows*!"

"What do I know, Mom?" I asked patiently.

"Sorry, what? Oh, I wasn't referring...hold on, dear." More fumbling and a sharp "No, I will not do that!" and she came back. "Did you get my text? Come to Marco's room ASAP?"

Como mark zoom sap meant come to Marco's room ASAP? I shook my head, thinking she really had to take advantage of her opposable thumbs and retire the voice-to-text feature on her phone. It wasn't doing her any favors.

"Are you busy, dear? Can you come over right away?"

I could, but I wasn't sure I wanted to. If the three of them had put their heads together, it couldn't be good. Plus, I now realized where all the shopping bags had gone. "I'm sort of busy," I told her. I planned to track down Don before Ramirez got back from the police station. And maybe I could find Whitney somewhere downstairs.

"Of course. I understand," Mom said, in a long-suffering tone that told me she didn't understand at all. "If you're too busy to spare a few minutes for your mother—"

I rolled my eyes. "I'll be right there." I didn't have the strength to carry that kind of guilt around all day.

It only took a few minutes before I was knocking on Marco's door. There was a pungent odor seeping out of his room that made my nose wrinkle. I heard rustling sounds, and then the door opened, and Marco pulled me inside. The heavy drapes were tightly closed, leaving the room in near darkness, but the flickering light from dozens of burning candles planted on every surface was bright enough to see that they were all wearing some sort of native getup that included grass skirts and bare feet. Mom and Mrs. Rosenblatt wore theirs over their street clothes, but Marco had gone the extra mile, painting indecipherable figures on his chest and stomach in something that looked like blue Sidewalk Chalk. He also had a strange feathered headdress and wore a corded necklace that might or might not have featured a chicken bone as a pendant. He'd amped up the eyeliner to complete the effect. I stifled a laugh.

He motioned with one arm. "Come in, come in. We've been waiting for you."

I thought maybe I'd heard that line in a few horror movies, right before things started going south for the heroine. I could feel my eyes widen as they adjusted to the dimness, and I was able to see that the furniture had been pushed aside and an army of small black tiki idols arranged in a circular pattern on the floor, their jeweled eyes gleaming in the candlelight.

Oh boy.

I took shallow breaths but I couldn't keep the acrid scent out of my nostrils. My eyes were watering. On the plus side, my sinuses were completely clear. "What's going on here? What's that *smell*?"

"It's incense," Mom said cheerfully. "Welcome to your juju cleansing, dear!"

Mrs. Rosenblatt stepped forward, the rustle of her plus-sized grass skirt sounding like a hurricane blowing through the palm trees. "Here. Hold this." She thrust something into my hand.

I glanced down to see a tiny alligator head and immediately dropped it on the carpet. *That's* what they'd gone shopping for? No wonder they hadn't wanted me rooting through the bags. Eww! I wanted no part of this. Plus I was about thirty seconds from passing out from the stench.

"You shouldn't have done that," Mrs. Rosenblatt said sternly. "That's for protection."

"Don't worry, dear, it's not real," Mom added. "We couldn't find a real alligator head. So we bought a toy alligator and lopped him in two. But you can hold this instead." She handed me a little cloth bag tied with ribbon. Judging from its earthy scent, there were some kinds of potent herbs inside. "It's a mojo bag," she explained. "You keep it with you at all times."

I tried to give it back. "I really don't—"

"No, no, you mustn't let anyone else touch it!" She scurried backward, out of my reach and grazed a tiki idol with her foot. It rocked and fell over, its faux emerald eyes glittering up at us in accusation.

"That could be a problem," Mrs. Rosenblatt said, looking at it.

"No problem," Marco said. He seemed unusually happy. Maybe he'd inhaled too much incense. "I'll just stand the little guy back—ow!"

"Told you," Mrs. Rosenblatt said.

"The chicken bone jabbed me in the throat," Marco said, rubbing just above his collarbone.

I rolled my eyes.

"Shall we begin?" Mrs. Rosenblatt asked. "Betty, do you have the pre-sacrificed chicken ready?"

My mouth fell open. "The *what*?"

"Well, we weren't going to sacrifice one ourselves," Mrs. Rosenblatt said with great patience. "That would be strange."

Oh, *that* would be strange.

Mom turned her back, and I heard the crinkling of a plastic bag. When she turned around, she was holding a roasted Cornish game hen. "It's the best I could do," she said apologetically. "I got it at the supermarket. I couldn't find a Boston Market."

"It'll have to do," Mrs. Rosenblatt said in an aggrieved tone. "Set it in place."

Mom stepped carefully among the tikis on the floor, giving the emerald-eyed one a baleful look and a wide berth, and set the Cornish game hen in the center.

"Now we all join hands," Mrs. Rosenblatt instructed.

"What, with all this Cornish hen grease on me?" Mom shook her head. "I'd better go wash up. You never know when salmonella may become a problem. Does anyone have any sanitizer that I can—?"

"Go use the bathroom soap, Betty," Mrs. Rosenblatt said wearily.

Mom hurried off into the bathroom. We stood and listened to the water running and the slippery squishing sounds of hand washing and Mom humming *Black Magic Woman*, and then she was back, salmonella-free.

"Now we all join hands," Mrs. Rosenblatt said. "And *all* means *all*."

"Let me, let me," Mom implored her. She sounded like an excited six-year-old at Christmas. I didn't have the heart to dampen her enthusiasm, so I clasped hands with Marco on my left and Mom on my right.

"Do you remember the words?" Mrs. Rosenblatt asked her.

"Of course I remember the words," Mom said. "This isn't rocket science, Dorothy." She closed her eyes and took several deep breaths. Marco and Mrs. Rosenblatt closed their eyes, too. I didn't dare close my eyes on this bunch.

Then Mom began chanting, too low at first to be understood, then louder and louder. "*Laissez les bons temps rouler! Laissez les bons temps rouler!*"

Mrs. Rosenblatt's eyes snapped open. "Betty."

"*Laissez les—*"

"Betty!"

My mom's eyes flew open. "What? Did it work?"

Mrs. Rosenblatt shook her head. "You got the words wrong! You said you remembered the words!"

My mom blinked. "What'd I say?"

"You said, 'Let the good times roll,'" Mrs. Rosenblatt told her.

"Oh, dahlings, I'm *all* about that," Marco said with a delighted smile. "I think she got the words just right. *Ow!*" He whipped his head around to look behind him. "My grass skirt just pinched me in my—"

"Okay," I said, dropping both hands and backing out of the circle of craziness. Tears were running down my cheeks from the incense. Or maybe suppressed laughter. "I'll leave you all to figure this out, and I'll be back later, alright? I just want to take care of something first." And I turned and bolted.

The last thing I heard as the door slammed shut behind me was, "*Laissez les bons temps rouler!*"

CHAPTER FOURTEEN

———

"What is that smell?" Ramirez asked a couple of hours later. We were at the Lost Aloha Shack, grabbing a quick bite to eat. Ramirez had a burger with the works while I'd gone with a simple tropical fruit salad. Truth was, I couldn't taste my food anyway. The odor of incense and candles was still clinging to the inside of my nose and, apparently, the outside of my body. We had a ring of empty tables around us, but probably that was just coincidence.

I opted for the casual approach in my answer. "It's incense. From the juju cleansing."

Ramirez froze mid-bite. "Come again?"

I popped a piece of papaya into my mouth. Nope, no taste. "Mom and Mrs. Rosenblatt thought my juju needed a good cleansing, and they convinced Marco to help. Although I doubt it took much convincing. He seemed pretty happy about the whole thing." I still hadn't figured out where he'd gotten the feathered headdress and the chicken bone necklace.

"Your juju," Ramirez repeated.

"Yeah, it's a whole thing." I shrugged. "Something to do with pre-sacrificed chickens and alligator—"

Ramirez held up his hand. "Stop right there. If I hear any more, I might have to arrest someone."

"Suit yourself." I tried a juicy piece of mango. Tasted like a lot of nothing. I sure hoped that was a short-term side effect. "Speaking of arresting someone, did you find out anything useful this morning?"

Surfer Dirk threaded his way among the tables in our direction, balancing a serving tray at shoulder level and moving in time to music that only he could hear. "Hey, chica, what's going on? The pageant dudes must be keeping you busy. Haven't seen you here lately." He lowered the tray and leaned in toward me. "I heard about Miss New Mexico. Major bummer, huh?"

I glanced at Ramirez. He was glaring at Dirk as if assessing the breakability of his nose. I wasn't used to seeing this kind of reaction from Ramirez. It was flattering and a little scary. For Dirk. I put a calming hand on Ramirez's leg. "Dirk, I'd like you to meet my husband, Jack Ramirez."

Dirk's eyebrows shot upwards and disappeared under his shaggy pelt of blond hair. "This hombre's your husband? Hey, it's very cool to meet you, dude." He stuck out his hand.

"Dirk the surfer," Ramirez said, shaking it.

"That's me," Dirk agreed. "If you got the time, I got the waves. Come see me whenever."

"Yeah," Ramirez said, "I'll do that."

I shot him a frown that he ignored.

"Cool," Dirk said. "You guys all set with the libations?"

"We'll call you if we need you," Ramirez told him, and Dirk and his tray floated away, oblivious to Ramirez's irritation. Ramirez watched him leave through narrowed eyes. "I think you can toss that guy's card. I'm not sure he can *find* the ocean, let alone surf it."

"Already done," I said. I'd tossed it right into my bag last night, along with Detective Whatshisname's and Jeffries' signed photo. "So about this morning?"

Ramirez turned his attention back to his plate. "The autopsy report was in for Jennifer Oliver. She suffered blunt force trauma to the back of the head, most likely a lava rock taken from the landscaping near the pool. They found trace amounts of blood and hair on it."

My stomach twisted. I pushed my remaining fruit salad aside. "That's horrible."

"Murder always is," he said. He ate a fry. "There was something else. The M.E. found some sort of cheap emerald ring stuffed into her mouth. He thinks it happened post-mortem." He took a bite of his burger, chewed and swallowed. "Looks like someone was sending a message."

"An emerald ring?" My voice was faint.

Ramirez looked hard at me. "Yeah, that's what he said. Did you know about the ring?"

"It was hers," I said. "It was a promise ring."

"A promise ring," he repeated. "I thought that was a high school thing."

"In this case," I said, "it was a secret boyfriend thing."

"Xander Newport gave it to her?"

"Not that boyfriend." I shook my head, explaining about the mysterious lover with the green eyes. "And Mom and Mrs. Rosenblatt talked to some locals who said Xander had been partying and flirting with other women at a bar in town, the Curling Wave, the night Jennifer was killed," I finished.

Ramirez polished off his burger and shoved his plate aside. "Funny, I don't remember reading that in the report. It seems Mr. Newport omitted a few details in his statement."

I wasn't surprised. "He showed up at the hotel looking for a room after her body had been found," I said. "Making a commotion at the front desk like he'd just arrived on the island."

"Don't suppose you talked to him," Ramirez said.

I nodded reluctantly. "I caught him in the bar. He was sitting alone, acting like the grieving boyfriend. He told me he knew Jennifer had been seeing someone else. But he wanted to win her back."

"Or have her die trying," Ramirez said. He drained his beer. "I'll follow up with the detective in charge. See just how solid Newport's alibi is."

"It doesn't look good for him, does it?"

"No," he said. "It does not."

I fell silent as thoughts of Jennifer's secret lover flooded into my mind. Had he been the one to stuff the ring into Jennifer's mouth in a fit of jealous rage over her ex's efforts to reconcile with her? Or had it been Xander, the not so grieving boyfriend, out for revenge after she'd dumped him in favor of someone else?

But what reason could either of them have had to then kill Desi?

It seemed like the more I found out, the less I knew.

* * *

After lunch, Ramirez wanted to talk to some of the hotel staff to get an overview of what they might have seen and heard throughout the week, so I decided it would be a good time to call home to check on the kids. When I stepped off the elevator on the twelfth floor, I saw the housekeeping cart sitting across the hall from my room, outside of Maxine and Whitney's. Their door was propped. I slowed and took a peek inside. No sign of the maid. No sign of Whitney or Maxine, either. They were probably still doing their bathing suit walks for the judges. Which meant the room would be void of beauty queens for a while longer...

And would provide a perfect opportunity to look through one of my prime suspect's things.

I hesitated, fingering the keycard in my pocket. Every instinct was telling me that snooping through Whitney's stuff was a bad idea. At the very least it was an invasion of privacy. It might even be illegal.

What would Ramirez do?

I shook my head. Unfair question. Ramirez was a cop, and cops operated under a different set of rules. Cops had probable cause and search warrants.

I had an open door.

As I stood there trying to talk myself either out of or into the idea, the maid appeared in the doorway lugging an armful of plush bath towels, which she deposited in the laundry bag on her cart. I nodded and smiled at her while I pretended to be listening to the voicemail on my cell phone. She was preoccupied enough with her work that she barely seemed to notice me, which was just what I'd hoped for. If she barely noticed me, she couldn't describe me later. She took her time gathering fresh towels before going back into the room to restock the supply.

Immediately I stuffed my phone into my pocket, slipped into Whitney's room behind the maid and ducked into the closet. It was a large closet with two doors and enough room to park a Fiat. That is, if it hadn't already been stuffed with enough clothes to fill a small department store. Just my luck, either or both of the queens were gross over-packers. Judging by how little room I had to maneuver, they'd brought their entire wardrobes. All sorts of fashion flotsam was underfoot: pumps, flats, wedges, belts that had slipped from hangers, two laundry bags in differing stages of fullness. Then there were the clothes on hangers, many of them covered in drycleaners' plastic: cocktail dresses and gowns and skirts and jackets and tailored walking shorts. There was too much of everything, but at least the clothes provided cover. I knelt down behind a seafoam green gown with a chiffon train—I sure hoped it didn't belong to Maxine, considering her tendency to trip—and waited for the maid to finish up her duties.

After she'd given the vacuum a perfunctory push across the floor a few times, the maid packed up her cart and moved off down the hall. I emerged from the closet, careful not to disturb whatever organizational system Maxine and Whitney had going on in there. I took a moment to survey the room, deciding where to start. I knew I had a limited amount of time, but I hoped to find some proof that Whitney had it in for her fellow contestants. Specifically Jennifer's stolen bikini top. I had my doubts about Whitney, and while not finding the bikini top wouldn't dispel them, finding it would definitely confirm them.

I started with the dresser, quickly figuring out that the girls had divvied up the drawers evenly, two apiece, but that was where their compatibility ended. These two were the Odd Couple of the beauty pageant circuit. Whitney was as precise as a surgeon in her placement of items in the drawers. All the items that could be folded were folded. Everything else was rolled into balls or cylinders. Colors were coordinated. Like purpose went with like purpose. Even her cosmetics were carefully arranged into categories on top of the dresser: eye and brow makeup separate from foundation and blusher separate from lipsticks and lip stains. Hair care off to the left. Skin care to the right. I lingered at the skin care products for a second, taking note of the labels on the various jars and tubes. A girl could always improve her skin, right?

Unfortunately, along with the name of a good moisturizing serum, the only thing I learned was that Whitney was not hoarding Jennifer's bikini top. At least not anymore. She could have stolen it and immediately thrown it away. I had no way of knowing.

I bit my lip and looked at the remaining two drawers. Maxine's drawers. There was really no need to continue with my search. I'd done what I'd set out to do and come up empty. There wasn't much point in subjecting myself to Maxine's chaos theory method of unpacking. Not even the maid could have made order out of this mess, and she was paid to try.

Still, I didn't like to leave a job half done. My plan had been to search the room, and Maxine's belongings were in the room.

That was enough to convince me to open the first drawer. And almost recoil from the horror show inside. Maxine had none of Whitney's freakish neatness. Her personal items were shoved randomly into the space provided, rolled into lumpy balls where possible, stretched into wrinkled planes if need be. As far as I could tell, there was little order to any of it. What couldn't be squished into the dresser was in a tangled leaning pile on top, with a random blouse sleeve and a single leg from a pair of pantyhose sprouting from the pile and hanging toward the floor. I did a small shudder on behalf of her clothes. Even bargain brassieres didn't deserve to be treated that way.

Her cosmetics weren't any better. Everything was jumbled together, some of the jars and lipsticks left uncapped. Hairspray cans mingling with mascara tubes. It was a miracle that Maxine managed to pull herself together so well.

I bit my lip as I opened the bottom drawer. I expected more of the same, and I got it. I did a quick search through bra and panty sets and Spanx—what in the world would a tiny thing like Maxine need with Spanx?—and swimsuits, trying not to feel like a perv and failing miserably.

My search was so quick that I almost missed the one bikini top that had no matching bottom. I tugged at it gingerly, pulling it from beneath the layers so I could take a better look. Definitely too small for Maxine. I thought back to Desi's description of Jennifer's pilfered bikini top: white bandeau style with a seashell embellishment. And that's exactly what I'd found. But what was it doing among *Maxine's* things? That made no sense. Maybe it was Maxine's, mistakenly purchased in the wrong size and discarded in favor of another. But what were the chances that two contestants in the same pageant would own the same unique suit?

I put it back where I'd found it, buried beneath a rumpled pile of undergarments, and slid the drawer shut, my mind racing.

I'd honestly expected to find it in Whitney's possession, if I found it at all. Did I have Maxine all wrong?

I was lost so deeply in thought that I almost didn't hear the female voice on the other side of the door. "I'll just be a minute," someone called out.

I gasped. It was Maxine's voice.

"It was so silly of me to forget my earrings. I really appreciate your coming up with me. I get so nervous..."

She hadn't yet finished her sentence when the door began to open.

CHAPTER FIFTEEN

———

I swung a panicked look around the room. I'd never make it back over to the closet in time. The bathroom was out of the question. That left only one option. I dove under one of the beds, wriggling forward on my belly to pull my feet completely out of sight. A colony of dust bunnies billowed up into my face, and I pinched my nose to stifle the sneeze that rose in my throat. It was clear that the maids at the Royal Waikiki didn't live for their jobs.

I peeked out from beneath the bed skirt and caught sight of a killer pair of Gucci stiletto sandals, nude suede with crystal embellishment. Maxine might be a train wreck in the grace department, but she had impeccable taste when it came to footwear, I had to give her that.

After a few minutes of muttering to herself and clomping around in search of her earrings, Maxine found them and hurriedly left the room again. I gave her two minutes' lead time in case she'd grabbed the wrong earrings. When she didn't come back, I hauled myself out from under the bed and across the hall into my own room. That had been much too close for comfort, and it had served me right. I shouldn't have been in Maxine's room in the first place. Even though I had found Jennifer's stolen bikini top and gotten a great idea for a new shoe design.

I slapped the dust off of my clothes, splashed some cool water onto my face, and stood on the balcony looking at the ocean until my heart stopped pounding and I felt like myself again. I wasn't sure what I'd accomplished across the hall, other than to further muddy the waters by adding yet another suspect to a list that already seemed to include most of the people in the hotel. And I knew Ramirez would not be happy about my methods. With any luck, he wouldn't have to know about it for a while. Tonight was the final night before the pageant, and it was being celebrated with a private luau on the beach. Tomorrow I'd be tied up with the pageant itself. If Ramirez took his time interviewing hotel staff, I might be able to avert full disclosure until we were on the plane heading home.

I turned away from the ocean with a sigh and noticed the alert light blinking on my cell. I picked it up and saw I had a voicemail from Ramirez. He was going back to the police station to accompany Detective Whatshisname to check out Xander Newport's alibi.

I placed a quick call home to check on Livvie and Max and assure Mama Ramirez that everything was perfectly fine in paradise, before heading down to the auditorium for my afternoon of scheduled fittings. With the televised pageant set for tomorrow, it was a whirlwind of stilettos and slingbacks as I quickly fit in the last of the remaining forty-nine ladies. Though, the fact that Laforge had decided to cut out the talent portion of the competition to compensate for the lack of rehearsal time did cut down on the number of shoes per girl. I was just finishing my last one, Miss Wyoming, when I heard a text message coming through. I grabbed my cell phone, hoping it was Ramirez with some news from the police station. No such luck. Instead, it was Dana, letting me know the judging session was over, and she wanted to recover with a drink. That sounded like music to my ears, so I grabbed my purse and headed up the escalator.

I found Dana at the Lost Aloha Shack, getting a head start on the drinks. Considering her sagging shoulders and drooping head, I guessed the last couple of hours hadn't gone so well for her. I slid onto the stool beside her and noticed that in addition to the libations, she had what looked like a slice of chocolate cake (not carob or soy product but actual chocolate!) in front of her. Whoa. Things must really not be going well. "Tough day at the office?"

She dredged up a dramatic sigh. "Hey, Mads. I swear, I don't know what I'm doing here."

I eyed her half-empty Lava Pit and had some idea.

"This was just supposed to be a fun little pageant," she went on. "Judge some beauty queens in the usual categories, admire some evening gowns, blah, blah, blah. There's nothing fun about it. There's nothing *real* about it."

I saw Dirk headed our way and warded him off with a tiny head shake. He lifted his chin in acknowledgment and veered off to take care of a group in duck shirts farther down the bar.

"Have the judges gotten any more instructions about how to score it?" I asked her.

She shook her head. "And we probably won't. As things stand now, Whitney is clearly the front-runner. That's what everyone wants, right?"

I didn't know about everyone, but it seemed that it was what *someone* wanted.

"For this I gave up two weeks with Ricky?" Dana slurped some of her drink through a straw. "I don't know what I was thinking. I'm never getting involved in a pageant again. I don't want to be asked. I don't even want to get an invitation to *attend* one."

"Well, it's almost over," I told her. "The telecast is tomorrow. And then we can all go back to our regular lives." All except for Jennifer and Desi, that is.

Dana removed the straw, lifted her glass, and motioned to Dirk for a refill. "So what's going on in your corner of paradise?" she asked me.

I gave her a rundown of the latest developments, glossing over the juju cleansing fiasco and focusing on my suspicions about Xander and the discovery of Jennifer's stolen bikini top, though I remained sketchy on the details of exactly how I'd come to be in the room in the first place. Dana had enough problems. I wanted to give her plausible deniability. She remained quiet, but that might have been because the couple of drinks had left her a little sleepy.

"I knew there was something about Xander," she said when I was through.

"We don't know anything for sure," I hedged. "Ramirez is looking into his alibi."

She stared moodily into her fresh drink. "The only thing is, why would Xander want to kill Desi?"

While I disagreed it was the *only* thing, it was a *big* thing.

"I can't find any connection between Jennifer and Desi," I admitted.

"Except for Miss Hawaiian Paradise," Dana said. I nodded. "That's a lot," she said. "But then maybe it isn't."

"Exactly." I eyed her Lava Pit, which was already half gone again.

"None of it makes any sense. The only thing they had in common is they're both dead." She sucked another quarter inch through the straw. "I'm sorry—I'm just in a lousy mood. I think I'm going to go grab a nap before dinner. Maybe everything will look better after some sleep." She stood. "You'll be at the luau tonight, right?"

I nodded as I watched her wind her way along the path toward the hotel lobby, and I couldn't help but think this pageant couldn't end soon enough for everyone.

* * *

With a couple of hours before dinner, I decided to enjoy my last days in paradise poolside. I texted Marco to see if he wanted to join me, but he said he was busy with "a project." Considering his last project involved chicken bones and juju war paint, I didn't ask. Instead, I'm proud to say I managed to conquer my skittishness about being in the vicinity of the pool all by myself. Mostly. I still avoided the chaise where I'd found Jennifer's lifeless body. It almost seemed like the experience had left an unpleasant imprint in that precise spot, and to even look in the direction conjured up the image all over again. Luckily, it seemed a number of families were at the pool today, and the energy and boisterousness of the splashing kids playing Marco Polo left me feeling relaxed and safe. If I closed my eyes, I could pretend I was listening to Max and Livvie at play. That happy thought, coupled with the warm sun on my skin (slathered in sunscreen) and the gentle, soothing breeze, soon lulled me to sleep.

When I woke up, I was shocked to see it was nearly six. The sun had shifted from overhead, sliding farther across the sky as the afternoon waned, and the kids were gone. Only a few couples remained at the pool, and the immediate area had quieted down considerably. I gathered my things and headed back to my room to shower and dress for the evening. In all honesty, I wasn't 100% looking forward to it. The celebration luau for pageant contestants and staff was generous in concept, but I wasn't sure how celebratory the general mood would be. From what I'd seen during the past week, everyone was either frightened or suspicious or both, and the mood was grim.

I settled on a gauzy sapphire blue sarong, spent twenty minutes blowing out my hair and doing a light makeup, and by seven thirty, a far less gloomy Dana, Marco, and I were making our way down to the beach.

The dining area had been closed for the evening to all but the pageant personnel, most of whom seemed to be already in attendance. Jeffries and Ruth Marie were chatting, sipping cocktails, their heads close together, his arm draped protectively across her shoulders. I spotted Laforge playing the part of the attentive host as he roamed, dressed in island chic white with his shirt unbuttoned halfway to his navel and his trademark sunglasses in place. Ashton Dempsey had affixed himself to Whitney, likely trying to align himself with a winning contestant again, talking in her ear as his bulging belly in a screaming Hawaiian shirt nearly brushed against her hip. Even from a distance I could see he was wearing more makeup than she was. Surfer Dirk chatted with himself as he circulated, serving food and drinks. From the looks of it, he was the happiest person on the beach.

Most of the contestants stood in nervous-looking clusters, occasionally glancing outside their private circles like frightened deer watching for a predatory mountain lion. Whether their nerves stemmed from the next day's pageant or fear for their personal safety was anyone's guess. I found it interesting that only Whitney didn't seem to share their apprehension. Was it because she knew she was the front-runner now?

A live trio was set up on the stage, providing a soothing musical backdrop while native dancers swayed in mesmerizing rhythms to the beat. Despite the laid-back island vibe, no one seemed particularly relaxed or festive. In fact, there was an air of somberness layered over the entire affair.

"Doesn't feel much like a party," Marco commented, glancing around.

"Can you blame them?" I sipped my drink. "I know I don't feel like celebrating."

Dana nodded. "I can't believe I'm anxious to leave Hawaii." She paused. "Uh-oh."

I looked at her. She was staring over my shoulder with a mixture of amusement and horror.

"I've been looking for you, dear!"

I turned to see Mom and Mrs. Rosenblatt making their labored way toward us through the sand. They were impossible to miss. Mom was wearing a basic black twinset with two leis draped around her neck and enough flowers in her hair to plant a garden. Mrs. Rosenblatt was in a flesh-colored muumuu that for a moment was scarier than anything else that had happened during the week. "You know this party is for pageant personnel only," I told them in a mock scolding tone.

Mrs. Rosenblatt shrugged. "As if we'd miss a good luau. And this—" She tipped her nose up in the air and sniffed. "—is a good luau."

Mom studied me. "How are you feeling, dear?" She leaned in closer. The scent of frangipani washed over me. "Are you carrying the mojo bag?"

I'd forgotten all about the mojo bag. I think I'd *accidentally* left it in the wastebasket in my room after the juju cleansing. From what I'd seen of the housekeeping service, it was probably still there.

"What's a mojo bag?" Dana asked.

"Well, let me tell you—" Mom began.

"Look, here come the fire dancers," I cut in. "We should find a seat."

As we made our way to a viewing spot, I couldn't help but cast another casual glance over the beach. Assuming that Xander Newport's alibi held up—and if it didn't, chances were good that he was now at the police department—my instincts were telling me that the killer had to be among the assembled group here at the luau. It was an unsettling thought. It wasn't easy to put it aside and trust that there was safety in numbers, but eventually I found myself lost in watching the performance of the skilled fire dancers. The breeze was warm and gentle, the ocean calm and unhurried as it rolled onto the beach in frothy ringlets. Overhead, the palm fronds rustled quietly in answer to the breeze. It was an idyllic night.

Until my cell phone buzzed with a text. I tried to ignore it, but my curiosity got the better of me. After all, it might be Ramirez with news of the arrest of Xander Newport. Shielding the phone from Mom's curious eyes, I stared at the message on the screen, which I noted had been sent from an unavailable number:

I know who the killer is. Meet me by the pool at midnight.

My head shot up, and I quickly scanned the group, hoping to spot the source of the text among our companions. While the gathering darkness and shifting shadows created by the fire dancers made it difficult to read faces, I saw several cell phones out. Most pointed at the stage, taking pictures and videos. My gaze whipped from one beauty queen taking selfies to a coach intently hunched over his smart phone screen. The text could have come from anyone here. They all had a copy of the pageant personnel contact list. I scrutinized anyone with a phone, but no one looked back or paid me the least bit of attention.

Dana nudged me. "Are you alright?"

I gave a start and dropped the cell phone back into my purse. "I'm fine. It's just a…shoe thing." I forced a smile, and Dana's attention went back to the dancers. But my concentration was broken. I wished it was a shoe thing. That, I could handle. It was familiar, comfortable ground. But this was unnerving. Any one of the people surrounding me could have sent the text. I had no way of knowing, and no one seemed to be jumping up to volunteer the information.

Unless, that is, I showed up at midnight as requested.

CHAPTER SIXTEEN

———

I tried not to look like I was checking out every single patron at the luau for suspicious signs as I listened to the pounding drum beat and watched the spectacular finale of the dancers' performance. I was careful to keep a neutral expression, trying my best to imitate Ramirez's blank cop face, even though I couldn't, my gaze straying again and again to the assembled crowd. Of course, it was possible that someone not in attendance at the luau had sent the text, but as I catalogued the pageant personnel, there didn't seem to be anyone missing.

Which made me wonder if it had come from someone not involved with the pageant at all. Someone like Xander Newport, or Donatella Curcio. Had they seen something that pointed to Jennifer and Desi's killer? Possibly something that hadn't even made sense until now? I felt like I'd talked to everyone involved with the pageant about Jennifer's death at this point. Maybe something I'd said or a question I'd asked had jarred loose a memory.

Then again, there was always the possibility that the text had come from the killer himself, and this was his attempt at getting victim number three alone. I fought back a chill at that thought, despite the warm evening.

A few minutes later, the dancers hurried off into the night to hearty applause, and dessert was brought out to even more applause. Mom and Mrs. Rosenblatt decided to take theirs back to the room to enjoy on the balcony. Dana and Marco went to refresh their drinks, leaving me alone with my thoughts. I watched absently while the other attendees slowly started to disperse, some forgoing the desserts entirely, others carrying their plates back into the hotel with them. Before long, the group had thinned considerably.

I was so deep in thought that I didn't notice Maxine until she fell into the chair beside me, unsteady in the sand in the Gucci stiletto sandals I'd admired from underneath her bed. They looked just as good from out in the open, and I took a moment to admire them while she tried to corral her long blonde hair extensions in the ocean breeze. "It's pretty out here, isn't it?"

I nodded. "Very pretty." Although the fire dancers had departed, the flickering tiki torches circling the area continued to provide a peaceful, intimate ambiance.

"I just can't help but think about everything that's gone on." She pointed with her chin out beyond the tiki torches to the darkness. "How do we know someone's not out there watching us right now?" She shuddered. "I'm not going to be the last to leave tonight, I can tell you that."

"Did you come with Whitney?" I asked.

Maxine nodded. "You bet I did. I don't go anywhere alone now. And I don't think you should, either."

I gave her a sharp look. Was that honest concern or a threat? Maxine was staring out toward the ocean, her eyes narrowed against the breeze so that she looked almost...calculating. I wondered for the first time if perhaps Maxine wasn't as dumb as she seemed, if she *had* actually been the one who'd sabotaged Jennifer by stealing her bikini top, and maybe even killed her to get a leg up in the competition. Maybe she wasn't even as clumsy as she seemed. Maybe it was all an act to deflect suspicion while she murdered her way toward the top of the pageant rankings.

The thought sent a chill shimmering up my spine. I fought the sudden urge to leap from my seat and get as far away from her as I possibly could. "I'm not taking any chances," I said, choosing my words carefully.

"Good." She nodded her approval. "I like you, Maddie. I'd hate to see something happen to you."

Now *that* sounded like a thinly veiled threat. I was finding it hard to swallow. My mouth was dry.

"Well, it's just about curfew time. I think Whitney's waiting for me to head back upstairs." She pushed herself out of the chair, her heels stabbing into the sand as she stood. "I wouldn't want to get in any trouble on the last night."

"No," I agreed, my voice faint. "You wouldn't want that."

She tottered off in her stilettos with a cutesy little finger wave. I forced myself to stay put and give her a five-minute head start before I called it a night myself and hurried back into the hotel. I was halfway through the lobby on my way to the elevators when I realized Don still hadn't made an appearance since the discovery of Desi's body in the auditorium. Kind of strange, considering she hadn't missed a single day prior to that. It made me wonder again if a guilty conscience was keeping her away.

I took the elevator to the twelfth floor, but instead of turning toward my room, I went in the opposite direction, toward Marco's, where I hoped my husband would be. I hadn't seen Ramirez all day, and I wanted to hear what he'd learned about Xander's alibi.

Luckily, I found Ramirez alone in the room, wearing jeans and little else. No shirt, no shoes...and with the way he looked, there were no complaints from me.

"Hey, babe," he said, before pulling me into his arms and giving me a lingering kiss that went a long way toward calming my nerves.

"Hey, yourself," I replied when we finally came up for air. "That's the best greeting I've had all day."

Ramirez shot me a grin. "It better be."

I glanced around the room and noticed that the TV was on in the corner, tuned to ESPN. It seemed that he'd been lying on his bed watching some sports highlights. There was a half-empty bottle of beer on the nightstand.

Ramirez hit the *mute* button on the remote as I sat on the foot of his bed. "So how was the luau?"

My mind shot straight back to Maxine's strange comments and their potential hidden meaning. In the bright, comfortable hotel room with my homicide detective husband, I now felt like maybe I'd been reading too much into them. "Oh, you know. You've seen one luau, you've seen them all."

"Uh-huh." He studied me. "You want to tell me about it?"

"The luau?" I shrugged. "A pig, some alcohol, a lot of desserts. The end."

"Maddie…" This time he snapped off the television and tossed the remote on the bed. "What happened?"

He knew me so well. And just, maybe I *wasn't* reading too much into the beauty queen's words. Maybe Maxine was crazy as a loon and planned to mow through all the remaining states to snatch the Miss Hawaiian Paradise crown. I did a deep breath. "I think Maxine might have sabotaged Jennifer. Or maybe Whitney did. But one of the two, for sure, but I'm leaning toward Maxine."

Ramirez's expression didn't change. He'd traveled this road with me before. Plus he was way better at the cop face. "And you think this why, exactly?"

Uh-oh. Not sure I wanted to confess to sneaking into their room and hiding in the closet and under the bed, not to mention going through their things. Even though I had found the bikini top, the search itself had been a tad in the gray area of legal, and Ramirez was a cop, first and foremost. Well, also a stud muffin, but mostly a cop. And I wasn't in the mood for a lecture on the legalities of *not* breaking and entering.

I thought fast. "Just some comments Maxine made at the luau," I said with deliberate vagueness.

"Like *I sabotaged Miss Montana*?" Ramirez asked.

I grinned and swatted his arm. "She wants to win. It's not outside the realm of possibility that she'd do anything and everything she could to beat the competition."

"So what you're saying," Ramirez said slowly, "is not that she sabotaged Jennifer. It's that she might have killed her."

"That's what I'm saying," I agreed. "Only I didn't say it—you did."

He took a drink from his beer and offered me the bottle. "And you're *not* saying it why?"

"Things she said to me at the luau," I said. "Like telling me to be careful. That she liked me and would hate to see something happen to me."

"Sounds vicious," Ramirez joked.

I shot him a look as I took a sip of beer. "It's not only what she said, it's how she said it."

"And how did she say it?"

I thought about Maxine's narrowed eyes, staring out over the ocean. Like she was considering the best way to bump off Miss Nevada or something. "Almost too sincerely," I said finally.

Ramirez just looked at me. "What a witch."

"You had to be there," I told him.

"Guess so." He took his beer back and drank some.

"Then there's the clumsiness," I went on. "She falls all over the stage during the dance numbers. She fell over Desi's body! And she fell into the chair on the beach tonight. I mean, no one can be that clumsy, can they? It's got to be an act."

Ramirez tilted his head to look down at my heels. "How high are those things?"

I pulled my feet under the chair, mostly out of view. "Four inches. But we're not talking about my heels."

"Fine. How high are *her* heels?"

At least five, maybe even six inches. Compared to some of the other girls, Maxine was a little vertically challenged. She wore stilettoes on steroids. I glared at him. "What's your point?"

"I think I made my point." Ramirez sipped his beer.

I crossed my arms. "Okay, it's not just what she said. Maybe there's something else."

"Thought there might be."

His smugness irritated me. "Maxine has Jennifer's stolen bikini top in her dresser drawer," I blurted out before common sense could stop me.

That got his attention. He lowered the beer bottle, his eyes fixed on mine. "How would you know that?"

No way was I admitting to breaking and entering. He could glare at me all night long. I wasn't cracking. "I was on my way back to the room earlier," I said, "and the maid was working in there and she had the door propped open like they do, and—"

"And she had the dresser drawers open, too," he prompted. "And the bikini top was lying right on top with a 'Jennifer' nametag on it?"

I rolled my eyes. "Okay. So I *might* have slipped in and looked around for a *few* minutes. It was worth it, though, don't you think?"

"No," he said flatly, "it was not. What if she or her roommate had come back to the room and seen you?"

"She didn't see me," I said. "I was under the bed." Oops. Well, I don't know how *that* slipped out.

Ramirez didn't say anything for a while, but I could see the muscles in his jaw working. "You were under the bed," he said finally.

I nodded. "And let me tell you, the housekeeping in this place leaves a lot to be desired. You should've seen the amount of dust under there."

He wasn't amused. "Maddie, I'm beginning to get the feeling you actually like putting yourself in harm's way."

I shot him a dirty look. "Oh, come on! That is so unfair. Not to mention sexist. You go chasing after killers on a daily basis, but do I lecture *you* on safety? No."

"Not the same thing. I'm a *trained* homicide investigator."

I ground my teeth at the emphasis he put on the word trained—after all, this was not my first murder rodeo either—but considering I'd yet to decide what to do about the potential midnight meeting by the pool, I decided to let it go. "Fine. So how did your very official police investigation go today?" I asked instead.

"Maddie…"

"What? I can't even *ask* about an investigation?" I blinked my eyelashes up and down in mock innocence.

"Fine." He shook his head, his expression softening finally. "Xander Newport was at the Curling Wave until closing time. So unless he hired someone to do his dirty work, he's in the clear."

My shoulders slumped a little. "He has witnesses?"

"Only every female in the bar," Ramirez said. "He hit on all of them, including the transgendered one. Turns out the guy's a creep but not a killer."

I was disappointed, but not totally surprised. Xander might have had a motive to kill Jennifer, but there had never been a reason for him to murder Desi. And I doubted that there were two killers on the loose. "So Xander's in the clear," I said, mostly to myself.

"Sad, but true." Ramirez stood up and pulled me to my feet, his hard, bare chest pressing against me. "Happy now?"

"Not quite," I told him, tipping my face up to his. "But maybe you can fix that." I gave him a suggestive smile.

"You better believe it," he agreed, lowering his mouth to mine. His arms tightened around me, fitting me more closely against him, and I wound my hands into his hair, breathing in his musky scent as a little sigh of satisfaction bubbled up and escaped me.

"You two need to hang a sock on the doorknob!" Marco called out from the doorway. "Give a boy a sign, already!"
I groaned, and Ramirez reluctantly pulled away. I erased my lipstick from his lower lip with my thumb, seeing the frustration evident on his face.

Trust me, right there with you, pal.

Marco took off his floppy beach hat, tossing it on the nearest bed, and bustled across the room, waving a drink in his hand. "I just heard the funniest story from Ruth Marie. You would not believe what she did to become Miss 1962—" He stopped when he noticed our expressions. "Wait, was I interrupting something? 'Cause I can go amuse myself for a while." He took in Ramirez's bare torso. "All night, if need be."

Ramirez opened his mouth, but I said, "Don't worry about it, Marco. I'm beat, anyway." I stood on my toes and gave my husband a quick goodnight peck on the lips. "See you in the morning."

"I'll make it up you, dahling," Marco called after me.

I heard Ramirez grunt and open another beer as Marco continued his tale. "Anyway, as I was saying, Ruth Marie is such a card, she told me..."

For a moment, I almost thought Ramirez had the shorter end of the roomie stick on this trip.

* * *

I wasn't being entirely dishonest with my husband. I was beat. But as the minutes ticked toward midnight, I felt myself getting reenergized. Or maybe that was just the anticipation building. Okay, I knew Ramirez wouldn't approve of me showing up at midnight alone to meet the potential murder witness. And, honestly, I had no intention of waltzing into the deserted pool area by myself at midnight, exposed and vulnerable to who knew what. But I also had no intention of letting this potential lead slip through my fingers. What if someone really had seen something? With the televised pageant tomorrow, time was running short to find Jennifer and Desi's killer. If I went down to the pool early, and I could find a satisfactory hiding place, I could wait until the texter showed up, get a definite ID, and then question him or her in the light of day, preferably in the middle of all the beauty queens and judges and a security guard or two. Maybe the plan wasn't Einstein brilliant, but it was the best I could do on short notice.

I briefly thought of calling in backup, but as I mentally ran down my list of possible backers I dismissed each one. There was no way Marco could slip out without Ramirez catching wind of it. If Mom and Mrs. Rosenblatt came with me, we had about as much chance of keeping hidden and quiet as an elephant in a public library. Dana would've been a great co-conspirator, but her phone was turned off for the night. I tried to tell myself I would just be hiding in the shadows and watching. Totally not in any danger. Totally not out in the open. Totally fine without backup.

Though I didn't totally believe myself.

I went through my usual bedtime ritual for Mom and Mr. R's benefits, pulled on a pair of shorts and a T-shirt and climbed between the sheets, but sleep was the last thing on my mind. I stared at the ceiling, waiting while the minutes passed. Mrs. Rosenblatt must have forgotten her breathing strips as her snoring provided a metronome of sorts to mark the excruciating movement of the clock. By 11:45, she and Mom were finally doing a lumberjack duet. Perfect. In fact, they were loud enough that I could slip out of my bed and out of the room—and probably away in a helicopter if I chose—unnoticed.

In my flip-flops and a sweatshirt, I rode the elevator down, passed through the lobby without encountering a soul, and went out the back entrance. A minute later I was approaching the pool. The breeze had stiffened, rearranging the clouds so that they obscured the moon. Someone had stacked up the lounge chairs for the night and lowered the umbrellas, lending an air of abandonment to the area. But the cabanas were open. I slipped inside the closest one to wait, ducking down behind a gauzy curtain. With my cell on silent mode this time.

Minutes continued to tick past with agonizing slowness. Midnight finally came and went, and I was still waiting. No movement at all, save for the palms and the occasional lizard that darted along the pool apron. Even the surface of the water was still as a mirror. I stretched the kinks out of my legs and settled in again. I'd give it fifteen more minutes before chalking the whole thing up to a hoax. Or maybe the texter genuinely had information but had developed cold feet about sharing it.

Either way, by the time my cell finally read 12:15, I'd had enough. I emerged from the cabana to go back to my room, disappointed that nothing had come of what might have been a promising lead.

I'd only taken a few steps up the path when I suddenly felt a presence behind me. I turned.

But it was too late. Blinding pain shot through my skull, and the shadowy palm trees and lava rock waterfalls slid into blackness.

CHAPTER SEVENTEEN

———

"Maddie!"

Someone was jostling me, lifting me off the hard concrete and placing me onto something softer and warmer. I didn't want to be jostled. Jostling hurt, mostly my head, but my back felt tight, and my right elbow was sore, too. I wanted to be left alone, right where I was, to go back to sleep.

"Maddie, wake up!"

I forced my eyes open. Ouch. That hurt too. They took a second to focus, but then I saw Ramirez bent over me with a look of such deep concern that it was gut-wrenching. He had tiny beads of perspiration dotting his forehead, but it wasn't hot. It was actually cool, cool enough that I couldn't seem to stop shivering.

Ramirez drew in a quick breath and muttered, "Thank God," before pressing a kiss onto my forehead. I tried not to wince at the contact and struggled to sit up. He pressed me back gently but firmly onto a lounge chair and sat on the edge so he could hold me there. "What happened?" he asked. "Can you remember?"

I took a look around at the still water of the pool, the stacked lounge chairs, the empty cabanas. "I don't know," I said honestly. "I don't have a clue. I thought I was alone, but then I felt this...*pain*...and now you're here." I tried to smile at him, but it only made my head hurt.

"Did you see anyone?" he asked.

I tried to think about it, but I didn't really want to think. I wanted to sleep. And I wanted a blanket. Why was I so cold? "No. No one," I said. Who had been there? Had my witness turned on me? Or had the killer followed me here and tried to take me out before I found the witness?

"I'm taking you to the hospital." His eyes shifted to the top of my head. "You need to be checked out. You've got a pretty good egg up there."

"I'll be fine," I said, reaching up to touch my scalp. Which was a mistake. A lightning bolt of pain slashed through my head, setting my teeth on edge, yanking me right out of my lethargy. "By the morning," I added. I looked at my fingers. No blood. No blood was a good thing.

"You could have a concussion," he said, his harsh tone contradicting the compassion etched into the lines of his face.

"I don't have a concussion. I just have a headache." A monster headache. The mother of all headaches. Then something suddenly occurred to me. "What are you doing out here, anyway?"

"Thank your mother," he told me. "She woke up and found you missing and shot me a text. She's worried sick about you." He gave me a faint smile. "The text made absolutely no sense, by the way, but I gather she doesn't think your juju cleansing did the trick. Apparently you're still cursed."

I managed to roll my eyes.

"And because your juju is cursed," Ramirez went on, "I'm putting you on the first plane home in the morning."

"I can't go home," I protested. "Tomorrow's the pageant. I mean today." I stopped myself as I was about to shake my head. I wasn't ready for head shaking quite yet. "Besides," I added, "I'm almost sure someone knows something about the murders. Maybe."

Ramirez's dark eyebrows drew together. "This isn't a game, Maddie."

"I don't think it's a game."

"Then exactly what where you doing out here alone?"

"Uh—"

"Here we go!" Marco hustled down the path toward us, carrying a lumpy ball of hand towel in both fists. "I couldn't find an actual ice bag so I did the next best thing." He unfolded a corner of the towel to reveal a mound of ice cubes. "I raided the ice machine. This might be a little sloppy." He handed it over. "Sorry it took so long. How are you feeling, honey?"

"She's feeling like she wants to go home," Ramirez said firmly.

I placed the makeshift ice bag gingerly on my head. I didn't have the energy to fight him. At least not yet. "I don't suppose you brought aspirin with you?"

Marco whipped a small tin from the pocket of his shorts. "Voila. My tiny travel companion. Here." He shook three of them out and handed them over. "But I didn't bring any water."

"This is fine." I swallowed the aspirin dry, cringing at the sharp taste that lingered on my tongue. Then I closed my eyes and laid my head back, perfectly willing to sleep the rest of the night away right where I was.

But Marco was having none of it. "Come on, Sleeping Beauty. We're putting you to bed."

"She's coming back to our room," Ramirez said.

I allowed myself to lean on Ramirez as he slid an arm around me. He supported me back along the path to the hotel and up to his room, with Marco dancing ahead to open doors and push elevator buttons and pull back covers. Despite practically carrying me the last few feet to the room, Ramirez wasn't even breathing hard when he laid me down on his bed. He leaned over to kiss my forehead. "We'll talk about this in the morning," he whispered.

A few minutes later I was vaguely aware of him sliding into the other side of the bed, but then someone shut off the lights, and I drifted away.

When I opened my eyes again, sunlight was slanting through a gap in the drapes, and I was able to think coherently again, even if I was still tired from my ordeal. The headache had subsided into a dull aching sensation in the back of my head. I glanced to my left at Ramirez's rumpled empty side of the bed, and to my right, at Marco's tidy fully made one. Alone again. But wiser in the light of day. I closed my eyes again, trying not to freak out at the idea of how close I'd come last night to being in Jennifer's shoes. Ramirez was right about one thing—this was no game. And I was tired of playing. In the light of day, I was feeling more than happy to leave the investigative heavy lifting to the big boys.

I threw aside the covers and swung my legs over the side of the bed. My back registered a minor complaint at the movement, but nothing felt too badly out of whack. Today was pageant day, and I intended to fulfill my responsibilities. I pushed myself to my feet and went to check the damage in the mirror. Not terrible, but I would require some make-up to look presentable. I took a quick shower, letting the warm water cascade gently over my head without doing any actual rubbing with my fingers. Even the water splashing on my scalp set off prickly little bursts of pain like tiny electrical shocks.

At the sink, I squirted toothpaste directly into my mouth, and blew dry my hair while finger-combing it into something if not couture, at least less frightening. And with a dip into Marco's skin care collection, I wasn't looking half bad. I had no choice other than to put on the prior night's clothes, but they looked no worse for my lying on the ground for who knew how long before Ramirez found me.

My phone was Vouge-ing when I emerged from the bathroom. I hurried across the room to snatch it up.

"Oh, thank God you're safe, dear. You can't imagine how worried I was."

"How worried we were," Mrs. Rosenblatt yelled in the background.

"What on earth happened to you?" Mom asked. "Marco just told me that they found you by the pool. Why would you go down to the pool at night?"

"Something came up during the luau," I said. "I thought I had a credible lead. And I took precautions." I should have taken an armed guard.

"Oh, honey, with juju like yours, you know you shouldn't be wandering around anywhere by yourself, especially at night."

Geez. "I don't think it's my juju, Mom," I told her. "I think there's a killer on the loose."

There was a beat of silence. Then, "And this is supposed to make me feel better? Having you running around alone in the dark with a *killer on the loose*?"

"Tell her to come down to the buffet," Mrs. Rosenblatt yelled. "Tell her I found a real chicken."

"Dear, Mrs. Rosenblatt said—"

"I heard what she said," I cut in. "But I'm sorry, I'm super busy. I have final fittings for the pageant today."

"Well, be careful. I'm your mother, dear. I worry about you."

"I doubt I'll get a moment alone all day," I promised her. "I'll be surrounded by pageant people."

"Still, make sure you carry the mojo bag. You need all the protection you can get."

"I haven't forgotten the mojo bag," I told her. I'd never forget the mojo bag, or the rest of the juju cleansing fiasco. No matter how I tried. "I have to go, Mom. I've gotten change."

"Tell her we have the right words!" Mrs. Rosenblatt was calling out as I hung up.

I was still shaking my head when Ramirez came in. He was followed by Marco, wheeling a room service cart draped in a white linen tablecloth. "Good morning, sunshine!" Marco rolled the cart over to the glass doors and threw the drapes open wide. I blinked at the brightness. "We brought you a little breakfast. We didn't know what you'd want, so we have a little of everything." He whipped off the tablecloth with a flourish, and I gaped at the spread beneath. A coffeepot, glasses of apple, orange, and cranberry juices, stacks of toast, a few muffins, some croissants, and whatever entrees lay beneath the metal covers. Everything looked incredible and smelled even better.

"Looks like you cleaned out the buffet," I said. "I hope you two haven't eaten yet."

Marco quickly spread the tablecloth and transferred the food onto the table, arranging it so artfully it looked like a catered meal. The only thing missing was a centerpiece. While we settled in, Ramirez asked, "So how's your head feeling?"

I shrugged, trying to play it off. "Not bad. I washed my hair and everything."

Marco's eyebrows lifted as he appraised the finished product, but he didn't say anything.

"Then you'll have clean hair for the trip home," Ramirez said. "There's a flight out at two o'clock this afternoon."

Marco's eyes went wide and shifted from my hair to Ramirez and back to me.

I took a bite of a croissant. "I can't leave on the day of the pageant," I told him. "I have work to do."

"And you signed a contract," he finished. "Yeah. You said that last night." He sliced into his Western omelet with a vicious slash.

Did I? I didn't remember. "Right, well, it's true. I have to honor my contract," I said. "Especially today." I gave him what I hoped was a charming smile. "Why don't you stick around and play bodyguard?"

"I'd love to," he said, "but I can't. I'm heading to the station as soon as we finish eating. I'm hoping they can track down that text."

I paused. "Did I tell you about that last night, too?" I asked. Huh. Maybe I'd hit my head harder than I'd thought.

But Ramirez shook his head. "No," he ground out. "But like any good investigator, I checked your phone."

I should have felt violated, but considering I *had* been keeping something from him, I just sipped my juice instead.

"But all things considered," he continued, "I really don't want to leave you alone."

"I won't be alone," I said. "I'll be with everyone from the pageant."

Marco did a little hiccupping sound around his mouthful of orange juice, like a peal of laughter was stuck in his throat. "Honey, aren't those the people you need to stay away from?"

"He's right. You need to have someone else with you," Ramirez said, his expression grim. "And it should be me." He glared at his omelet in frustration.

Marco patted the corner of his mouth with his napkin. "I'm free as a bird all day. I'd be happy to be Maddie's shadow. Hey, maybe I can even pick up some fashion tips backstage. As if I need them," he added with a giggle. I watched him slather butter on a slice of toast and take a dainty bite from the corner.

I grinned. "That's a great idea. Marco will be my assistant today, and when the pageant's over, I'll get on the next plane, no questions asked."

Ramirez's eyebrows lifted. "Regardless of the status of the investigation?"

"Regardless," I agreed. "I don't even have to report downstairs for a couple of hours. I can stay right here, and we can play—"

"Ladies of leisure?" Marco asked.

"I was going to say cards," I said. "But I like your idea better."

He did a little hand clap. "I'm so in, I've practically ordered the mimosas."

Ramirez considered it. "It's not perfect," he said finally, "but it'll have to do." He pointed his knife at Marco. "Do not leave her side. For any reason. I don't care what she tries to tell you."

"Hey," I said in mild protest.

"And miss seeing all the shoes and gowns and glam up close?" Marco shook his head. "Dahling, you couldn't *pry* me away from her."

We managed to get through breakfast without another mention of the assault, although it seemed obvious that Ramirez wasn't entirely comfortable leaving me under Marco's protection. That didn't surprise me. But he knew as well as I did that the text I'd gotten last night was the best solid lead toward finding the killer that we'd gotten yet. Plus, I got the feeling that finding this guy, or gal, had just become personal to Ramirez. I assured him that I fully intended to keep my word. Once Miss Hawaiian Paradise was crowned, I'd be on my way to the airport.

After Ramirez left, Marco accompanied me to my room (which was thankfully empty) so I could change my clothes and put on some makeup. My finger-combed hair wasn't exactly pageant-ready, so I took some time working it over with a round brush, careful to avoid scraping the bristles over the bump on my head. The finished result wasn't perfect, but it wasn't going to induce pointing fingers and laughter, either, so I called it a win.

We grabbed two quick lattes at the coffee shop in the lobby before heading down to the auditorium for a full day's worth of last minute fittings and dress rehearsals.

While the telecast was still several hours away, the backstage area was already bustling with activity and crackling with nervous energy. Marco took it all in with a gleam of glee in his eyes. "This is so exciting!" He squeezed my arm.

"You can find yourself a seat and watch the rehearsals if you want," I told him. "There's no point in following in my footsteps. I'll be perfectly safe with everyone here."

He shook his head. "Nope. No way, honey. I promised your hubby I'd be your personal assistant, and that's what I'm going to be."

"Suit yourself." I shrugged. "It won't be much fun for you to watch shoe fittings."

He propped his fists on his hips and stared at me, incredulous. "Are you *kidding* me? They're *shoes*."

I led him into Dressing Room A, and his jaw dropped at the sight of dozens of shoeboxes lining the walls. They'd been joined today by two racks filled with belts, scarves, and other leftover accessories from wardrobe. "I think I'm in heaven," he whispered. "How dare you keep this from me?" He scurried over to peek inside some of the boxes, occasionally pulling out a shoe to admire it. "You are a true visionary," he told me.

I grinned. "You are a nut. Grab a seat. The first fitting is in a few minutes."

My first fitting of the day was with Whitney, who seemed unusually subdued as we made last minute adjustments to her assortment of shoes. I chalked it up to pageant nerves and quickly made the changes—leaving out the pair we'd had set aside for the talent number which had been cut—while Marco looked on, occasionally wiping drool from the corner of his mouth.

After we repeated the process with a dozen of other girls, I stood and stretched. "I'm going to grab a cup of coffee. Want some?"

He shook his head. "I'll just wait here and watch over the shoes." He narrowed his eyes at me. "You're not leaving this immediate area, right?"

"Just to the break room," I assured him. "I'll even leave the door open so you can see me the whole time." The truth was, I didn't mind if Marco kept an eye on me. I had something of a case of nerves myself. Despite my earlier assurances, being surrounded by pageant personnel wasn't exactly a source of comfort when I knew one of them was likely a killer. I just hoped Ramirez finished up at the police station quickly.

I headed for the refreshment table to pour myself a cup of coffee with lots of cream. (Hey, it wasn't a latte, but it would provide the much needed jolt.) I was stirring sugar into the Styrofoam cup when Laforge stepped up beside me. He'd lost his customary swagger and seemed worn down, even defeated. It was clear that the week's events weighed heavily on him. Beyond that, he looked *different*. It took me a moment to realize that he wasn't wearing his uber fashionable sunglasses. I'd grown so accustomed to seeing them in place that he didn't seem like the same person without them.

He gave me a rueful smile as he reached for a cup. "I don't know about you, Maddie, but this can't end soon enough for me."

"I am right there with you—" I stopped mid-sentence, staring at him. Laforge had gorgeous eyes. Startling eyes. Emerald green eyes. Jennifer had raved about her lover's green eyes. And I hadn't seen any other man all week whose color could hold a candle to his.

"Do you know all the cutting I've had to do to fit the time?" He sighed. "Add to that losing two of our contestants. What a nightmare."

I could hardly believe it. I blinked at him, taking in his tight, pale yellow leather pants, sleek silk shirt, and faux fur vest. Was it possible that Laforge was Jennifer's secret lover?

"We've had to totally redo the choreography," he was saying. "I hope Miss Arkansas can handle it. I have my doubts." He took a sip of coffee. "To tell you the truth—"

"You were sleeping with Jennifer," I blurted out.

Laforge gave a start, splashing coffee over the rim of his cup and onto his hand. He winced and reached for some napkins.

"What are you talking about?" he asked, his voice an octave higher.

I shook my head, still trying to make sense of it. "You gave her the promise ring. You're the guy she told all of the other contestants she was in love with."

He paused. "She said that?" Something in the tone of his voice completely confirmed what my brain was having a hard time wrapping itself around. He took a quick glance around us then hustled me into a quiet corner.

"Look, there's no need to alert the press. This can stay between us."

"I never noticed your eyes before," I said. They really were lovely—clear and bright, rimmed in long, thick lashes. I couldn't blame Jennifer for raving about them.

He frowned. "My eyes?"

I nodded. "They're green."

The frown deepened.

"Jennifer loved your eyes," I explained. "She talked about them all the time."

He tossed the used napkins into the wastebasket, his expression reflective. "I didn't know."

"So...you were just pretending to be gay this entire time?"

He stared at me. "What do you mean, pretending to be gay?"

I felt a flush creep up my neck into my face. "Nothing. Never mind." I did a mental forehead thunk. I'd totally bought into the stereotype of the ultra-fashionable man being gay and never even considered the possibility that Laforge and Jennifer had been having an affair. But it made perfect sense, really. The pageant was a workplace, and workplace affairs weren't uncommon.

"We met earlier in the year on the circuit," Laforge said quietly, staring into his cup. "New York, maybe, or Chicago. Doesn't matter. She was magnificent. It was instant attraction for both of us."

I raised an eyebrow. While Laforge did have nice eyes, there wasn't much else about the guy that screamed instant attraction to me.

"But it was more than that," he added. "Of course, with me being the Miss Hawaiian Paradise pageant director and she being a contestant this year, we couldn't exactly take it public."

"Plus there was her boyfriend, Xander."

I watched Laforge's expression closely as his jaw clenched. "Right. Him."

"He wouldn't exactly take kindly to the fact he was being cheated on."

Laforge shook his head. "It wasn't like that. Jennifer didn't love him. Heck, she hardy even saw him lately, with all of the traveling she did for pageants. She was just using him as the perfect cover for our relationship until we were ready to go public."

"And the ring?"

Laforge nodded. "It was my promise to her that we'd go public as soon as I stepped down as director."

I blinked. "You were stepping down?"

He nodded. "After the Miss Hawaiian Paradise Pageant. It was all arranged. Ashton Dempsey was set to take my place. I told him I was leaving over drinks the night that Jennifer..." He trailed off.

Which is why he'd been seen being uncharacteristically cozy with Dempsey that night at the bar. I was quiet for a moment. "Did he know about you and Jennifer?"

Laforge took a sip of his coffee. "No, only that I was leaving. We weren't ready to tell anyone. But then when she...well, everything changed. Then there was no point in stepping down without her. There was no point in anything."

I noticed the slight tremor in his hands and more muscles tensing in his jaw. His grief seemed genuine and palpable.

Then I thought of Ashton Dempsey ratting out his first client, Donatella, and getting her disqualified for much the same infraction committed by Jennifer and Laforge. "How did he take it when you changed your mind?" I asked.

He shuddered. "Not well at all. He made it clear that he saw me as just a roadblock to his lofty ambitions."

Given what I knew about Dempsey, that wasn't hard to believe. I couldn't help but wonder if he'd thought that removing Jennifer from the picture would push Laforge's exit as pageant director and his own lock on the position he coveted. But was a directorship worth committing murder?

But of course, Jennifer had had another even more glaring loose end. "What about Xander Newport?" I said. "Did Jennifer tell him you were seeing each other?"

"That Neanderthal?" Laforge snorted. "I don't know what she told him except that it was over. I don't know why he flew all the way out here when she didn't even want to see him."

I had an idea why he might have done it. Now that it seemed clear Laforge would have no reason to kill Jennifer, it was more likely than ever that Xander Newport had come to Hawaii with revenge on his mind. But according to Ramirez, Xander had a solid alibi.

Which pretty much left me at square one again.

CHAPTER EIGHTEEN

———

The rest of the afternoon was a frenzy of last-minute fittings and frayed nerves with a few wardrobe crises thrown in for good measure. Miss Alaska's zipper broke. Miss Virginia had lost some strategic sequins from her gown. Miss Ohio stepped outside for some fresh air and returned with a head full of frizz. I helped out where I could while staying out of the way in the dressing room, gathering a needle and thread to work on the zipper, digging in Miss Virginia's wardrobe bag for extra sequins, and eliminating Miss Ohio's frizz with a flat iron and a can of hair spray. All of which gave me little time to think about Laforge and Dempsey and murder. Which was probably better for my own nerves.

By three o'clock, I still hadn't heard from Ramirez, so Marco and I grabbed a quick bite to eat in the dining room before returning to the auditorium. By then the audience was starting to file in. I spotted Xander Newport seated alone in the back, half hidden in shadows since the house lights weren't fully up yet. I wondered what he was up to. It seemed unlikely he'd have an interest in the pageant now that his ex-girlfriend was no longer part of it. I decided to give him the benefit of the doubt and assume he was there for purely sentimental reasons.

Mom and Mrs. Rosenblatt had taken seats in the front row. I sent a reluctant Marco to join them, assuring him there was no way I'd be leaving the confines of the backstage area throughout the course of the night. I waved to Mom, and she waved the plastic alligator head back at me.

Contestants scurried about backstage, getting outfitted and putting final touches on hair and makeup while Laforge stood in the wings, directing their individual onstage entrances. Ashton Dempsey lingered backstage, practically taking notes as he watched the proceedings. It seemed to me he still had his eye on a pageant directorship despite Laforge's decision to stay. Dana was in place at the raised judges' table, right in front of the stage, comparing notes with Jeffries and Ruth Marie.

Finally lights flashed backstage, signaling the live show was about to start. Beauty queens lined up, the host went onstage, and the cameras started to roll. I stood off to the side as the opening music swelled, and the contestants danced onstage to their first choreographed number.

I was so preoccupied with watching Maxine stumble her way through a dance number, hoping that if she fell it wouldn't be because of my shoes, that I almost missed the text when it came through with a subtle vibration in my pocket. I pulled my phone out.

A chill ran through me when I saw the word *unavailable* again instead of a phone number. My first impulse was to delete it without reading it. Anonymous texts had meant nothing but trouble for me. But if I deleted it, Ramirez might not be able to track it. And if I wasn't going to delete it, I might as well read it.

I held my breath and swiped my finger across the screen.

Dressing Room A. Commercial break. I know who the killer is.

My eyes immediately bounced upward, scanning the dark wings. The girls were filing off the stage in groups. I noticed Whitney and Maxine were among the first. Had one of them sent the text as soon as they'd danced offstage?

I glanced at the time on my cell, noting the first commercial break was now only five minutes away. Not enough time for Ramirez to get here, assuming I could even reach him on his cell.

I peeked out into the audience and spotted Marco. His attention was riveted to the host as he introduced Miss California and her aspirations of becoming a brain surgeon...and a fashion model. I did a little discreet wave, but he didn't notice me. I took a step back, deeper into the wings, and tried an odd little kabuki dance of arm waves and leg kicks, anything I could think of to draw attention. Which I did, from the very old gentleman sitting in the end seat of the first row. He stared at me with huge eyes through his thick glasses, elbowed his very old wife, pointed my way, and they both gaped at me with open mouths.

I ducked back into the shadows.

I dialed Marco's number on my cell. It rang three times before switching to voicemail. Of course he'd turned the ringer off for the show.

Frustrated, I typed out a text to Mom: *Need Marco's help backstage*

I pressed *send* and waited. And waited some more. No reaction from Mom. Marco didn't leap from his seat and come racing to my side. Her cell was off too. How polite of her.

I blew out an exasperated sigh. I looked at my cell. Three minutes left.

Time for Plan B.

While the bump on my head ached at the thought of a repeat of last night, the fact that my potential witness was texting again said he or she was desperate. Okay, let's think logically about this. The commercial break was short—three minutes tops. What could happen in that time? Plus, I was backstage at a pageant, with an auditorium full of people, which meant it was highly unlikely anyone would try to physically harm me even if I did meet Mystery Witness. I mean, there were TV cameras here for crying out loud. No one would be stupid enough to make a move like that.

Would they?

Just in case, I dashed toward the dressing rooms, searching for anything I could use as a weapon. Unfortunately we weren't attending a law enforcement convention, it was a beauty pageant.

I snatched up the closest thing I could find, which was a hot pink flat iron that I yanked right out of the outlet on my way to Dressing Room A. Not the most practical weapon, but it was dangerously hot and could inflict a nasty burn. Or produce incredibly smooth hair, depending on how things turned out.

I reached the dressing room with a minute to spare, surprised to find it dark. I was pretty sure I'd left the light on when I'd finished up the fittings. Which meant someone had come in behind me and turned it off again for some reason.

I didn't want to think what the reason was as I frantically felt for the light switch.

My spine started to tingle, and I suddenly decided this was a bad idea. I should never have come back here without Marco. I turned to leave when someone said, "Close the door."

I jumped and let out a little yelp that would never be heard over the obnoxiously loud dance number winding down before the break. There was only a sliver of light filtering through the open door, not enough to see who'd spoken, but more than enough to see the horrifying muzzle of a gun emerge from the shadows, pointed directly at me.

Not good.

Holding the flat iron at my side, half hidden behind my leg, I prayed it wouldn't cool down before I might need to put it to use. I reluctantly did as I was told and pushed the door shut.

"Lock it. We don't want to be disturbed."

I fumbled with the doorknob as if I were locking it with shaking hands. The shaking hands weren't a pretense. Adrenaline was surging through my veins, leaving a metallic taste in my mouth and little sparkling starbursts of light in my field of vision.

"Now turn on the light."

Not sure I wanted to do that. On the one hand, it would give me a good look at whoever was on the other side of that gun. On the other hand, it would give them a better look at me. A better look meant better aim. The gun already provided an insurmountable advantage over a flat iron. I'd rather take my chances in the dark.

"I said turn on the light *now!*"

Okay, so I was dealing with a short fuse. Good to know. My hand trembled when I reached for the light switch, patting the wall a few more times than I needed to before I found it and switched it on.

And turned to see Jay Jeffries. Distinguished pageant judge Jay Jeffries. Sleazy womanizing Jay Jeffries, beloved by hundreds as Dr. Calvin Drake in *Island of Dreams*. He looked every inch a sophisticated TV star from the neck down in his custom fitted tuxedo. But from the neck up, he looked like a loon. His lips were peeled back from his teeth like a Rottweiler on the attack. His eyes were narrow and mean looking. A thought flitted through my brain: *He'll be missed from the judges' table.* But would he? How long would it take for him to shoot me then get back to work?

I touched the flat iron to the back of my leg. Still hot but not the blazing heat that I needed. But it would have to do.

"Maddie, Maddie, Maddie." He shook his head in mock sadness. "You just couldn't leave things alone, could you?"

"It was you all along?" I stared at him.

"Step into the center of the room." He gestured with the gun. "Away from the door."

I shuffled forward a few steps. I didn't want to give him a glimpse of the flat iron. Not yet. "*You* killed Jennifer and Desi?"

"I tried to warn you off," he went on, as if he hadn't heard. Maybe he hadn't. He probably couldn't, over the voices in his head. "How's your skull, by the way? I have to hand it to you—you can really take a hit. I gave you a pretty nice one." He seemed proud of himself.

My stomach did a slow roll. "I don't understand. Why did you kill them?"

"Why does anyone kill anyone?" He shrugged. "Jennifer got in my way. She threatened to turn me in to that twit Laforge and the Hawaiian Paradise Corporation. I couldn't have that, not after what happened two years ago. They'd have cut me loose for sure this time. Plus, with the scandal, I could have lost my role on *Island.* I can't lose my role. I'm Dr. Calvin Drake!"

"Wait—turn you in for what?" I asked.

He rolled his eyes. I almost expected them to keep spinning. "For Whitney, naturally."

For *Whitney?*

"You're surprised," he said, his tone almost genial, like we were chatting over drinks at a cocktail party. "I can't imagine why, but let me see if I can't clear it up for you. I've been doing the Hawaiian lei with Whitney since we got here. Turns out Miss Delaware thought she could sleep her way into the crown." He smirked. "And I was happy to let her think it. Everything was going along just fine until Miss Law and Order noticed Whitney sneaking out to meet me one night."

That must have been the night Whitney had claimed to be going to the vending machine. She'd just been worried about getting caught violating curfew and reached for the most convenient excuse. She must have known that if her affair with Jeffries had been discovered, she'd have been out of the pageant for sure. And she deserved to be. I felt a surge of anger at her self-serving lie.

"Jennifer actually had the nerve to confront me," Jeffries said. "*Me*! Didn't she know what I could do for her career? Silly girl." He made a *tsk'ing* sound. "I met her on the beach, and I tried to convince her how far she could go, how far I could *take* her, if she just kept her mouth shut, but she wouldn't give in. Said she was giving me one chance to resign before she went to Laforge with it all. So I followed her back to the hotel to make her see she had it all wrong."

"Which she didn't," I said. "She had it exactly right."

He shrugged again. "It was all her fault, really. Turned out the glamour girl had a temper. She thought I was threatening her, and she didn't like that. She came at me. I grabbed the lava rock. And the rest is history."

I tried to squelch the horrible reel that was playing in my head. I knew all too well how it ended. "And you stuffed the promise ring into her mouth."

"That stupid thing." He snorted. "That's what she gets for rejecting me. No one rejects me."

I tapped the flat iron against the back of my leg. It had gone from Broil to Bake. I didn't have much time if I hoped to use it as a weapon.

"What about Desi?" I asked, hoping to distract him and the surprisingly level aim of his gun. "Why did you have to kill her?"

Jeffries looked surprised at the question. "You said it yourself. I *had* to. Desiree followed Jennifer when she left her room that night. Nosey bitch saw the whole thing go down. And then she had the nerve to blackmail me! These women had no *respect* for Jay Jeffries!"

It was coming into sharper focus. "Desi blackmailed you into putting her in first place."

"Very good." His smile was brief and chilling. "She knew I had no choice. I had too much to lose. So I passed along the rumor to pad her scores. No one bothered to ask where the order came from. Only, you know women. Can't keep their mouths shut."

I gritted my teeth but decided now was not the time for a lecture on sexism.

"Desiree was no exception," he continued. "She was too chatty. Especially with *you*." He narrowed his eyes my way. "It was only a matter of time before she'd have said something to someone and *poof!* Goodbye, Dr. Calvin Drake."

It looked like Dr. Calvin Drake had said goodbye a long time ago. This guy was off his rocker.

"I couldn't have that kind of notoriety." His lips flattened into a slash. "So I got her here into the auditorium by telling her I'd slip her a preview of her final interview question. It was pathetic, really, how eager she was to become Miss Hawaiian Paradise. Then I hit her on the head and killed her."

His matter-of-factness was terrifying. And so were his next words.

"And now we come to you. Little Maddie Springer, the shoe designer. The bit player who just couldn't let it go. I thought for sure my little love tap would scare you off, but you just kept poking and prying to get to the truth." He lifted the gun. "Congratulations. Now you have."

The gun had been horrifying in the dark. It was even worse in the light. Especially when he pointed it at my heart. I'd heard about your life flashing before your eyes in the face of imminent death, but I shoved those thoughts down. I was focused on the fact that the flat iron was almost completely cooled and wouldn't even be able to singe a piece of paper. I needed an alternative, and I needed it fast.

I grabbed the power cord with one hand and the flat iron itself in the other, whipping it toward Jeffries like I was Lara Croft raiding a tomb.

It struck him in the side of the head, catching him completely by surprise. He grunted, his free hand going instinctively to his face.

I charged toward the boxes of shoes stacked behind him against the wall, yanking them down in bunches, as many as I could manage, as fast as I could manage it, hurling them toward him. Lids went flying, and shoes came tumbling out along with their paired gel inserts and leftover anti-slip sole pads that fluttered to the floor like dead autumn leaves.

He staggered backward away from the onslaught, holding up his hands to ward me off. But I was out of shoe boxes. I looked around wildly and spotted Miss Ohio's can of hair spray, still sitting on my work table. I snatched it up and lunged forward, wielding the hair spray straight out in front of me, the nozzle fully depressed. The cloud of hair spray hit Jeffries smack in the eyes. He slipped on a stiletto, losing his grip on the gun, and went down on his back. I watched the air rushing out of him at once, his eyes squeezed shut. Or maybe glued shut by the Extra Firm Hold.

He rolled onto his right hip, fumbling for the gun amidst the dozens of shoes.

I took aim again with the hair spray.

But the thing about beauty queens is that they use a lot of hair spray on a daily basis. At a pageant, they use cases of the stuff. In fact, somewhere beyond the dressing room's closed door I was sure there was plenty of fresh aerosol ammunition. But in this room, I had just the one can.

And it was empty.

I stared at it in disbelief, shook it, and pumped the nozzle. Nothing.

Suddenly Jeffries' leg whipped across my shin, sending a searing pain up my right side and knocking me off my feet. I went down on both knees, my teeth clacking together hard.

His arm was moving, coming out from beneath him. Groping again for the gun.

I grabbed the nearest stiletto and lunged forward on my knees, hammering it at him like I was driving a stubborn nail into wood. He yelped and covered his face with both hands, which would have left vulnerable areas like his heart exposed if he'd had one.

The stiletto broke off.

I gulped in some breaths and reached in the mess for another.

A squishy sort of slap hit me on the arm.

Jeffries was slapping at me with gel inserts, left, right, left, right, in a hard crisscrossing motion, like he was dusting a piece of furniture with a rag. His eyes were still shut, and tears trickled from beneath his lids. Still, he whacked away blindly. Had I not been fighting for my life, it would have been comical.

I grabbed the broken heel and stabbed at him with it, aiming for fleshy, body parts like his face. I was furious. Furious that he'd killed Jennifer and Desi, furious that he wanted to kill me, furious that he'd made me waste months of work and ruin dozens of pairs of shoes.

The heel slashed into one of the gel inserts, slicing it open, and gobs of purple gel bled out onto Jeffries' hands. He threw it aside in disgust and tried to cover his face from my onslaught. But gel was dripping from his fingers, and when he tried to flick his hand to shake it off, the stiletto slipped through his defenses and gashed his cheek. He let out a high pitched shriek and rolled onto his side, away from me.

That was all the opening I needed. I had to get to safety. I needed out of that room like I needed my next breath. I sprang to my feet and scrambled for the door, sliding on the multiple shoes, boxes, lids, and flotsam strewn across the floor, ignoring the pain in my shin as I tried to kick a path ahead of me so I could move faster. I had to move faster—

I was a step away when I felt a strong hand clamp onto my shoulder, yanking me back onto the floor like a rag doll. Jeffries stepped around me, in front of the door, blocking my exit. He smirked down at me, looking like a deranged character from a horror movie, blood mixed with purple goo dripping down his torn cheek, his eyes wild with rage.

His gun now firmly in hand and aimed at my head.

I wanted to close my eyes as thoughts of Max and Livvie and Ramirez flooded my mind. As if that would somehow keep those thoughts more private and sacred. But like a train wreck, I couldn't look away, my gaze locked on the barrel of the gun.

I heard a loud bang.

And it took me moment to realize it wasn't a gun ending my life but the door flying open, knocking into Jeffries. He went sprawling one way and the gun flew another.

I ignored his grunt of pain. I dove for the gun just as I saw Maxine rush in.

"Maddie, I'm so sorry I broke your—" Her blue eyes widened comically when she saw the mess, a pump with a broken heel dangling from her hand. "What happened?"

I pointed the gun directly at Jeffries, proud to see my hands weren't shaking a bit. "Call 9-1-1," I told her. "This pageant is over."

CHAPTER NINETEEN

———

Ramirez and Detective Whatshisname took only minutes to show up. Ramirez left the detective to Miranda-ize Jeffries and haul him away in cuffs, bawling and clutching his injured cheek with gel-slicked fingers. Jeffries didn't look my way. I resisted the urge to kick him when he passed, even though it seemed like the least I could do for Jennifer, and Desi, and even Laforge, who'd lost the woman he truly loved.

As other investigators and plain clothed officers trickled in, Ramirez led me to a relatively quiet corner backstage. My bravado dropped away when I fell into his arms. Being held by my husband felt like home, and it was a place I didn't think I would ever be again. I clung to him, buried my nose in his chest, and breathed in his familiar musky scent. I felt as much as heard the low rumble of his voice while he promised me I was safe and it was over. I stayed right where I was until I began to believe it.

"I should have called you," I told him. "I should have sent you a text or tried to call the station—"

"Shh." Ramirez stroked my hair. "I'm just glad you're alright. If he'd hurt you…" I heard him swallow hard. He didn't want to finish the thought anymore than I did. "I should have been here," he finished.

I shook my head. "If I'm not at fault for not calling, you're certainly not at fault for not playing bodyguard." I paused. "But just out of curiosity, where were you all day? I thought you'd be back sooner."

"Waiting on some lab results," Ramirez said. "Turned out as the forensic evidence started coming in, it was pointing straight to a pageant insider. We were actually back here at the hotel waiting for this fiasco to end so we could talk to a few people again. One of them Jeffries. Turns out skin cells underneath Desi's fingernails matched the DNA from his hair sample."

I shuddered. "He kept telling me he's Dr. Calvin Drake."

"Not anymore," Ramirez said. "And by the way, I'll be looking to talk to Marco next. He promised me he'd stay by your side all day."

"Don't blame him," I said. I'd turned my face back into his shirt, and my voice was muffled. "I sent him to sit with Mom and Mrs. Rosenblatt. I didn't think anything could happen to me here, with all these people around."

Ramirez snorted. "All what people? Half the audience left after they came back from commercial break. One judge was missing, and Miss Arkansas practically took a header into the first row when the MC tried to introduce her."

Maxine. Her clumsiness had saved my life.

"Doesn't look like he's taking it too well," Ramirez said. I looked up at him, questioning, and he tipped his head toward the wings. I turned to see Laforge slumped in a folding chair, hands on knees, head hanging low. "I don't blame him. Even before the break it looked like a grade school musical out there."

"That bad?" I asked.

Ramirez shrugged. "What do I know about pageants?"

I grinned.

"But," he added, "the woman in a duck shirt sitting next to me called the director there LaFail. And considering the live feed went dead halfway through when the authorities arrived, I'd guess most people are going to agree."

So Laforge might be out of a job after all. I couldn't help but feel sorry for him, losing both his girlfriend and his career in the same week.

Of course, the pageant hadn't gone spectacularly for yours truly. I wasn't sure how it was going to play in the press that one of my stilettos was responsible for catching a homicidal soap star.

We suddenly heard the crash of breaking glass coming from the refreshment table, and I jerked up to find Maxine hovering over a shattered water pitcher. I couldn't help a grin.

Maxine could be forgiven for a few dozen broken water pitchers, as far as I was concerned.

She angled away from the table and made wild arm gestures to the young police officer at her side, probably describing how she'd barged into the dressing room, knocking Jeffries over. The officer nodded, took notes, and sneaked furtive glances at her. I couldn't blame him, either. Maxine had been in the middle of her intro number, and she was a knockout in her tightly fitted sequined minidress.

I took Ramirez's hand and pulled him along with me as I went over to thank her.

"Maddie!" She turned away from the officer to wrap me in a bear hug. "I'm so glad you're alright! I wouldn't be able to stand it if something had happened to you!"

I felt a little ashamed that I'd ever suspected her of anything. She was probably the most genuine participant in the pageant. "Well, your great timing saved the day."

She grinned from ear to ear. "That's the first time anyone has ever said *I* have great timing."

* * *

"They're killing Dr. Calvin Drake," Dana said the next morning at breakfast. We were outside under a brilliantly blue sky. The full heat of the day hadn't settled in yet, and the mild ocean breeze took the edge off the warmth while carrying the heady scent of the flowers in its wake. Finally, Hawaii felt like the paradise I'd expected it to be.

"Who is?" Mom asked, buttering a croissant.

"The *Island of Dreams* writers. When Ricky called this morning, he told me it was in *Variety*. They're killing off his character by having him accidentally fall into an active volcano while hang gliding."

"Ouch. What a way to go," Marco mumbled around his mimosa.

"I lost a husband that way once," Mrs. Rosenblatt said, nodding solemnly.

All heads at the table turned to her.

"Into a volcano?" Ramirez asked.

"Well, not *exactly* that way, but Lenny did have a nasty accident with a hot barbeque one summer while flying a box kite."

I stifled a laugh.

"Anyhoo," Dana said, changing the subject, "as of this morning, my judging duties are officially over. The Miss Hawaiian Paradise Corporation had Ruth Marie and me pick a winner based on our preliminary scores. And, you'll never guess who won the crown." Her eyes twinkled mischievously.

"Miss Vermont," Mom said. "She had the most beautiful carriage."

"Miss Pennsylvania," Marco said. "She had the most beautiful skin."

"Miss Arkansas," Ramirez said. "She had the biggest—"

I narrowed my eyes at him.

"—heart," he answered, giving me a mock innocent look.

"Ramirez got it!" Dana cut in. "It was Maxine, Miss Arkansas. Can you believe it?"

I almost couldn't.

"How on earth did that happen?" Marco asked.

"Well, since the top three contenders were all either killed or disqualified, and also because she saved our Maddie, Miss Arkansas won the crown." She bit her lip and frowned. "Of course, it's probably the last one ever. No network will touch the Miss Hawaiian Paradise Pageant after this kind of scandal. It's become the laughingstock of the pageant world."

Didn't I know it. The first thing I'd done that morning was check the online tabloids for their take on the pageant debacle. While just about every single one had some take on the mess, the *L.A. Informer*'s site had called it "the best reality TV scandal since the latest Real Housewives arrest." The only bright spot in the article had been that they'd called my shoes "killer fashion," citing that if women wore a pair of my stilettos they wouldn't need their mace for protection. Already this morning, my online orders had doubled. Who knew that fashion as a weapon was such a selling point?

"Well, good for Maxine," Mom said, popping a mango chunk into her mouth. "She seemed like a sweet girl."

"Even better for her, Ashton Dempsey has agreed to stay on permanently as her coach. He told me she might even have a shot at Miss America next year," Dana added.

I took a sip of my fruit smoothie. It tasted wonderful. Everything seemed to taste or smell or sound wonderful after my brush with death the night before. "Wait, did you say one of the top contestants was disqualified?" I asked. "What happened?"

"Didn't you hear?" Dana put down her spoon. "Turns out Whitney *had* been lying about her age to stay in the pageant, and somehow Jeffries found out about it. But because she looks like that and Jeffries is, well…"

"We know what he is," Ramirez said flatly.

Dana nodded. "Let's just say she used her feminine wiles to convince him to let her stay on and compete."

"Wonder how she did that," Marco muttered.

"Ruth Marie told me that she broke down and admitted everything when the police questioned her," Dana continued. "She even admitted to trying to sabotage the other contestants before the pageant started."

"So she was the one who stole Jennifer's bikini top," I said. I'd mostly moved beyond anger at Whitney to something more like pity. She must have known the pageant world was moving on without her and had been desperate to compete one more time.

Dana nodded. "She said she stole it and hid it in Maxine's dresser drawer while she was asleep. Talk about catty. Poor Maxine didn't even realize it was there, although I can't imagine how."

I could. I'd seen Maxine's dresser drawer.

"Whitney played dirty, for sure," I said, "but she didn't actually have a hand in killing anyone, right?"

"No, that was all Jeffries," Ramirez said. "I called the station earlier. He confessed to everything last night. Didn't even bother to ask for a lawyer. He said he wanted to get it over with so he could get to a plastic surgeon about his cheek before his career was ruined." He leaned over to give me a kiss. "Good job there, by the way."

I smiled at him. "I'm just glad it's all over with," I said. "This pageant has been a nightmare from the start."

There were murmurs of agreement around the table.

"While we're playing guessing games," Marco said, "you'll never guess what my plans are for today." He pushed aside his cantaloupe with a huge smile. "I'm taking our little fashion tragedy Donatella Curcio out for a salon day." He held up his juice glass in a toast to his own genius.

Forks and spoons clattered to the table. Except for Ramirez, who kept eating his pancakes with serene indifference. I gave him a pass. Ramirez hadn't met Don and couldn't appreciate the enormity of Marco's accomplishment.

Marco nodded. "I ran into her while I was shopping the other day. Honestly, I almost didn't recognize her. She was wearing something that used to be a dress back in the '90s and shoes to die for. *Women's* shoes. At least our Don has impeccable taste there. Who knew?" He frowned. "Anyway, turns out my subtle hinting—"

I stifled a laugh. There was nothing subtle about Marco, especially when it came to fashion.

"—struck a nerve with her. I mean, I doubt she'll be rejoining the pageant circuit any time soon, but we did end up doing a little shopping tour together and picked out some uber cute stuff."

"So she was your 'project?'" I grinned at him, realizing now that Don hadn't been absent due to guilt but a change of heart. Or, change of clothes, as the case may be.

He nodded. "She's still got that unibrow thing going on, though. We've gotta do something about that today." He shrugged. "Anyway, she decided that there was nothing wrong with a happy medium where femininity is concerned. I'm kind of proud of her, actually. She's like a new woman. Or she will be, when I'm through with her."

"Good luck with that," I told him.

"I don't need luck, dahling," he said. "Underneath that corduroy and polyester, there's a diamond waiting to be polished. I've seen the proof."

He had a point there. I just hoped he had the patience.

"I like this game," Mom piped up. "Guess what Dorothy and I are doing this afternoon?"

"They'll never guess," Mrs. Rosenblatt said. "You'll never guess," she told us.

"Cleansing someone's juju?" I asked, trying not to be snarky about it. Especially since I could taste my food again.

"Oh, no, dear." Mom did a little dismissive wave. "We're clear in that department now. This is much better. We're taking a private surfing lesson with Dirk from the Lost Aloha Shack!"

Mrs. Rosenblatt nodded. "He's cleared his whole afternoon to work with us."

"He's going to teach us how to wax our boards and everything," Mom added.

This time Ramirez was the one to drop his fork. He looked up in alarm. "Don't they wear wetsuits to surf?"

Marco did a wolf whistle. "You go, girls!"

"That's why our lesson is this afternoon," Mom said. "He said he'd need some time this morning to scare up the right sizes for us. Can you imagine how darling we're going to look in wetsuits?"

I didn't want to imagine. I didn't even want to *think* about Mrs. Rosenblatt in a skintight wetsuit. But I knew *darling* wasn't the way I'd describe it. Poor Surfer Dirk didn't know what he was getting himself into.

"This year, our first lesson," Mom said. "Next year, we hang ten at the Pipeline!"

"Well, I don't have that kind of energy," Dana said. "This experience has been exhausting. I plan to park it on the beach all afternoon and work on my tan. Without judging a soul." She pushed aside her bowl of brown rice and raisins. "I'm done with the pageant world for good. I'm sticking to kinder, gentler Hollywood, where all the violence is make-believe."

Mom looked over at me, blotting her lips with her napkin. "What about you, dear? What are your plans for the afternoon?"

Out of the corner of my eye, I saw Ramirez glance my way with a hopeful expression. "I don't want to sound like a wet blanket," I said, "but I need to catch up on some rest after the past few days. I haven't been sleeping too well."

"It's the snoring, isn't it?" Mrs. Rosenblatt said.

"Of course it's the snoring," Mom told her. "You sound like a road grader when you sleep."

Mrs. Rosenblatt's mouth twisted. "Well, I bought those breathing strips."

"Yes, you did, and I haven't seen you use them since the first night you bought them," Mom said. "They've been sitting on the bathroom counter. The bathroom counter doesn't snore, Dorothy."

Mrs. R harrumphed but let it go.

"After that," I cut in, "I thought I might as well start packing. It's going to take me awhile."

"I know just what you mean," Marco said. "I don't know how I'm going to fit my grass skirt into my suitcase."

Ramirez raised an eyebrow at him.

"Well, I'm not leaving mine here," Marco said, defensive. "You never know when a grass skirt might come in handy."

"I was just thinking that last night," Ramirez said

Marco's face lit up. "See? I knew there was hope for you!"

* * *

The knock on my door came almost as soon as I got back to the room.

I opened it and grinned.

"Alone at last," Ramirez said. He stepped inside, closing the door behind him and slipping the chain. When he turned around, his eyes were dark and liquid, slowly going over me in a way that made me shiver. In a good way. A really good way.

"What took you so long?" I asked him. "I've been back here for two minutes already."

He grinned. "Had to listen to some fashion tips from Marco. He thinks I've turned over a new leaf."

I looked him over. Faded jeans, pale blue tee, and general air of studliness. I thought the old leaf was just fine. "You don't need fashion tips," I told him. "You just need to be wearing less fashion." I wiggled my eyebrows suggestively.

He kicked off his shoes and stripped the T-shirt over his head, leaving his hair in a very sexy tousle. The panther tattoo on his bicep flexed and stretched as he moved. His jeans were slung low, riding below the curve of his hipbone.

I admired the chiseled planes of his chest and abs. I think my mouth was starting to water. "But I have to pack. My plane leaves in..." I trailed off as he took a step closer.

"Five hours. The drive to the airport only takes thirty minutes, security and check-in an hour. I can help you pack in twenty." He leaned in, nuzzling his lips against my neck.

"Which leaves?" I was having a hard time keeping up with the math through my sudden hormone haze.

"Three hours," he said, kissing a trail down my neck. "Without work, kids, moms, pageant contestants, or murderers. Just you, me, and a big, empty bed."

Now *that* sounded like paradise.

ABOUT THE AUTHOR

Gemma Halliday is the *New York Times* and *USA Today* bestselling author of the *High Heels Mysteries*, the *Hollywood Headlines Mysteries*, the *Jamie Bond Mysteries*, the *Tahoe Tessie Mysteries*, as well as several other works. Gemma's books have received numerous awards, including a Golden Heart, two National Reader's Choice awards, and three RITA nominations. She currently lives in the San Francisco Bay Area with her boyfriend, Jackson Stein, who writes vampire thrillers, and their three children, who are adorably distracting on a daily basis.

To learn more about Gemma, visit her online at
www.gemmahalliday.com

Connect with Gemma on Facebook at:
www.facebook.com/gemmahallidayauthor

CPSIA information can be obtained at www.ICGtesting.com
Printed in the USA
LVOW06s1319170315

430898LV00001B/20/P

9 781500 846855